DUTY
AND THE
BEAST

Published by JFP Trust
2018 First Print Edition

ISBN: 978 1 9843484 3 2

Printed in the United States of America.

www.chelseafieldauthor.com

To every person who has ever been screwed over or shoved around by forces bigger and nastier than them.

I hope this book helps a little.

But I'd also advise chocolate.

Copious amounts of chocolate.

SERIES INTRODUCTION

If you've never read an Eat, Pray, Die mystery, here's what you should know about us poison tasters:

Harry Potter got a letter inviting him to Hogwarts to become a wizard. My offer was less exciting, but no less top secret. In fact, they didn't even tell me the truth until I was weeks into the training.

Welcome to the Taste Society.

A secret organization where you'll only be told what you absolutely need to know.

Throughout recorded history, wherever there was power, there was poison alongside it. As the use and knowledge of poison became more sophisticated during the rise of the Roman Empire, the role of food taster, known then as *praegustator*, was introduced.

Both poisoners and tasters still exist today. But instead of poor, untrained slaves putting their lives on the line every time someone important wants a meal, you have Shades like me. Poisons are more advanced but so are the antidotes and job training. And while I don't have magic in my blood the way Harry Potter does, I do have the rare gene mutation

PSH337PRS, which gives me increased resistance to toxic substances. That's why the Taste Society recruited me in the first place.

So why haven't you heard of any of this?

The same reason I hadn't until I'd jumped through a thousand hoops and commenced my training. Because both the authorities and the Taste Society go to great lengths to cover it up.

There's a scary logic behind why the rich and powerful elite favor poison over more direct methods. It's discreet, versatile, hard to protect against, and damn near impossible to trace back to the person responsible. Nobody wants to popularize poisoning among the masses.

But beneath the falsified news stories? The climb to power and fortune is a war zone, and poison is the weapon of choice. And around a third of those accounts you see about yet another public figure dying from a drug overdose or ruining their careers while under the influence are, in truth, carefully planned sabotage.

Oh, and Shades like me are the only means of protection.

1

TEN DAYS EARLIER

SIX MONTHS AGO, I'D WALKED into a job interview that I would've done anything to win. This time as I walked through the extravagant hall on the heels of a maid to meet my potential client, I planned to sabotage it.

The man I was meeting—Mr. Lyle Knightley—was looking for someone to protect his son, who happened to be the accused in a multimillion-dollar fraud case. A fraud case that was fast becoming a nationwide spectacle. But that wasn't why I was trying to sabotage it.

His son Richard—the dirtbag who'd lied and cheated over a hundred senior citizens out of their retirement funds—was by all accounts a privileged, self-entitled brat who hadn't shown a shred of remorse. But that wasn't why I was trying to sabotage it either. Most of my clients were on the undesirable side.

No, the reason I wanted to sabotage it had walked me to my car this morning and was waiting to take me to dinner later tonight. I could still feel the lingering touch of his lips on mine. The way one strong hand pulled me toward him while the other caressed my cheek. The look in his gray eyes as I left that begged me to do something his words never would: "Don't take this job."

The maid's staccato footsteps on the tile floor came to a halt, and I almost crashed into her back. "One moment," she said before slipping through a polished timber door and shutting it in my face.

I waited a moment, then another. My mind sifted through possible strategies. Play dumb. Nope, Mr. Knightley might like dumb. His son had allegedly enjoyed pulling the wool over the eyes of scores of people he considered of inferior intellect. Incompetent then. Except it would be hard to demonstrate my poison-tasting skills in the parameters of this interview, and incompetence was one thing that might warrant immediate dismissal by my employer. I needed to disappoint the client, not the Taste Society. That left me to play uncooperative and difficult. Maybe nosy too since I was guessing the Knightleys wouldn't want me poking into their affairs. Half the nation was already doing that.

The door opened. "Mr. Knightley will see you now."

The maid scurried away, her heels clattering on the tiles, giving me the impression she was glad to leave.

Like I would be doing in a few short minutes. I hoped.

Mr. Knightley Senior was seated behind a desk large enough for a woolly mammoth to shelter under. Bookcases encircled the walls, which might have endeared him to me if the titles hadn't all been the yawn-inducing nonfiction variety. He rose when he saw me. High-society manners ingrained into him from birth rather than any true courtesy.

He was a tall, austere man with pronounced cheekbones, scholarly black frames, and neatly trimmed gray hair. Despite being in his own residence on a weekend afternoon, he was wearing a suit and tie.

Given I'd let my own unruly mop hang loose around my shoulders and wore a casual white tank top, an old pair of jeans, and runners, I was expecting his reception to be cold, unimpressed. The way I intended.

But for the first time since I'd moved to Los Angeles—land of the image-obsessed, medically enhanced, sun-kissed actresses, models, and pop stars—the stranger in front of me was ecstatic at what he saw.

"You're perfect."

I was too dumbfounded to speak, and he took my silence as a request for more information.

"You look so wholesome. So innocent. Just what my son needs to improve his public image."

Dammit.

And in another first since moving to LA, I wished I'd

gotten a spray tan and stuffed my bra with . . . well, whatever those who couldn't afford surgery stuffed their bras with.

This was not a good start to sabotaging the interview.

"I'm not sure how I feel about being used for public relations, Mr. Knightley. It's not part of my job description."

"Then we'll pay you more for it."

Ugh. One thing I'd learned after keeping company with the rich and famous was that their knee-jerk solution for everything was to throw money at it. Worse, most of the time it worked. If only the rest of us had it so easy.

"I don't do this for the money," I said. A blatant lie. That was the sole reason I did this gig.

A smile spread across his face like an ink stain over a page.

Actually, it was a nice smile. If his son's was anything like it, I could see how it might have conned so many out of their hard-earned cash. Except, come to think of it, the stories I'd heard said the scam had been played out over the phone.

"That's even better," he told me. "Your naïveté is more than skin-deep. The press will love you."

Crap. Everything was backfiring. What other reason would people do this job?

I wandered over to the bookshelf and pretended to snoop. Pretended I was apathetic toward this whole conversation. "The truth is, the one thing I'm interested in is rubbing shoulders with celebrities," I lied again, borrowing the motive from a few of the other Shades I'd trained with. "And your son isn't very interesting to me."

Surely that would offend his ego and make him rethink his assessment.

Instead, he looked as if I'd given him a freshly baked plate of cookies. "Excellent. My son isn't taking his safety seriously, so I need a Shade who won't be swayed by his charisma or pushed around by his strong personality. Listen, I'll sweeten the deal for you. We both know this fraud case is the talk of the country. Think about how getting an exclusive, inside account will give you an in with those stars you admire. They'll want to hear what you have to say, and they'll remember you for it."

This guy was a gifted negotiator. If I hadn't intentionally misled him about my motives, he would be pressing all the right buttons. I supposed his son had inherited the skill.

I pushed a book—*Investment Banking: Institutions, Politics, and Law* by Alan Morrison, a gentleman who must've been the life of every party—back into its place on the shelf. Then thought better of it and reshelved it in an empty slot farther down. As if I hadn't already failed my objective to sabotage the interview and this tiny act of defiance would change Mr. Knightley's mind.

"Plus I'll match whatever the Taste Society's paying you," he added, ignoring the misplaced book. "You might not need the money, but everyone likes to have more. And remember, the assignment will be over in three months or less. What do you say?"

My brain blank of ideas to turn the situation around and my heart heavy with the thought of breaking the news to Connor, I walked back to that polished door. "I'll think about it," I said.

———————

NOT WANTING TO GIVE Connor the bad news, I retreated to my Corvette to make my final attempt at getting out of the assignment.

It was a lovely spring afternoon in Los Angeles, one of the first of the season. The kind of day where the air felt more breathable, the crowds less oppressive, and that had neither winter's rain nor summer's smog to mar its blue skies.

I rolled down the windows and tried not to feel unseasonably glum. This was my last chance.

I phoned my Taste Society handler.

Jim greeted me in his usual warm and friendly fashion: "State your ID."

Since I wanted him on my good side, I didn't try to engage him in conversation. I'd learned several hours into our acquaintance that any attempts at befriending him only pissed him off.

"Shade 22703," I said.

"What was the outcome of your interview?"

"The client offered me the job." The words were bitter on my tongue—not unlike many of the poisons Shades were trained to detect. "But I was thinking I might turn it down."

"You're kidding." Jim didn't say it with surprise the way

most people would. He stated it with obvious displeasure—strongly suggesting that I better damn well be kidding.

"Um."

"Let me give you a piece of advice." Again, he didn't say it with genuine concern the way a normal person would. He said it with a you're-too-dumb-to-live intonation. "You've already turned down two jobs in the past two weeks. You're getting a bad reputation with the assignment team. And you don't want to get a bad rep. They'll make sure you get the worst clients."

"But . . ." The thing was, I couldn't tell him the real reason I'd refused the last two jobs. Connor's and my relationship wasn't strictly prohibited, but it was understood within the Taste Society that your job came first. You could have relationships so long as they didn't interfere with your assignments. Easier said than done when those assignments required you to adopt a girlfriend-boyfriend relationship as a cover story or travel around the world as a rock star's groupie on a six-month tour.

"You only get one more refusal this year," Jim said. A fact I was excruciatingly aware of. "Do you really want to waste it on an assignment this short?"

No I didn't. That was why I'd tried to sabotage the interview. But I was limited in how far I could take that sabotage without landing in trouble with my employer. And my attempt had failed dismally.

If I accepted the job, Connor and I would have to publicly break up. The assignment necessitated that I pretend to date Mr. Knightley Junior to give me plausible reason to spend long hours in his company and taste his food in public. Which meant the whole freaking country would think I was dating one of the most despised men of the month.

Far worse was that Connor's family and my friends would believe it too.

The one potential upside was that the job might be over in two weeks. The trial was scheduled to begin in just eleven days' time. After that, Mr. Knightley Junior was either going to prison or leaving the country.

If he went to prison, my duties were over.

But if he won the case, he'd be going on a daddy-financed trip to Japan, and I'd be dragged along with him. One more piece of carry-on luggage for the spoiled rich kid.

The overseas move was designed to give Knightley Junior a fresh start. Somewhere his face hadn't been splashed across every news outlet for the past weeks insinuating his guilt in the biggest fraud case of the year.

Okay, we were only a couple of months into the year, but it was a big case. One that tugged at the heartstrings of millions of Americans. Even if the jury concluded there wasn't enough evidence to convict him beyond all reasonable doubt and he won the trial, he'd never recover if he stayed here.

The single perk to that much publicity was the Taste Society would avoid assigning me another "girlfriend" cover story for a while; that way nobody would get curious why I was dating one powerful person after the next. A valuable gift with just one refusal left until my first twelve months of employment ended in September.

It was like gambling, and I wasn't a gambler by nature.

But I was guessing Richard Knightley was guilty. Why else would a chief federal prosecutor and dozens of elderly folk around the country point the finger at him? And justice would prevail, right?

Except I wasn't so naive as to believe that anymore.

"Take your time," Jim said, sarcasm dripping like the fat from a pork belly roast. "I don't have anything better to do than wait for your answer."

The assignment might be a horrible one, but it was a maximum of three months long even if Knightley Junior did win the case. What if I used up my last refusal and the next job offered would steal me away from my loved ones for an entire year?

I felt my shoulders slump. "I'll do it."

"Gee, your enthusiasm could use some work," said the pot to the kettle. "I remember how excited you were to get your first assignment not so many months ago." He sounded pleased with the change. "Welcome to reality, kid. You start tomorrow."

———

THE THING THAT SUCKED MOST was my failed sabotage attempt wasn't the worst thing that happened to me that day. I returned to my apartment—a tiny place in

Palms I shared with my affable British housemate—to find Connor in my bedroom. Usually, I was ecstatic to have Connor and bedrooms in the same place at the same time, but since my bed was a single and the walls were thin, *my* bedroom was not where we tended to hang out.

Plus my mood was dampened by the knowledge of our impending fake breakup.

I drank in his familiar features. No-nonsense short, dark hair, gray eyes the color of an overcast wintry morning, and an unreadable expression that was the envy of poker players everywhere.

He was sitting on my bed. If it had been me, my back would've been resting against the wall, my legs slung over the bed covers, and my housemate's cat, Meow, would've been sprawled on my lap. Meow *was* sprawled on his lap, but the man I was loath to give up for the spoiled Knightley kid was sitting at the edge of the mattress, straight-backed, strong, controlled, unbending. A stark contrast to the ball of fluff stretched over his knees.

Connor was like that. All hard edges except for a splash of softness reserved for a select few. It gladdened my heart every day that he'd allowed me to become one of those select few.

I walked over to him, leaned down so he wouldn't have to disturb Meow, and kissed them both, hoping to bring out some of the warmth in his eyes that I loved so much. Sometimes I thought Connor was a bit like a cat. Proud, dignified, aloof until you've won him over, and meticulously well-groomed. Not like me.

I was more a dog kind of person.

But his lips against mine were different, restrained.

"I need to tell you about Sophia," he said.

My mouth went dry. The woman he'd loved, the one who'd died. He'd promised to tell me the story someday but had been reserving this unprecedented level of opening up to me for our upcoming trip to Australia. It was less than three weeks away and one of the major reasons I didn't want to be dragged off to Japan.

Connor had surprised me with the plane tickets a month earlier, showing me how much he'd cared, how much he'd been paying attention. I'd been pining for a visit home ever since I'd landed in LA, and so he'd made it happen. Simple as that.

So why did he *need* to tell me about Sophia now? In my *apartment* of all places? And didn't he want to hear how the client interview had gone first?

"Okay," I said, sinking to the bed beside him.

Part of me was squirming with curiosity, the other part jittery with nerves, and a third part anxious for Connor whom this was sure to be a painful conversation for. And having to fake break up just after he bared his soul to me was hardly good timing. But I wasn't about to argue with something he felt he needed.

"I met her through work. She applied for a position with Stiles Security and Investigation."

That made sense. His whole life was work, so where else would he spend enough time with a woman to fall for her?

"She was a professional bodyguard. Ex-military. Had a sharp mind for strategy, was proficient at close combat, and could outshoot me nine times out of ten. I gave her the job because she was the best applicant by a mile."

I swallowed a pang of jealousy. Stupid. To be jealous of a dead woman. But she was everything I wasn't, and she sounded perfect for Connor. While he and I fit together like . . . well, I wasn't sure *how* we fit together exactly, they would've worked like a well-oiled machine. And now I was thinking of them moving together with oil in a different way. I was an idiot.

Connor's face was strained. A tiny ripple on the surface that hinted at turbulence deep below. It was hurting him to tell me this, and my mind was busy conjuring the green monster.

"We understood each other. The job. The demons. The release of someone to share it with. We got engaged. A month later, she was killed. The job we shared—the one that brought us together—killed her."

My stomach dropped, and the green monster vanished without a trace. "I'm so sorry."

Connor went on as if I hadn't spoken. "She was trained to anticipate and defend against physical threats, and she was an expert at it. The Taste Society had a VIP client who needed a traditional bodyguard as well as a Shade, and so I gave her the job. But the assassin found a way around both of them. I believe it must have been Stalenburg."

Goosebumps pricked along my arms, and my mind

dredged up the day I'd first heard the name Stalenburg. The sweat-soaked hitman who'd spoken the three syllables in a reverent whisper. Connor telling me she was regarded responsible for every fatal poisoning of Taste Society clients protected by Shades in Los Angeles over the past fourteen years. That she never made mistakes, that no one had anything on her.

He hadn't mentioned she'd also killed his fiancée.

"I'm so sorry," I said again, feeling like a broken record. But no words would fix this, soothe this. Nothing could.

"I'm telling you what happened because I love you, Isobel Avery."

If I didn't know better, I'd swear Connor choked up as he said those astonishing words.

"You do?"

He started as if *I'd* shocked *him*. "Of course. Isn't it obvious? I thought you knew."

"Um—"

"Why else would I work so hard at being a suitable life partner for you? Someone who opens up to you, is less than hopeless at communicating, and—God forbid—tries to make you smile by making stupid jokes?"

"Wow." I could barely get the word out. My eyes were wet, and my heart was expanding like somebody had hooked it up to a helium pump.

"But I can't be with you when you recklessly throw yourself into danger without even taking precautions."

And just like that, my balloon popped. And plummeted

to the ground. Where it was torn to shreds by a passing lawn mower.

"What? What are you talking about?"

"I ran into Levi today, and he told me about your plan to confront that human-trafficking doctor. Inadvertently that is, he assumed I already knew."

Oh no.

Desperation to save the girls had driven me to lengths I'd never thought I'd go to. I would've done almost anything to get Doctor Dan to talk, to tell me where they were being held. But it wasn't the line I'd been prepared to cross that bothered Connor. It was the danger I'd put myself in to cross it.

This was going to be bad.

"It's one thing for you to be a Shade. I mean, that's bad enough, but fatalities are very rare and you're trained for it. But this?" His gray eyes met mine, and they were raw with anger. "This is another thing entirely. Why would you take that risk alone? Why wouldn't you tell me?"

He wasn't going to like my answer, but I had to give him the truth. "Because . . . you would've stopped me."

"You're damn right I would've stopped you. It was an insane risk!"

I opened my mouth to explain, but Connor lifted his hand. "It's done now, and I didn't bring it up to argue about it." There was a long pause. Maybe the longest of my life. "You asked me to communicate with you, to trust you and be vulnerable with you. Well, this is me being vulnerable and communicating. I'm asking you to stop this reckless behavior because I've already lost the love of my life once, and I can't go through that again. Can you promise me that?"

"Yes, of course!" I wanted to shout.

I wanted to cry.

I wanted to fall on my knees and beg his forgiveness.

Yet I sat there frozen instead.

Just yesterday I'd received a postcard from one of the girls I'd saved. How could I promise not to put myself in danger if the cost was other people's lives? Innocent people's lives. I might not be overly qualified, but I kept finding myself in positions where I was the only one around to help.

Connor's mask—the one I'd been so honored he'd let down for me—slammed into place. He carefully slid Meow off his lap and stood. Then he reached into his breast pocket and withdrew an envelope, giving me a déjà vu moment of the first day I'd ever met him. He handed the envelope to me.

I cracked it open. Inside were the plane tickets he'd bought for us to fly to Australia together.

"Maybe Etta would like to go with you," he said quietly.

Then he walked out of my apartment.

2

PRESENT DAY

BEFORE CONNOR HAD FINISHED walking out
of my life, I'd resolved to win him back. Pity it wasn't just
a matter of cooking him a roast the way it would've been
to return to Meow's good side. The same trick worked for
my roommate, actually. Alas, Connor was a harder nut
to crack.

It had been a full ten days since he'd walked out of my
apartment. Ten days since I'd seen him. I'd tried to change
that, but my new client was selfish and demanding, which
meant I'd had no scheduled time off whatsoever. On the
few occasions I'd had a surprise hour to spare and driven to
Connor's house or workplace, he'd been out. But this wasn't

the kind of thing that could be resolved with a phone call, no more than with the aforementioned roast, and so it was that I was formulating a more sophisticated plan.

But right now I was at a candlelit dinner with the wrong man.

I rolled the tiramisu around my mouth. The powerful flavors of the coffee and liqueur, the sweetness of the sugar, and the bitterness of the powdered cocoa, formed an ideal combination for concealing poisons.

"Got plans after we finish dessert?" the wrong man asked me.

He was twenty-four years old with a round, boyish face, disproportionately full lips, and hair that was supposed to be windswept but had in fact been attentively tousled. It would've been a pleasant enough face to have dinner with if familiarity hadn't soured my perception of it.

"Not with you," I said, pushing the tiramisu over to him.

Safe. I was almost disappointed it was free of dangerous substances.

Rick the Prick, as I'd nicknamed him, smiled. "Really? You'd think with what my father's paying you, you'd put out too."

I resisted the urge to slam my dessert fork into the hand that began fondling my leg under the white linen tablecloth.

Only because I didn't want my own tiramisu to taste like blood though.

"For babysitting you? I should've asked him to pay me more." My acerbic reply trailed away to a whisper as someone neared the table, and I pasted a smile on my face. We were supposed to be a happy couple.

Rick the Prick made a strangled noise in his throat, and for a second I thought I'd made good on that dessert fork after all, but then I realized the person approaching was walking fast and clutching a steak knife.

I stood up.

Rick darted behind me. The bastard.

The guy with the steak knife was over sixty with a shock of white hair and bushy eyebrows. Those eyebrows drew down farther when he was faced with me instead of Rick.

"Hide behind your woman, will you? You cheating, chicken-livered sonofabitch!"

His face was flushed. His hands shaking. I was guessing he was one of the unfortunate retirees who'd been scammed by Rick the Prick, and I was tempted to let him have at it.

Tempted, but not overcome.

I held out my hands in a placating gesture that doubled as a ready self-defense position. "Please, sir, put the knife down, and then you can yell at him all you want."

Being a physical bodyguard wasn't part of my job description, but I had a feeling Knightley Senior wouldn't be very happy with me if I allowed Knightley Junior to get stuck (or sawed at) with a steak knife on my watch. More compellingly, I didn't want this poor old guy to wind up with criminal charges on top of his other problems.

"He's going to court tomorrow anyway," I reminded him. "Is it really worth your freedom?"

My words weren't getting through. I glanced around for one of the waitstaff. A waitress was standing almost within reach, her face frozen. The steak knife guy turned his head to see what I was looking at, and she dumped her tray and its contents with a shriek and fled.

That was helpful.

Lucky I'd been keeping up with my self-defense lessons ever since I'd been abducted by a stalker and then narrowly escaped being strangled and stabbed by a human-trafficking scumbag. I was sick of feeling helpless.

"Please, sir," I said again.

He was gripping the steak knife hard enough that his knuckles were white but hadn't moved closer. Undecided whether he wanted to go through me. "How can you stand there and protect that piece of human excrement?" he asked, gaze fixed on Rick.

Good question. One I didn't want to examine too closely. I took a risk and snatched up the stainless steel tray the waitress had dropped. It would make a decent shield if it came to that.

But my sudden movement pushed the assailant into action. He swung the knife —not really at me—maybe just at the world in general. This guy wasn't an expert by any stretch of the imagination. I got the tray up in time and smacked it into the blade. The unexpected force of my blow startled him into dropping the makeshift weapon.

Moving fast, I grabbed his now-empty hand and twisted it until he was kneeling on the floor. "Sorry, sir," I whispered. And I was. I was filled with pity for him. His arm was trembling from shock and adrenaline. His bank account was presumably empty, and I knew what it was like to be desperate for money with debtors breathing down your neck.

Plus I'd been thinking about stabbing Rick with the cutlery myself.

The piece of human excrement, as this gentleman had so aptly labeled him, was looking cocky and self-congratulatory now that I'd neutralized the threat. "I want this man arrested immediately! Somebody call the police."

I winced and considered letting the man go so he'd have a chance to escape.

The would-be assailant spat in Rick's direction. "Enjoy your moment, pond scum. You'll get what's coming to you tomorrow."

I shifted my grip on the guy's wrist to ease the ache in my back from bending over him and tried not to glare at Rick too.

"Definitely should've asked for better pay," I muttered.

———————

I RETURNED HOME from my night protecting Rick the Prick and wanted nothing more than to crawl into bed and feel sorry for myself. This was officially the worst assignment I'd had as a Shade. Even including the one where I got shot.

The apartment was empty except for Meow's welcome company, and I breathed a sigh of relief. She trotted up to me, and I snuggled her into my chest, unsure whether running my hand over her sleek black-and-gray stripes was more soothing for her or me.

Meow wasn't particularly interested in people problems, unless they were the kind that had me coming home smelling of seafood, but she was a great cuddle buddy. And she didn't ask questions. A trait I appreciated more than usual since I'd prefer to stab *myself* with a dessert fork than think about my life right now.

I'd managed to convince Rick not to press charges by pointing out it made him look weak to be scared of an old man with some cutlery, and that being gracious about it might garner him some brownie points with the jury tomorrow.

That was the highlight of my week.

I fed Meow, watered the houseplant that was starting to die despite my best efforts, and had just changed into my cupcake pajamas when I heard a knock at the door. Praying it was somebody selling something so I could tell them to get lost, I trudged across the new blue-and-gray-flecked carpet and then the ancient ugly linoleum to answer it.

Two women stood on the landing. One was spirited, slender, stylish, and in her seventies. That was my next-door neighbor.

The other was in her fifties and had a mild, forgettable presence—a leftover trait from her days as a PI. An extremely misleading leftover trait. That was Connor's mother.

Both of them were better than me at shooting, scheming, and just about everything else, and the pair of them were as thick as thieves.

Etta would probably like to try her hand at thievery, but I was pretty sure Mae had more scruples.

My neighbor slipped past me through the door. "Mae came by to visit you, but nobody was home, so I invited her to wait at my place. We need to talk."

Oh boy. Had any good conversation ever kicked off with those four words?

Mae shared a smile with me behind Etta's back and offered a quick hug. "It's nice to see you. Is now an okay time?"

I returned the hug and stepped aside. "Yeah, come on in."

Connor may or may not have told Mae about our breakup, but Etta certainly would have. She'd been unimpressed by the news and threatened to "slap me until I came to my senses" before I explained that he'd been the one to end it. Still, that didn't explain why Mae was here. A silly part of me hoped Connor had sent her.

"I'll put the kettle on. I think there are some cookies around here somewhere too if Oliver hasn't polished them off."

I went to the kitchen to get things started, and they took seats at the white IKEA dining table. Did they know that Connor had assembled that for me after thugs fire-bombed the apartment? He'd assembled almost everything in the living room: the coffee table, the muted blue couches, the TV cabinet except for two of its drawers (I'd been preoccupied with stopping Meow running off with the screws). Which meant I couldn't sit anywhere without being reminded of him. Mae had been a huge help too, helping me wash every single thing that was washable to get rid of the reek of smoke and the ash that had infiltrated every nook, cranny, and cupboard.

Great, we hadn't even begun "the talk," and I had a lump in my throat.

I brought the mugs over along with the few measly cookies Oliver had left me. When we were all nursing steaming cups of tea, Mae studied me. "How are you?"

"I'm . . ." My mind ran through all the things I wanted to say. Determined to get him back. Missing him so much. Still clueless about how to work things out between us. "Okay," I finished lamely.

Judging by the pity on their faces, they didn't believe me.

"Oh, hon," Mae said.

Etta shook her head and snagged another cookie.

"I'm sure he wouldn't want me telling you this," Mae went on, "but Connor isn't doing well either. That's kind of why I'm here . . . I mean, I try not to be one of those mothers that meddle in their kids' affairs, but sometimes Connor *needs* someone to meddle. He's too hardheaded for his own good. So I was thinking that maybe I could assist you in helping him come around. If you wanted him to come around, that is."

Cripes. The lump in my throat swelled, and I could barely swallow my tea. I wanted more than anything to accept her help. Mae knew Connor better than anyone, plus she'd experienced her own deep personal loss and had gone on to conquer the resulting fear and pain, at least mostly. And Etta, well Etta had racked up more experience with men in her lifetime than a dozen other women combined. I would've loved to benefit from their collective wisdom.

But the decision was out of my hands. It had been from the moment I'd taken on Knightley as a client.

I'd informed my friends about the breakup as soon as I'd pulled myself together enough to do so. Not because I hadn't been holding out hope that Connor would change his mind, but because if he did, we'd still be forced to fake our separation so as to not compromise my cover story with Rick the Prick. Even so, I'd delayed announcing my "new boyfriend" to anyone. With the media coverage focused on the scandal and Rick lying low in the lead up to trial according to his daddy's orders, I'd figured my exact relationship with the accused could stay undefined for as long as possible.

Unfortunately, "as long as possible" had just arrived.

With the first big day of trial tomorrow, the secret would be out. Cameras weren't allowed in the courtroom, but Mr. Lyle Knightley wanted me up close and personal with his son in the desire that my innocence would somehow extend to him. I'd have to be by his side as he entered and exited the building—where the media circus would be lying in wait.

So as much as every fiber of my being wanted to accept

Mae's offer, and as much as I wanted to avoid Etta's certain ire, and as much as it pained me to utter the words, I had to tell them.

"I'm sorry," I mumbled into my mug, "but I'm seeing someone else."

"Who?" Etta spat. The ever-elegant woman actually spat.

I wiped a few damp cookie crumbs off my face. "Richard Knightley."

I hid a cringe as I waited for them to react. Etta would explode. Mae would be disappointed. I wasn't sure what was worse.

Instead, they exchanged a significant look between them, and when Etta spoke again, she was calm.

"You mean the Richard Knightley who's stolen millions from old folk around the country?"

"Allegedly." The words came out through clenched teeth. I couldn't believe I was about to defend him. As far as I was concerned, Rick the Prick could rot in prison. Just so long as he wasn't poisoned before he got there. "He's not as bad as the media likes to make out," I said. *He was worse.*

Etta and Mae exchanged another glance.

"Is this the Richard Knightley who had suspicious relations with those Russian students?"

"Nothing was proven."

"The one the media has dubbed the Silver Spoon Scammer?"

It was a nicer name than I'd given him. "As I said, the press seems to have it out for him."

"This is the same man whose friend posted a YouTube video of him kicking a cat?"

I winced. "That was a year ago. He's changed."

They looked at each other again. "I see," Etta said, still calm. It was like she was channeling Connor. Gosh, I missed him.

Mae reached across the table and patted my hand. "We understand, hon. I guess I'd better let you get to bed then. The first hearing's tomorrow, isn't it?"

Maybe I should've been relieved, but their quiet acceptance knocked me for a loop. I wanted desperately to be able to take it back. To beg them for help with Connor. To explain everything so I could undo the damage I'd just done with the woman I'd been considering as my future mother-in-law.

The Taste Society's demands for secrecy had never cost me so much as in this moment.

"Uh-huh," was all I managed to get past my teeth.

They rose together, and I stood automatically and walked them to the door.

What had just happened? I'd dreaded being grilled mercilessly, but their lack of questions was worse. Like they'd given up on me.

Before they left, Mae gave me a final hug. I clutched her in return, wanting to cry. "I'm so sorry," I whispered.

Then they walked out of my apartment too. Just as Connor had.

CONNOR

It had been ten days since I'd last seen her. A situation that should've gotten easier, but hadn't. So I'd been working long hours and coming home only when my body demanded rest. Like now.

I slipped into bed, ignoring the drawer full of her clothes that I should've returned already. As if by holding on to them I could keep a piece of her for myself.

Idiot.

But I still didn't ask Maria to post them back to her.

It took me longer than usual to fall asleep.

3

AFTER ETTA AND MAE HAD LEFT, I'd been too out of sorts to do anything other than read. I read until the book fell out of my hands, and I escaped reality in sleep instead of fiction. So I was pretty sure I was still dreaming when I woke to my phone ringing, and my blurry vision told me it was Connor.

Energy jolted through me, and I almost dropped the phone in my haste to answer it. I didn't have a chance to clear my throat, so I hoped my voice would sound sexily husky rather than like a zombie's after an all-night bender.

"Hello?"

"Isobel?"

It was him!

"Yes," I sang. *Oops, too enthusiastic.*

"Your client's been killed."

"Oh." I noticed then that it was still dark outside. The clock read a quarter past one.

"Can you come to Hermosa Beach to see if there's anything you can tell us before the scene is cleared away?"

Oh sure. I loved seeing dead bodies. Especially in the middle of the night. And it was just the thing to get Connor in the frame of mind to take me back.

"Of course."

Connor gave me the address, his tone all business.

I allowed myself a self-indulgent groan before hauling my ass out of bed and grabbing the first clothes I found. Then I remembered this was the first time Connor would see me in a week and a half, and I might do well to remind him what he was missing. Then I remembered my client was dead and decided my romance plans would have to take a backseat.

I mashed my hair into a semblance of a ponytail, washed my face, and was good to go.

The address Connor provided brought me to a residential cul-de-sac illuminated by streetlamps and not much else. But I didn't have to squint to spot the house numbers. The front of 2439 was buzzing with police and the grim sight of an ambulance with its lights turned off.

There was no one here they still had a hope of saving.

I parked as close as I could, which wasn't all that close, and got out. The salty, kelp-infused scent of the ocean washed over me along with the cool night air. We weren't near enough to the beach to see it, but the smell alone was a luxury in a city that so often smelled of exhaust fumes, pot, and urine—among its other more desirable scents. I breathed in a few lungfuls to brace myself and headed for the hive of people.

Despite the hour, there were a few gawkers in nightwear and a couple of journalists too. I gave the journos a wide berth, offered my name to a guy in an LAPD uniform, and he waved me under the crime tape. Gosh. Somehow in all my recent brushes with the law, I'd never crossed crime scene tape. Maybe it was the sleep-deprived two-in-the-morning thing, but it felt surreal.

The house in front of me was narrow but modern, with a gently arched roof and floor-to-ceiling windows on the second story. I passed shadowy trees and hedges to reach the door and found it ajar. A sign read:

AI security is active on these premises. Enter at your own risk.

It seemed whatever that meant, it hadn't been secure enough to save Rick the Pr— No. Richard Knightley, I amended, the weight of his death settling on me like a sodden blanket. The door squeaked as I pushed through it, and then I heard a feminine automated voice say, "Authorization complete. What can I do for you, Officer Mendez?"

A uniformed officer was sitting on the floor with a laptop and a frown. "Tell me what happened in the ten minutes before you called the police today."

"There was a security breach," the feminine automated voice replied. "I followed protocol and administered vitrazolam to the intruders to sedate them until law enforcement arrived."

"Explain your protocol in more detail."

"When my security mode is set to active, I monitor the house using motion and visual sensors. If there is a human inside that does not match my database of allowed persons, I estimate height and weight using visual diagnostics, calculate the most probable amount of vitrazolam to sedate them with minimal risk, and fire a projectile injection to administer it with the nearest robotic air gun. I also simultaneously alert law enforcement to the security breach."

Far out. That was one high-tech security system. *Maybe I should look into one of those.*

"Then why did you fire at Isaac Anand?" the officer asked. "He owns the house you're protecting."

Or maybe not then.

"Sorry, but I do not recognize the person you're referring to."

"I've provided a photo for you to scan."

"There is no person with those visuals on file."

The officer rubbed her face, muttering to herself, and caught me gawking. Her glare reminded me I had my own job to do.

"When were you last updated or restarted?" she asked behind me as I walked into what appeared to be half living room, half office. My brain was processing what I'd just heard and wasn't prepared for the shock of seeing two bodies on the ground. One I recognized. Rick—Richard.

The other was a male stranger around my age. Isaac Anand, I guessed.

My empty stomach did its usual trick of threatening to heave, so I forced myself to concentrate on the rest of the room. Along the entire length of one wall ran a desk of monitors and computers, with a single lonely ergonomic chair suggesting they were all for the same person. The other half of the space was taken up with the sorts of things you'd generally find in a living room: a collection of armchairs, a coffee table, and a giant flat-screen TV. There were also two more law enforcement personnel I didn't know and one that I did.

I'd expected Police Commander Hunt to be here—he was the secret LAPD liaison assigned to the Taste Society, and it was a case involving one of their clients after all. But his scowl still hit me like a cold hose to the face. It seemed I wasn't the only one who'd been dragged out of bed and wasn't thrilled about it. No doubt having to cover up Taste Society secrets from his colleagues—secrets that included the reason for my presence here—wouldn't help his temper.

Connor's presence would be easier for Hunt to explain. He at least was an experienced investigator, and most officers at the 27th Street Community Police Station knew he was called in to consult on certain cases. They just didn't know the real reason for that was because Connor worked for the Taste Society and people high above both men had arranged discreet cooperation between the two organizations.

In contrast with me and the commander, Connor would no doubt look as if he'd been styled by a professional team and awake for hours: alert and immaculate in his tailored clothes and ever-ready haircut.

I wondered briefly whether I could pull off that haircut. Then I saw Connor.

If Hunt's scowl had been a cold hose to the face, Connor's presence was like a flash storm. An instinctive rush of warmth and electricity followed by the cold, drenching reality of our separation.

It had only been ten days, but he looked different. I was used to his face being more familiar than my own, and I didn't like the milliseconds it took to catch up.

Against my expectations, he wasn't immaculate. Not quite. There were new circles under his eyes, and the state of his shirt suggested he'd been wearing it all day instead of picking it out from his perfectly ordered wardrobe an hour prior. Had he not gone to bed?

"Hi," I said. There was so much more I wanted to say, but this was not the time nor place.

"Hey."

"What happened here?" No need to gesture to the bodies I was avoiding looking at.

He seemed relieved to jump straight into work mode. "It appears the artificial intelligence security system shot these guys with tranquilizer darts. Or someone else shot them with tranquilizer darts and is trying to make it look as if the security system did it."

"Does the security system have a woman's voice? Because I just heard her . . . I mean *it* talking to Officer Mendez in there, and the system confirmed it was the one to shoot the darts. But the darts were supposed to sedate, not kill. The computer or robot or whatever it is estimates their weight to get the dose right."

"Yes. And I'm guessing it wasn't supposed to shoot them at all since Isaac Anand—the second victim here—is the owner of this house and the designer of the security system. Can you tell what was in the darts? Maybe someone switched them with a more lethal substance."

I'd only been trained to identify drugs that could be swallowed and absorbed through the stomach, but many poisons could be administered by both injection and ingestion, so it was worth a try. Connor unscrewed the tail end of the dart and handed me the rest of it, complete with the pointy needle attached. A needle that was a good 1/16-inch thick and over an inch long. Ouch.

I sniffed it before doing anything else. A faint bitter chemical aroma. Nonconclusive. I ran my pinkie finger around the inside edge and carefully tasted the tiniest amount I could manage. First on the tip of my tongue, then allowing it to mix with my saliva until it coated my whole mouth. It tasted the way it smelled, except with the added pleasure of a mild, rotten citrus-like tang. "Yes, it's vitrazolam or a very close relative, which is what the system said it was."

"Hmm," was all Connor said.

"Does that mean that this . . . their deaths . . . could really be the result of some technical glitch?"

"It's possible. Mendez told us the security system is a working prototype that is being tested before it can be released on the market. But if that's vitrazolam, the dose would've had to be more than double what it should've been to kill them so quickly. The LAPD was here within ten minutes after the AI system called nine one one, but both Knightley and Anand were dead on arrival."

"Oh." That changed the picture substantially. Vitrazolam was a slow-acting sedative, taking a solid fifteen minutes to reach full strength when injected intramuscularly. Not that a person wouldn't be sluggish and dopey within a minute or two, but to be beyond resuscitation after just ten minutes? I chewed my lip. "I mean, someone could be unusually sensitive to vitrazolam and lose respiratory function on a low dose, but two of them?"

"Exactly. The odds are astronomical that they'd both have abnormal reactions."

"So either the artificial intelligence isn't that intelligent and its calculations are way off, or somebody tampered with something to make sure they died."

"Yes. That's why I phoned you. When did you last see your client? Do you know what he was doing here?"

"No. I left him hours ago at a restaurant called Brago in Santa Monica. He told me he was having late-night drinks with his father before the trial started tomorrow." I remembered it was two in the morning. "Or today, technically.

They didn't want me there. Mr. Lyle Knightley was arrogant enough to assume no one could've spiked his expensive scotch, I guess."

"Have you ever seen Richard with the other victim?"

I forced myself to take a proper look at the second man. He was young, about my age, and his expressive dark eyebrows and neatly trimmed beard failed to make him appear any older. His face was relaxed as if sleeping, lips slightly parted. But those lips were tinted blue from lack of oxygen, and his rich brown eyes were fixed open, unseeing.

"No," I said.

"Heard him mention the name Isaac Anand?"

"No."

"Interesting." Whatever Connor was going to say next was interrupted by a phone call. "Will you excuse me for a minute?"

Left to my own devices, I looked around the room some more, trying to think of anything but the two dead men on the floor and failing miserably. What had they been doing when they'd been shot with lethal amounts of vitrazolam? Their awkward positions against the carpet suggested they'd gone down with little control over their limbs and didn't leave any clues. Richard was a prick—for all I knew he was here to scam Isaac—but it didn't make his death feel okay. I wasn't sure how professionals who dealt with violence or tragedy or death on a daily basis dealt with it.

Hunt must've seen I was alone, and like a predator

spotting the opportunity to kill off its prey away from the safety of the herd, he stalked up to me.

"Another person in your circles turns up dead, Ms. Avery."

I scanned his craggy features, every detail tough and dangerous. A sun-weathered face that lacked an ounce of fat to soften it, an ex-military, steel-gray buzz cut with a matching prickly mustache, and a swagger that'd make a western gunslinger wet their pants.

But so far I'd managed to maintain my bladder control during our acquaintanceship, and while he liked me no more than he ever had, we'd come to a bit of an understanding a month ago. So I was pretty sure his accusation had no weight behind it.

"Then either I'm a killer who's great at framing others for murder, or I'm moving in the wrong circles."

He huffed. Hopefully in an amused way. "I suppose you'll be working with Stiles on this case then? Unofficially, I mean." He didn't sound pleased, but there was less menace than there would've been before we'd come to that understanding.

The question made my brain hiccup. Would I be working with Connor on this? I'd been too preoccupied with the immediate circumstances to consider what might come next.

Would teaming up on a case help or hinder my efforts to win Connor back? Given how much trouble I'd had even seeing him, maybe it would be a positive thing . . .

Hunt was waiting for a response.

"Most probably," I agreed.

Connor returned to the room, and I was struck again by how much I missed him. That cemented my decision.

"I think we should work this case together," I told him as soon as he was near enough to hear me.

Although his features barely moved, he looked pained. "Really?" A full second passed before he added, "Why?"

Because I can't stand not seeing you every day. Because I want you to remember how good we are together. Because your mom told me you're struggling as much as I am with this breakup. Because I want you back. Duh.

"Because it's a complicated case and my insights might prove useful," I said.

He wiped a hand across his gorgeous face and exhaled slowly. "I'm going to get some sleep. I'll pick you up at eight."

4

SIX HOURS LATER, I was dressed, upright, and mostly awake. A good beginning to any investigation. Now I just had to hope that Connor would pick me up as agreed rather than think better of the whole idea after a night's sleep.

I shouldn't have wasted energy worrying about it. Connor was a steady sort. If he told you he'd do something, he'd do it. At eight sharp his black SUV rolled up outside my apartment building.

At one minute past, I climbed into the passenger seat, and he handed me a thermos with real, honest-to-goodness coffee in it. I could've kissed him for that.

Okay, his citrus and leather scent underneath the heavenly aroma of my espresso flooded me with memories, so my body was looking for any excuse to kiss him, but that's beside the point. I was touched he'd gone to the trouble of bringing it for me.

He handed me his phone next. "Have you seen this?"

It was a news article with the headline:

Artificial Intelligence Security System Kills
Homeowner and Guest!

"No." I hadn't seen it. I'd barely managed to wake up yet, let alone start any research.

The article went on to outline how a suspected malfunction had caused the AI security system to fire the darts with lethal amounts of vitrazolam, not telling me anything I didn't know beyond the fact that Isaac Anand was a respected mind in artificial intelligence and robotics.

"They're wrong," Connor said. "It wasn't a malfunction, it was murder. Police analysts found that the AI code had been tampered with to delete Isaac Anand from the system. That in itself wouldn't have done anything worse than put him to sleep, but whoever did it also changed the formula the AI used to calculate the quantity of tranquilizer so that instead of point zero one milliliters per pound, it was point one milliliter per pound. Then they just needed to set the AI's security mode to active while their intended victims were in the house."

"Geez." We'd kind of assumed it must have been murder last night, but having it confirmed in the light of day still hit hard. And it was scary to think that two simple changes to a code could be enough to turn a security system into a killing machine. Literally.

Connor had yet to pull away from the curb. "If we're going to work together on this, we need to lay out some ground rules. I won't be party to you putting yourself in danger—so you have to swear you won't see a single person connected to the case without me."

He was holding his jaw in such a way that I knew there'd be no negotiation on this. "That's fine," I said. And it was fine . . . probably. I had no attachment to Rick, so it shouldn't be too hard to avoid putting myself in harm's way for his sake.

Connor wasn't finished. "And we can't allow our personal relationship to interfere with the investigation, so while we're working, we're working."

"Sure." I'd expected him to insist on that, and despite my feelings or lack thereof toward Rick, I didn't want to jeopardize the case either.

Connor didn't look happy about my ready agreement. Perhaps he'd been hoping to get rid of me. It brought up memories of the first case we'd ever worked together. He'd been appalled to have me tag along. Probably because he'd been fighting his attraction to me and didn't like that I was getting under his skin.

I hoped he was doing his version of a grimace now for the same reason.

Oops, focus on the case, Izzy.

"Where do you want to start?" I asked.

"Let's go over suspects and murder motives. For both victims."

"Okay. Richard Knightley is easy. He scammed so many people there are plenty who'd want him dead."

Connor passed me his phone again. "Like this guy?"

It was a YouTube video of Steak Knife Guy advancing toward Rick and me. *Oh no.* I felt my face go red even as I wondered how Connor had found it. Had he been keeping tabs on me? Or was it case research? He *was* very thorough.

In the video, Rick came off scared and weak hiding in my shadow. Good. I saw myself grab the waiter's tray and smack it into Steak Knife Guy's hesitant, half-assed swing, disarming him, then taking him down. I also noticed in the aftermath that I hadn't hidden my dirty looks at Rick as well as I'd thought. Oops. Acting had never been my strong suit; a fact made more apparent in LA where it often seemed that everyone and their dog had been in at least one commercial or television show.

The video ended, and I looked up to see Connor's lips twitch. "Nice moves, Avery."

I cracked a smile. "I was taught by the best."

"You mean Nick?"

He was referring to a member of his security team, the one he'd chosen to teach me self-defense. Was there jealousy behind the question?

I'd meant Connor, but my smile widened. "Yeah, Nick." I made him wait for a beat before adding, "And Spider-Man."

That made Connor smile too. The first time he'd taught me how to use pepper spray and a Taser, he'd made me practice on a full-size cardboard cutout of Spider-Man. He never had explained how he'd mysteriously happened to have one lying about his house.

The sight of his curved lips made my pulse speed up. Connor smiling more than a couple of times a week was unheard of for the first months of our acquaintance. The fact he'd slipped into one so easily now showed his guard was still lowered around me.

As if realizing the same thing, he visibly shifted back into business mode. "Is there any doubt in your mind that Richard's guilty of the scam charges?"

"No."

"Why not? You believe the best of everyone."

"I asked him about it once. Even with the Taste Society confidentiality contract, he wasn't dumb enough to admit it. But he said that when his dad cut him off, he'd had to come up with some creative business ideas. That he'd done it for years before anyone caught on. He was boasting as if it were something to be proud of. Something that proved he was smarter than everyone else. Plus he didn't show any guilt at all—despite the fact he must've seen the news stories about the lives he'd wrecked."

"I see."

"That's only part of it. From what I witnessed, he had zero regard for anyone but himself. Not even his father who, while I haven't warmed to the guy, obviously loved

Rick and was doing everything in his power to help him. Rick believed anybody who treated him well did it because he was so amazing, so there was nothing to appreciate them for. And anybody who didn't treat him well was dumb or damaged— or maybe playing hard to get if they happened to be a beautiful woman. He was an egomaniac. One who managed to ooze charm on occasion but only when it was to his advantage."

"Right, so he could've made a lot of people mad. But the trial against him was supposed to start today, wasn't it? Any reason you know of that would make one of his scam victims come after him now?"

I rubbed my face. The answer was something that had been bothering me all week. "Rumor said he'd hidden his money so well that even if he served time, he'd live like a king when he got out, and his victims would never get a cent. Plus the evidence wasn't strong enough for his conviction to be a sure thing." Richard had certainly seemed confident he'd walk away a free man.

Connor jotted a few notes in his trusty battered notepad. "Well, he'll never be convicted or acquitted now. Criminal cases are thrown out if a defendant dies before trial, and Hunt said the US Attorney on the case didn't have any leads for us. What about the class action lawsuit?"

On top of the criminal prosecution by the federal government, a group of victims had rallied together to sue for compensation and damages. I didn't know much about it beyond what I'd seen in the news. "I'm not sure, but so long as Richard was claiming to be broke, I can't see how they'd get any money out of that either."

In other words, they still had plenty of reasons to want him dead.

"Are there any other potential suspects you know of?"

"No, but I was only with him for a week and a half, and he was lying low, which meant I didn't meet many people who knew him. What about the other victim though? It was his house and his AI security system. Doesn't that imply he was the target?"

"Yes. Or that they were both targets. Or that the killer wants to throw us off course. Right now there are no obvious links between the two except a few phone calls Isaac Anand made to Knightley and the fact they were together when they died. Hunt and his team are doing the preliminary investigation into Anand, so for now, Knightley is our main concern. We need to work out what he was doing at Anand's home, and who else knew that's where he'd be. Then we can determine whether he might've been the target. Who would you say is most likely to have those answers for us?

"His father. Mr. Lyle Knightley."

"Then let's go speak to him."

———

MR. KNIGHTLEY SENIOR WAS IN A SUIT again, his silver hair neatly combed, his face clean-shaven. But the eyes behind his black scholarly frames were hollow.

Like his son's promises came my involuntary thought.

He received us in his office and listened to Connor's introduction with a blankness that was in sharp contrast to the man who'd conducted my interview. And when Connor broke the news that Richard's death was no accident, Lyle's gaze landed on me.

"You. You were supposed to protect him!"

Connor stepped closer to me, never mind the woolly-mammoth-sized desk was doing a fine job of keeping Lyle and me apart.

"Ms. Avery did her job, Mr. Knightley. Your son didn't die from anything he ingested."

"He wasn't supposed to die full stop! But he did, from poison. I want to lodge a complaint with the Taste Society."

"You're welcome to do that. But have you seen the video of Ms. Avery defending your son from a knife attack? It seems to me that she went above and beyond what you were paying her for."

Rather than diffusing the situation, Mr. Knightley grew more agitated.

"She talked Richard out of pressing charges so that lunatic went free. How is that protecting him? It sent a message to our rivals that the Knightley house is weak, that now's a good opportunity to strike because we're down and won't fight back. Where's that man now? Why are you wasting your time talking to me when the likes of him are out there?"

"Mr. Knightley, I can have Ms. Avery wait in the car if

you're unable to pull yourself together in her presence. But we're here to help. To find who did this. And it will be more efficient if she remains here."

Connor's suggestion of weakness was as effective as tipping a bucket of water over Lyle's head. He schooled his facial muscles into a polite—even friendly—mask. A Knightley was always in control.

"That won't be necessary," he assured us. "Tell me what you want to know."

Connor sat down, and Lyle and I followed suit.

"We're trying to understand what Richard was doing at Isaac Anand's house. Can you help?"

"Well, I don't know what he was doing there last night. He was supposed to be having a scotch with me." His eyes grew hollow with grief again. "But I know he'd been working with Mr. Anand in some capacity or another. Richard said Isaac was going to help him clear his name."

"How?" Connor asked.

"He never gave me any details. I told him not to get his hopes up, and I think that offended him."

How the heck could artificial intelligence and robotics clear the name of someone who was guilty? Or had Isaac simply been helping Rick to ensure any evidence stayed buried forever and the stolen money impossible to track down?

Connor remained impassive. "Did Richard mention anything about why he changed his plans? Why he wasn't going to meet you for that scotch?"

"No. He didn't so much as call to cancel."

"Is that unusual behavior for him? To stand you up without explanation?"

Knightley's lips thinned. "Unusual, but not the first time he's done it."

No, Lyle Knightley wouldn't like *anyone* standing him up. His son would be no exception.

"Any ideas why he did this time?" Connor prompted.

"He didn't tell me."

"So you said, but he's your son. Surely you can speculate."

Another man might have dropped his shoulders in defeat, but Lyle sat poised and upright in his chair. It was his eyes and the way he was allowing Connor to commandeer the conversation that showed the fight had gone out of him. "Something exciting if I had to guess. It would've had to be a better offer . . . But why does it matter? What does this have to do with his murder?"

"We need to determine if anyone could've anticipated Richard would be there. Or whether the real target was Isaac Anand and Richard was just collateral damage in the wrong place at the wrong time."

That snapped Lyle out of his listlessness.

"Of course Richard wasn't just collateral damage. Do you know how many imbeciles are accusing him of scamming them? Then the media goes and blasts his face all over national television. Look. I can give you a list of people who wanted him dead."

He pulled something up on his computer and printed it out. It was a list of every person in the class action lawsuit against Rick with their name and the corresponding figure of claimed losses.

Connor glanced at it, then tucked it out of sight. "That's all very well, Mr. Knightley, and we'll be going through this list, but we need to cover every possibility. How long had Richard and Isaac been collaborating?"

"I don't know. A few weeks maybe?"

"Is there anyone else your son might've told about how Isaac was going to help clear his name?"

"I have no idea, Mr. Stiles. My son is an independent adult, and I don't keep track of all his friends."

I thought that was debatable. Both that Rick could be called independent since he hadn't done an honest day's work in his life, resorting to stealing when his father cut him off, and that he had any friends to keep track of.

"Can you think of anyone else who might want to harm Richard?"

"No. Isn't that long list enough?"

"Just trying to be thorough, Mr. Knightley."

I got the feeling Mr. Knightley wanted us to go be thorough somewhere else.

Connor pushed on regardless. "Richard's phone records show six missed calls from you around the time of his death. Did you have an urgent reason to get ahold of him?"

"It was the night before the trial began, and he hadn't shown up when we'd agreed. I was worried he might be doing something foolish. Something that might negatively influence the outcome of the case."

Connor accepted the explanation with a nod. He'd probably gathered by now that it was a valid concern. "We have to ask, do you have any joint assets with your son, or does he hold any legal interest in your company?"

"You're asking whether I had any potential liability in this lawsuit or any financial gain in his death."

"Yes."

"No and no. I've been aware of my son's lack of . . . business acumen for some time, and I wouldn't expose my company to that kind of risk. His death wins me nothing but grief, Mr. Stiles."

"What about the scam money?"

"What money? If my son had any money, why would I pay his bills and spend the past three months researching and investing in a world-class horse-racing-and-breeding operation in Japan for him to manage when this court case is finally behind us?"

Oh yes, Richard had been extremely pleased with himself about that. Though he resented having to go to Japan.

"Were you so sure he wouldn't get any prison time?"

"I resent the implication of his guilt, Mr. Stiles. And no, I wasn't sure, but managers for such operations can be found, and I wanted Richard to have something to look forward to. A fresh start."

Lyle's eyes got wet. "He wanted to own a thoroughbred racing stable since he was a little kid, but I told him it was too blue-collar and he should set his sights higher. Maybe if I hadn't . . ." He trailed off.

"I assume this racing operation has been purchased in your name?"

"Clearly. And it was going to stay that way until both the trial and the ridiculous class action lawsuit were over. Now I'll be stuck offloading the useless thing."

"Thank you for your cooperation, Mr. Knightley. We'll be in touch."

We left Lyle staring at his desk and walked ourselves out.

———

AS CONNOR HAD POINTED OUT, when a criminal defendant dies before trial, the case is dismissed, so Richard would never be found guilty nor acquitted of the fraud charges against him. The class action lawsuit was another matter, and we needed to find out what Richard's death meant for the plaintiffs.

But first we needed to touch base with Hunt and sort out who was handling what. While the Taste Society pulled strings to allow Connor or their other chief investigators to work as a police consultant on any case involving the lethal poisoning of a client, Hunt and Connor had a relationship that was more competitive than cooperative. And the results had always been interesting.

Connor called Hunt, putting him on the car's speakers so I could hear too. "I'd like to talk to the attorney leading the class action lawsuit against Knightley. Want to send a uniform along so we don't double up, or will my notes suffice?"

Hunt took long enough to reply that I was wondering whether the line had dropped out when he spoke. "Look, Stiles, I'm going to level with you. We have so many cases piling up right now that my officers are never going to see their families again at this rate, and I'm sick of diverting resources and staff from equally important cases involving normal people every time some VIP shithead gets himself killed. So while I don't like you, I do respect your investigative skills, and I'm going to give you a longer leash than usual on this one. Just keep me in the loop and make sure you catch the bad guy, or my head's on the chopping block."

Connor didn't miss a beat. "As much as I'd like to see your head on the chopping block, Commander, I'd like to see the bastard who did this behind bars even more, so you can rest easy."

"I won't be resting, Stiles. Neither will you. Now get on with it." Hunt disconnected.

"Gosh," I said. "That was very diplomatic of the pair of you."

Connor gave one of his infinitesimal shrugs. "As he said, we don't like each other, but we respect each other on a professional level." He waited a minute before adding, "And I suspect old Hunt's going soft now he's got a girlfriend of his own to miss seeing."

That made me smirk. Until my thoughts turned to wishing Connor had a girlfriend of his own to miss seeing. Lucky we arrived at our destination soon after.

Jeffrey R. Dimond, the attorney heading up the class action lawsuit against Rick, did not look the way a prosecutor should. Midforties. Medium brown wavy hair that stopped shy of falling into his eyes. An oval face that was pleasant without crossing the line into good-looking or interesting. And a genuine smile that lit up his eyes.

He just seemed too *nice* to be in the profession that was the butt of so many jokes.

What do you call five hundred lawyers at the bottom of the ocean? My father had asked me once.

What? I'd asked.

A good start.

I couldn't imagine Mr. Dimond attracting that kind of sentiment. Then again, he wasn't prosecuting me.

We sat down in his office, a room that expressed the assurance of wealth but gave nothing away in terms of personality or taste. That was more along the lines of what I would've envisaged for an attorney. Connor explained why we were there, and Jeffrey nodded, his smile fading.

"I saw the news. It's going to be a blow to my clients."

"You don't think they'll be glad to see him dead?" Connor asked, blunt as my cousin's pug after it misjudged the dog door.

There was no surprise on Mr. Dimond's face. "I assumed since you're here that the police suspect foul play." He steepled his fingers. "I'm not saying they'll grieve his passing, but a conviction of fraud would've gone a long way toward the success of this class action. Now we'll have to convince the jury both that he committed the scam and that my clients suffered losses."

"So the lawsuit will go ahead?"

"Most probably, yes. Assuming we're allowed to proceed with the deceased person's estate being substituted for the defendant. But that's unlikely to help our cause."

"Where would you put the likelihood of the class action trial being successful before Mr. Knightley's death?"

"How much do you know about it?"

"The barest of bones. Enlighten us."

"All right. Cold call fraud cases are complex and difficult. The scammers behind them are sophisticated, changing their operation frequently, avoiding face-to-face contact, using overseas accounts that are much harder to dig into, and carrying it all out with technology designed to leave no trace or trail. That makes it near impossible for law enforcement to successfully investigate seeing as the scammers just dissolve everything and move on to the next scheme. Which makes prosecution difficult too since strong evidence is very hard to come by, and yet the onus is on us to provide it. If Mr. Knightley had been convicted of the criminal charges, our class action would've had an excellent likelihood of success—"

"What if he'd been acquitted instead?"

"It would've made things harder. But no harder than it will be now with the prosecution dismissed. A criminal trial needs to be proven beyond reasonable doubt while a civil case only needs what is called the preponderance of evidence—which in laymen's terms means enough evidence to make it more likely than not that our claims are true. Ultimately, I'd say this case will come down to who the jury empathizes with. But elderly victims like my clients have strong jury appeal, so I was optimistic."

"And with the defendant dead? How does that change things?"

"I would speculate that my clients will want to pursue the lawsuit anyway, but if anything, I imagine Mr. Knightley's premature death may make the jury feel more sympathetically toward him. The other side of all this is proving the defendant has money, and it's impossible to say whether it will make tracking that down harder or easier. As long as he was alive, there was a chance he'd give in to temptation and tap into his funds, which might allow us to prove they exist. On the other hand, his death puts an end to any further activities to hide them, and something may be found as his estate is sorted through."

"Any idea which of your clients might be more interested in revenge than financial recuperation?" Connor asked.

I guessed it was worth a try.

"Client-attorney privilege, Mr. Stiles. Besides, with the exception of Patty Wilkinson who's the lead plaintiff, I haven't spent much time with any of them. I suggest you speak with Ms. Wilkinson. I believe she's been something of a community leader and rallying point through all this and knows everyone in the class action."

"Thank you."

"I'm glad to assist. But if you want my opinion, the timing is off. Why attack Mr. Knightley now when the criminal case is finally about to go to trial? Most of them have been waiting twelve months or more for this moment, hoping to see him behind bars. I doubt you'll find the person you're looking for among my clients."

5

PATTY WILKINSON AGREED to meet with us in an hour, so we stopped for a bite to eat at a sushi place. I resolved to wait until our meals were half-gone before making my request to Connor.

The restaurant offered traditional Japanese decor with short, simple stools that made him appear larger than he was.

My hulking friend Mr. Black would've required one for each butt cheek.

Within a few minutes of us sitting down, an efficient waiter in a white uniform delivered our orders. I'd chosen raw salmon and avocado inside-out rolls and a matcha green tea milkshake. Connor had opted for one of their variety plates and freshly squeezed orange juice.

I let him eat in peace for a while, entertaining myself by imagining Mr. Black trying to balance on one of the tiny stools like an elephant at the circus.

Then I put down my chopsticks. "Connor?"

"Yes?"

"Um, how would you feel if I took lead on this case? Unofficially, I mean."

"That depends on why you're asking."

Fair enough. There were a lot of reasons. Primarily because I was thinking it might help his fears about my safety if he saw how much more competent I'd become since we first started out together. That maybe he'd realize my newfound confidence was a good thing.

Then again, Sophia had been more than competent and it hadn't saved her. But no one was safe, not really. I could die in a car accident tomorrow. In fact, I was probably *more* likely to die in a car accident than any other physical danger. Besides, how unlucky could Connor be? I mean, I knew it was *possible* for lightning to strike the same place twice, but to assume it would was like spending his life avoiding every location lightning had ever struck, just in case. It was irrational—and Connor was usually anything but.

Plus couldn't he see that I was taking on the same risk with him? His job in high-end security and murder investigations wasn't exactly a safe one.

I also wanted to take the lead because for our relationship to succeed, he was going to have to start treating me as an equal in our investigative work as well as the rest of our lives. If he hadn't had the ability to veto me on the human-trafficking case, I would never have needed to hide my plan from him. Both of us had to learn to work together on the same footing and with more consideration for each other's feelings.

But I didn't want to tell him any of that. At least not yet, so I told him my other reason.

"Because I'm not sure I want to be a Shade for the rest of my working life, and I'm exploring my options."

Yes, that's right, mister. I wouldn't always be putting my life on the line for rich strangers. Think about *that*.

It caught his attention. "Okay, I'll allow it. But the buck stops with me, so I'll be covering anything you miss. And you can't tell Hunt."

"That goes without saying."

"If anyone recognizes you from that YouTube video or any other press, we'll switch around and come up with an excuse for your presence. But other than that, she's all yours."

"Got it. Thank you." I was a little surprised—and touched—by how easily he'd agreed.

We lapsed into silence for a bit while we concentrated on our food.

"You don't want a dog, do you?" Connor asked.

"What?"

"Or know of anyone else who'd like one?"

"Why? What kind of dog?"

"I don't know, a medium-sized, mixed-breed kind. And it's a long story."

"I've got time."

"It's not very interesting. I've just acquired a dog against my will, and I'm trying to find a home for her."

"Well, what's she like?" I didn't know anybody who wanted a dog, except me anyway, but I was curious. Sadly, I didn't think it was responsible for me to adopt a pet right now. My life was too . . . Well, I was trying not to think about the state of my life. But it wouldn't be fair to bring a pup into it, no matter how much I might want to.

"She's brown. Sheds a lot. Eats a lot. Poops a lot. Likes to sit on your feet and hates classical music."

I tried to stifle a snort and wound up with milkshake in my nose for my efforts. "She hates classical music? How do you know?" I couldn't ask the question without breaking into giggles.

Connor scowled. "She howls whenever I play it."

Since it turned out I couldn't contain my mirth, I stopped trying. I clutched my stomach helplessly and laughed.

Connor was unimpressed.

"She h-howls when you play classical music?" I could barely get the words out, and people were starting to give me the side-eye. I didn't know who was responsible for this delightful twist of fate, but I wanted to throw them a party.

Connor made a show of looking at his watch and stood up. "Forget I asked. And for the record, I'm already second-guessing letting you take lead on this case."

THE LEAD PLAINTIFF Patty Wilkinson was in her late sixties, older than Mae, younger than Etta. She'd allowed her hair to go gray and was dressed for comfort in stretchy pants, a simple, loose-fitting top, and sturdy flats. But the effect was quietly dignified rather than sloppy. She received us in her formal dining room and served us strong black tea out of flowery teacups. The picture of innocence.

Except if Etta's "harmless little old lady outfit" had taught me anything, it was that the picture of innocence might only go skin-deep, and I knew better than to underestimate the older generation.

Even if they did live in a tangerine cottage with pink jasmine growing over the latticework.

To get around the problem of my lack of authority or credentials, Connor had introduced us at the door, truthfully saying he was a consultant with the LAPD, and I was his colleague. It was a handy loophole that implied I was working with the police without explicitly lying about it. He'd also revealed that Richard Knightley had been murdered since we'd have no reason to take up her time if he hadn't been.

As the attorney predicted, Patty didn't seem pleased about Rick's death.

"Sounds like he got off lightly if you ask me, and it's not going to help any of his victims, is it?"

She returned her teacup to its saucer and slumped against the backrest of the ornate timber dining chair.

"You know, when I started this lawsuit I was doing it for me and my kids, because I lost a bunch of money and I didn't work my tush off for fifty years to have my daughters' inheritance stolen by some lazy scoundrel. I was fortunate enough to have plenty left, but it was the principle of the thing."

I made the mistake of sipping my own tea and covered my grimace at the bitter, overbrewed tannin flavor by nodding sympathetically. With any luck, Patty would put my twisted features down to distress over the situation she was describing. And I was empathetic. According to Lyle's list, Patty had lost $70,000. Not as much as some, but a significant amount. A $100,000 debt had uprooted my entire life.

However Patty interpreted my twisted expression, she continued her tale. "But over the months of preparation, meeting other victims and hearing their stories, it's become about so much more than that. Some of these people lost everything, and this is their only hope of getting more than a fraction of it back. Many of them have experienced depression, some to the point of having suicidal thoughts, and there's a lot of self-loathing and blaming themselves going around. You have to understand—imagine staring down the barrel of ten, twenty, even thirty years of poverty, with your life's work ripped away from you and a workforce that doesn't want you anymore."

"Ouch," I said. I was supposed to stay objective, but it

was hard when the suspects were victims themselves.

Patty leaned forward. "Exactly. The criminal prosecution was good. We all wanted to see Knightley in prison. But it's this lawsuit that gave them hope, a purpose, a community of people who could understand what they've been going through."

That was good then, wasn't it? "From what I gather, your class action shouldn't be too disadvantaged by his death. Your attorney thought you still had a decent chance of winning if it came to a trial."

She pursed her lips. "Maybe we'll still win the lawsuit, but there are other repercussions. The media is going to stop talking about Knightley's scamming activity and start talking about his murder. I wanted to create public awareness. That's why I've been hitting up every publicity angle I can think of. It's the only way to effectively counter it, you know."

"Sorry, counter what?"

"The scamming of good, honest folk." Patty's words and hand gestures were growing more animated. "The police can't do it. The technology's getting more advanced, and the scammers are getting smarter and more numerous. It's estimated that older Americans lose over thirty-six *billion* dollars to financial scams and abuse every year. Not all of that's cold-calling schemes like Knightley's, but it's one of the more sophisticated ways to do it, and people have no clue how prevalent this stuff is. They say one in eighteen senior citizens are victims of financial scams, fraud, or abuse every single year, and that's just looking at those of us with our faculties all intact. It gets worse as folks' mental faculties start to decline."

"Wow. I had no idea it was such a big problem." I didn't have to ham up my response. I was so appalled by what I was hearing that I sipped my tea again in my distraction. *Ugh.*

Patty's tea sat forgotten on the dining table. Which seemed a shame when she was the only one enjoying it.

She nodded decisively. "You're not alone. That's the whole point; people need to know. Never invest in anything, never give out your personal details, and never transfer any money as a result of a cold call—no matter what the person on the other end is saying or how official they sound. You can't even trust a phone number they tell you to call for confirmation. Some people have been instructed to call the police or the credit card fraud number on the back of their card, spoken to someone who sounded official so it checks out, and then whoosh, gone. Scammers can temporarily hijack calls and phone numbers. So I wanted this class action to send a message to all the thieving lowlifes out there who think they can get away with it and, most importantly, raise public awareness that this stuff is out there."

Whatever Patty Wilkinson might be trying to hide from us, I believed her passion for spreading the word was genuine. She seemed to want to make sure *we* knew before we walked out her door.

Of course, being cheated raised a lot of strong emotions. She had wound up focusing hers on helping and educating others, but what about the rest of the victims? Or what if she found out that Isaac Anand was plotting to ensure Richard won both cases? That changed the game dramatically. But I wasn't ready to spill the beans on that one yet.

"Thank you, Mrs. Wilkinson. Both for giving us a rundown and for your public service. But I'm afraid I have to ask, with the devastating circumstances you mentioned some of the victims have found themselves in, surely getting revenge would be tempting?"

She shrugged. "Sure, but murder for stealing doesn't make sense. It's better to get your money back. Look, I'm not going to pretend someone might not have thought about revenge, but we've talked about this in our group meetings and agreed that it's best to do everything through the proper channels. There's much more chance of getting our money, and the publicity is miles better this way too."

If she did know about Isaac and Richard's agreement, she was doing a convincing job of pretending otherwise.

"Even so," I said, "we'd appreciate it if you could tell us who among your group might have the skill set or connections to hack into a security system or enough money left to pay for someone else to do it."

She gazed at me in disappointment, and I got a fleeting idea of what it might've been like to be one of her daughters. I hoped they were high achievers. Was she upset that we weren't getting the message? Or did she feel it would be a betrayal to her fellow plaintiffs? Either way, after a moment of making my insides shrivel, she cooperated. "All right. I'll have a think and get their details for you."

She retrieved reading glasses and a well-used address book from a drawer in the china cabinet and started flicking through it slowly.

Connor shifted his weight, a sign of impatience.

"Maybe you could send the list through when you're finished?" I suggested.

She rested the book on the dining table and sent me a stern look over her glasses. "If that's what you want. But I hope you're considering other avenues, young lady. Someone immoral and ruthless enough to be capable of what Richard Knightley did is bound to have more personal enemies."

She was right. But how many of Rick's personal enemies had reason to kill Isaac Anand as well?

———

PATTY'S HOME WASN'T FAR from the 27th Street Community Police Station, so we stopped in to swap our early findings with Hunt. We needed any information the LAPD had learned about Isaac Anand, and Hunt needed to hear what we'd found out about Richard. Especially that Knightley Senior had said our two murder victims had been working together to clear Rick's name.

That little detail offered a plausible motive for one of the scammed parties to kill them both.

The police station was an uninspiring two-story gray brick building, made even more uninspiring because most of my memories here weren't happy ones. I'd never been on the top floor, but the ground level was fitted out with additional gray bricks, cold dark tiles, and an unnecessarily low ceiling. Connor and I entered the open-plan office area and located Hunt's workstation, one of the few in the room with enough space to fit three people around it.

His desk was less bare than when I'd last visited. First there was a photo of him and Etta in an unadorned wooden frame. It was a selfie of the two of them at a lookout somewhere, and it might've been the first time I'd seen Hunt smile without any meanness in it. Second, there was a half-empty plate of cookies next to his coffee mug. I peered at them, curious about what kinds of cookies he favored since he'd thrown the ones I'd gifted him in the trash (he'd cited police protocol around food items coming through the mail, but he'd taken a certain relish in telling me about it). They looked familiar . . . Like the chocolate-chip-and-salted-caramel batch I'd baked for Etta last week in fact.

Hunt caught me staring. "Etta made those for me, and I'm not sharing in case you were wondering."

Etta *made* them for him? I bit my tongue and tried for a blank expression. I'd never witnessed Etta bake anything in her life. I wasn't sure she knew how, which was kind of weird for a woman of her era, come to think of it. But if she was passing off my baking as her own to Hunt, I wasn't going to out her.

Connor took up the slack in the conversation while I sat there in bewilderment. I didn't interrupt. Hunt firmly believed civilians with no training ought to leave investigating to the professionals, and he'd be more receptive with the report coming from Connor. One of many reasons we wouldn't be mentioning how I'd taken the lead on Patty's interview.

When Connor got to the part about Isaac helping Rick clear his name, Hunt looked thoughtful.

"Hmm, that might explain why we found the prosecution's list of alleged scam victims on Anand's computer. I have people going through his files searching for links between them as well as anything else of interest, but that's all we've got so far. They've found some heavily encrypted files that we're trying to crack—"

He was interrupted by the arrival of another police officer. "Commander, there's—"

"Is this important, Baker? I'm kind of busy right now."

Baker swallowed but kept eye contact. "Well, sir, there's a guy who walked in off the street saying he killed Richard Knightley and Isaac Anand."

6

CONNOR AND I WERE ALLOWED to witness the voluntary confession through the one-way glass.

The tiny room with its featureless gray walls, chipped table, and three chairs wasn't where I'd want to spend my last hours of freedom, but then I'd never had the desire to kill two people either. I looked at the man who had.

He was an overweight fellow in his early seventies with thin, wire-frame glasses, a short mustache, and a head neatly divided front to back where his hair had quit growing or persevered. Not the image my brain had conjured up when imagining who might be behind the high-tech murder. His name was Stanley Cox, and he'd been in the tech industry for an impressive forty-two years.

Last year he'd been fighting retirement boredom, feelings

of uselessness, a strained relationship with his wife, and jealousy of his wealthier friends when Richard Knightley (under another name, naturally) had talked him into investing their life savings into a brilliant new investment scheme that would return triple the interest rates of their current savings account. Think how pleased his wife would be when he surprised her with the extra cash.

That had been the last he'd seen of their life savings.

His wife had been furious and kicked him out of the house—the single asset they still owned.

He hadn't been able to get welfare (due to the asset he still technically shared with his wife) or a job since. And so he'd apparently assigned himself the job of murdering the man responsible.

Connor passed me the list Lyle Knightley had given us. Stanley Cox was on it. He'd lost $800,000. I gulped. More money than I'd earned in my lifetime, let alone accumulated. Then again, I wasn't sure how meaningful that was since my current worth was approximately negative eighty grand.

"Tell us how you did it," Hunt ordered.

"It was dead simple." I winced at Stanley's choice of expression. "I just hacked into Mr. Anand's security system, wiped all known persons from its database, and changed the formula it used to calculate how much sedative to inject per pound. Then I kept a watch on the house till they were both in there and activated the security mode."

"Why'd you do it?"

Stanley threw back his head and laughed, his stomach

jiggling with bitter amusement. "Well geez, if you don't know that, it's no wonder the police department can't catch all those bastard scammers out there."

"I'm asking for your statement on the matter, Mr. Cox," Hunt growled.

Stanley tried to fold his arms before remembering they were cuffed to the table. "Right. I'm one of over a hundred trusting idiots that Knightley stole from. Lots were lucky or smart enough to only lose ten or twenty grand. I lost everything. Including my wife."

"Do you really think your wife will take you back now?"

"No. But it made me feel better."

"Why last night, just before the criminal trial began?"

"Why not? I know how these things work. The asshole who can afford expensive lawyers gets off scot-free—or at worst goes to some fancy prison nicer than where his victims are living nowadays. You call that justice?"

I thought about Patty's faith in the worthiness of her cause. She'd gone to a lot of trouble to convince everyone that there was a better way, including Stanley I assumed. But Stanley hadn't been persuaded.

Maybe he didn't like her oversteeped tea either.

Hunt's mind was on more practical matters.

"Why not just shoot him?"

"I thought he might have bodyguards. Figured I had one shot so I better do it cleanly. Besides, I've spent a lot more hours with a keyboard than a gun."

"Why take out Isaac Anand too?"

"Because he was helping Knightley rig the court cases somehow, and anyone who collaborates with that prick deserves to die."

Yikes. I hoped he hadn't seen that YouTube video.

But if Stanley knew about their collaboration, had Patty known about it as well?

Cox was still answering. "That and I read about Anand's new security system in an online tech magazine, and it seemed like a good opportunity if I could hack into it."

"Why walk in here and confess?"

"Because I want the world to know why the bastard died. And who stood up to him."

"You want to be a hero?"

"Your words, not mine. That guy needed to be killed. Now, are we done with the questions? I'm tired and I wouldn't mind getting acquainted with my cell bed. I suspect it won't be too much worse than the hovel I've been living in anyway . . ."

Yikes. For someone who'd presumably spent his first seventy-something years on earth without killing anyone, Stanley was very nonchalant about his double murder.

"No, Mr. Cox, we're just getting started," Hunt said. Then the questions began again.

———

THREE HOURS LATER, STANLEY COX got his wish to get acquainted with his new bed (a bed he was going to spend an awful lot of time in without any bail money, and one I'd tried out myself), and Connor and I left the station.

I felt flat, wrung out, and exhausted, which seemed foolish considering it was the easiest case we'd ever solved. But the whole situation left me saddened. Three lives extinguished or ruined forever, and for what? And selfishly, I was disappointed I'd lost my excuse to spend time with Connor in a casual environment—one where we could share jokes and experiences and remind him how much he liked having me around.

Of course, I didn't express any of that. Instead, I made myself smirk in his direction. "Not that I've been keeping track, but I think that's the quickest we've ever solved a case. Maybe you should let me take lead more often."

His face softened in amusement. "Arrogance doesn't become you, Avery."

"Why not? Do you have dibs on that status?"

That got me a glance. "My confidence is well-founded."

Unlike someone else's I know was the implication. Oops, dangerous ground. Time to change the subject. "So what are you going to do with your unexpectedly free evening? Take your dog for a walk?"

"Maria would have already done that, and she isn't my dog."

If it weren't for our breakup, I would've volunteered to walk her and then dragged Connor along with me.

I suppose that answered what *I* would be doing with my

unexpectedly free evening; with the case over, I could give my full attention to winning him back. On that note, now was an ideal opportunity to make the first move. He had free time. He was already with me. I just needed to figure out what my first move might be . . .

A few minutes of racking my brain later, I realized with a spurt of anxiety that we were turning onto my street. So soon. I had to buy myself more time to plan.

"I've got something for you that I think might make your life easier," I told him.

"Oh?" He pulled up outside my apartment.

"Hang on, I'll grab it for you."

Instead of waiting in the car, he accompanied me up the two flights of stairs. The familiarity of the occurrence brought a pang to my chest, reinforcing how much I needed to take hold of the opening Stanley Cox had afforded me.

I darted inside and rummaged around the kitchen while my mind continued to race. Connor didn't come in. My mental workout was interrupted by my phone buzzing. It was a text message from Etta.

Gee, for someone whose boyfriend died last night, you don't look too upset.

Okay, definitely ignoring that one. I found what I was after and sealed a generous handful of them in a ziplock bag, then went outside to where Connor was standing by the railing, looking out over the street.

"Here," I said, thrusting the bag into his hands. "They're

homemade dog treats I make up for Dudley: dehydrated chicken, beef, and lamb heart. You should try playing classical music quietly and for short periods of time—whatever you can get away with without making your dog howl—and reward her for being quiet with some of these. If you feed her a bunch of them while the music is on, she'll start to associate treats with it and might even end up loving Vivaldi as much as you do."

He eyed the contents doubtfully. "Thank you. But I'm not keeping her."

"Sure, but in the meantime. While you find her a good home."

Connor let out a slow breath and pocketed the bag.

I watched a pigeon strutting its stuff for a second and mustered my courage. "Have coffee with me. Please. We need to talk. I didn't get a chance to think or respond the other day, and you'd only just found out about what I'd planned with Doctor Dan. But you love me, right? And I love you. Surely we can work this out."

Beside me, Connor went completely still. "Are you prepared to refrain from any behavior I deem reckless?"

I'd thought about it, a lot, and I wasn't willing to give up on helping others for the sake of my own neck. Or heart for that matter. But Connor's real issue had been my not telling him about the plan or taking anyone as backup, and I was sure we could come to a reasonable compromise going forward. I just needed to convince Connor of that. "I can't, I'm sorry. But—"

"Then talking won't fix this." Without meeting my gaze, he turned and headed down the stairs.

No. He couldn't walk away from me again! "Then what will?" I demanded.

He stopped. Turned back. Met my eyes. "Do you really think if I had an answer to that, I'd be walking away right now?"

The pain in his words stole the breath from my lungs.

Then he walked away. Again.

My phone buzzed with another message from Etta.

Oh, well you look proper upset now. I'll come straight over.

7

I DIDN'T FEEL UP TO FACING Etta in my current state, especially since I couldn't tell her the truth. So in a moment of weakness (or strength, I wasn't sure which), I sent her a text.

Maybe tomorrow? I'm heading out and need to get ready.

As soon as I pressed the send button, I regretted it. I'd just banished myself from the apartment, which precluded me from curling up in bed with Meow. The one activity I felt up to. What the heck was I going to do with the rest of the day *now*?

I could visit Oliver at the Fox. But that would require me to get presentable, smile, and make conversation.

I could go to the library. At least there I wouldn't have to talk to anyone, but I didn't think they'd let me bring Meow.

Or I could wait half an hour to regain my composure, come up with an alternate version of events for Etta, then text her to say my thing had been canceled and invite her over for a movie. Yeah, that one sounded decent. The movie would stop her from questioning me too closely, and the half an hour I'd bought myself would do me a world of good. Yep, turned out my moment of strength or weakness was a stroke of genius.

I had just crawled into bed, paid the petting toll to persuade Meow to settle down with me, and opened a book when my phone rang.

My first thought was that it might be Connor calling to say he'd reconsidered.

I was so close and so far away at the same time . . .

It was Harper, Connor's sister. "Hey, Iz. I was wondering if you could help me out with something?"

"Sure, is everything okay?"

Despite her relation to Connor, she was nothing like him. Well, except for the physical resemblance.

"Yeah, I just need backup picking up a few things from an ex-boyfriend's place."

"As long as it doesn't involve stealing his car or anything." It wasn't an unreasonable caveat when it came to Harper. She was a mechanic who loved flashy sports cars and made a habit of "borrowing" clients' vehicles for "test drives."

"Pfft, spoilsport. I'll pick you up in fifteen."

"No, wait! What's the address? I'll meet you there." She also enjoyed pushing the cars she borrowed to the limits of their capabilities. Me and my motion sickness enjoyed it less. "I'm, um, in the mood to take the Corvette for a spin."

"You're avoiding getting in the car with me, aren't you?"

"You do go faster than I prefer." *Because I'm too young to die.*

"Fine. I promise to be good. It's the middle of the day, and there are no quiet, winding roads along the way, so I wouldn't have much chance to enjoy myself anyway. I'll pick you up in fifteen."

She hung up before I could argue further.

I guess it was only fair I'd have to pay for my lie to Etta by having to go out. I spent ten of the fifteen minutes with Meow then forced myself upright. Harper knocked on the door a minute later. Four minutes early.

She'd probably been driving like a demon.

The demon driver gave me a hug. She was tall and lean and dressed in her usual tank top and jeans, her long espresso-brown hair hanging down her back in a careless braid. "How are you holding up without my idiot brother?" she asked.

Guess that meant Mae hadn't told her about my "new boyfriend" then. I bit my lip. "I'd prefer not to talk about it."

"Sure." She waited for a beat. "Sounds like something Connor would say."

I shot her a dirty look, and she raised her hands in feigned innocence.

"Okay, okay. Less talk, more action. Let's get out of here then."

It was when I was clicking my seat belt into place that I noticed Harper had a gun holstered to her belt.

"Um . . . What did you say we were doing again?"

Harper followed my gaze downward.

"Well, you know how my dating strategy often turns out badly?"

"Yeah . . ." I thought strategy was a generous term for it. As near as I could tell, her method meant she selected her dates based on the cars they drove rather than any character traits they might possess. But as alien as that seemed to me, she'd admitted in confidence that her reckless dating life was a way of taking the edge off her appetite for excitement—an appetite she'd curbed for the sake of her mother and brother who'd worry themselves sick if she joined the Army.

So who was *I* to judge?

She started the car—it was a cherry-red Ford Mustang GT today—and pulled away from the curb. "This date wound up worse than usual. The bastard got violent and shoved me into a wall."

"What? Are you okay? Did you report him?"

"Ugh, I'm fine, but there's no proof, so it's my word against his and all that jazz. Anyway, I have a few things at his place I want back, and if I have to shoot the jerk, I need a witness who can confirm that he attacked me first."

Holy cow. "Um, are you sure you shouldn't get a more qualified backup partner?"

"What's wrong with you?"

A lot of things. But I was pretty sure she was asking why I was unsuitable rather than asking me to list out my problems. "Let's just say I'm not as handy with a wrench as you are."

Harper grinned. "Not many people are. But you'll do fine. Besides, who else am I meant to call? Connor? You know as well as I do that he'll overreact in his need to protect me." She glanced at me apologetically. "I'm really sorry about that, by the way."

"Not your fault. And I still don't want to talk about it."

"Noted."

Unfortunately, I couldn't argue with her logic. After all, it was the same reasoning that had led me to tackle the human-trafficking doctor alone.

"What about Mae?" I asked. She might be a lot older, but she was also a lot more experienced with guns and a host of other useful things.

"Mom's an even worse option. You know that. She'd pretend it was no big deal, then redouble her efforts to background check and keep tabs on every man I ever pass within ten feet of. I can't cope with any more."

Harper was exaggerating, but I could see her point.

She parked the car outside a basic bungalow-style home with a front yard that was more concrete than grass. It seemed the man we were going to see spent his time and money on his car and not much else.

"It'll be fine. Teddy probably won't even be here. But grab your Taser just in case."

"*Teddy?*" I muttered, rummaging through my bag for the Taser and tucking it into my waistband.

I thought wistfully of the Fox or the library, then climbed out of the car still grumbling. It wasn't fair that I got all the blame for being a danger magnet when half the time I was dragged unwillingly into it by the likes of Etta and now Harper. Somehow they managed to never get hurt though.

We walked up the concrete driveway. Weeds growing through the cracks had been sprayed but not removed, and the timber front steps were in need of replacing. Harper nimbly skipped the third one and rang the doorbell.

A well-built man opened the door, and I amended my assessment to thinking he spent all his time and money on his car *and* his muscles. His petulant expression as he addressed Harper seemed at odds with his physique.

"I hope you're here to fix my car. It's been acting funny since last night."

"Oh? Maybe it objects to violence against women," Harper said, shoving past him into the house.

"What's that supposed to mean?"

While he was distracted by her brazen move, I snuck inside too.

Harper was speeding toward a door on the other side of the living room.

Teddy trailed after her, looking more bewildered than angry so far. "Hey, you can't just barge in here and waltz around my house."

"It really seems like I can since I just did," Harper pointed out. She opened the door she'd reached and stepped inside what seemed to be the laundry. "Hey, Iz, can you help me carry some things?"

I skirted around Teddy, keeping as much distance as possible, and joined Harper where she was digging through a pile of washing. She wasn't being neat about it either. Jocks and socks were flying everywhere.

"Ah, there you are," she said happily to a pair of blue overalls she'd uncovered from the pile.

"Seriously?" I hissed at her. "We're doing this for overalls?"

She threw them at me and kept digging. "Do you know how hard it is to find overalls that fit me? No one likes a saggy-crotched mechanic."

Thankfully, Teddy was keeping his distance. For now. Harper thrust a few more pairs of overalls at me and then grabbed a toolbox off the bench. I held out my hand resignedly to take it from her and almost dropped the darn thing when she released its weight. The blue metal box must've been lined with lead and filled with rocks, but she'd picked it up as if it weighed nothing.

Teddy scowled at the new state of his laundry room. "You better be cleaning up that mess you made."

"I'm a mechanic, not a cleaner, remember?" Harper said sweetly. She brushed past him and into another room.

I followed after her, trying to appear cool and confident and like the toolbox was a handy weapon rather than something I was worried about dropping on my toes. How was I supposed to get to my Taser carrying all this stuff?

Harper had led us into a bedroom this time.

Teddy didn't look happy about it. "What the hell do you want in here?"

She didn't bother to answer. Just slid open a drawer on the nightstand, pulled out a book, and plonked it on top of the armful of overalls I was holding. The title read *Zen and the Art of Motorcycle Maintenance*. Harper saw me eyeing it. "If you want a book about Zen or motorcycles, don't read that one."

Huh?

She went to the kitchen next and opened the fridge.

Teddy was looking pissed now, his jaw set as he tracked Harper's movements, but I thought it was a positive sign he had his arms crossed. Not the posture you'd choose if you were considering taking a swing at someone.

Harper was either oblivious or superb at pretending to be. I was betting on the latter. She grasped a jar of jalapeños and held them up with a flourish. Grilled cheese and jalapeño sandwiches was a Stiles family favorite, and it was an effort not to think about the times I'd made them for Connor and myself late at night.

"Right," said Harper. "I think that's all my stuff. Thanks for your cooperation, Teddy. Let's hope our paths never cross again."

Teddy moved to block the front door, his arms still folded but his posture threatening. "You're not leaving until you fix my car. That's your job, isn't it? And you owe me something for all those dinners."

Harper added the jalapeños to my teetering armload with a nose wrinkle of apology, then marched over to face him. "You really want to trust me with your keys just now? You go right ahead and give them to me, honey."

"I'll supervise," he sneered.

"You sure about that? Because I'm just as good at sabotaging cars as I am at fixing them."

Teddy's cheeks went pink.

"You'll have to find someone else to service your parts now, dickhead. Think about that before you lay your hands on anyone in anger again."

I held my breath, releasing it only when Teddy shuffled aside, his face mulish.

Harper waited for me to exit first, then shut the door with a bang.

"That went well," she said cheerfully.

I supposed her assessment was accurate enough. At least no one had gotten physically aggressive.

But her grin was a little too victorious to be explained by that alone. "Lucky for us he's too stupid to have connected the dots between his temper tantrum, his mechanic ex-girlfriend, and his car acting funny."

I gaped at her. She might have mentioned she'd sabotaged his car in revenge *before* dragging me in there.

Harper misread the reason for my disbelief. "I know, it hurt me to tamper with that beautiful Lexus, but he was such a jackass of a man I couldn't help myself. Besides, it'll be going to waste without me around. I swear a woman pushing a stroller overtook us once while *he* was driving."

"You don't need to justify it to me," I said. At least not the tampering with his car part. Since we'd gotten out alive, I decided to let the other part go as well. "But would you mind carrying this toolbox?" The whole left side of my body was starting to ache.

"Oh, sorry." She took it from me like it weighed nothing at all. "Guess I should've grabbed that last."

———————

WE LOADED HARPER'S things into her borrowed Mustang, and she offered to take me out to dinner by way of thanks.

I was hungry but in no state to be out in public, so I requested takeout instead.

"What kind of takeout?" Harper asked.

I spotted a lurid red KFC sign up ahead. "That'll do."

She snagged a single drumstick for herself and handed me the delicious-smelling paper bag. "When I offered to buy your dinner, deep-fried chicken wasn't exactly what I had in mind. I don't suppose it'll be enough to buy your silence about the whole Teddy thing, will it?"

To not say anything to Connor or Mae, she meant.

I wasn't sure how I felt about that. Hiding my plans from Connor had caused a lot of trouble, but then this was in a very different league and wasn't my story to tell. Nor was there likely to be any further danger as a result of it.

"My silence comes cheap," I told Harper. "So long as you promise you won't go near him again. And will call me straight away if he puts two and two together about his car problems and threatens you."

She sighed at my final stipulation. "I suppose that's better than what either of my family members would've demanded from me. You've got yourself a deal."

"And you've got yourself some crotch-fitting overalls."

She grinned. "Good point. I should be thanking you. Thank you."

I pulled out the box of assorted deep-fried chicken and saluted her with it. "Glad to help."

Harper waited until I'd bitten into a delectable, crispy wing before speaking again. "On that subject, are you sure I can't be of help with you and Connor stuff? I know him pretty well, in all his frustrating glory."

My disastrous conversation with him came rushing back, and my bribery chicken suddenly seemed less delectable.

Since I didn't lose my appetite easily, I was forced to consider her offer. I needed to keep my cover intact given there was a high chance Mae or Etta would tell Harper about my supposed relationship with Richard Knightley at some point. But maybe I could ask my questions in such a way that it seemed as if I was trying to understand what had happened between Connor and me—rather than trying to win him back less than twenty-four hours after my "boyfriend" died. I'd been surprised today by the strength of his reaction, the depth of his pain. Perhaps if I understood more of what he'd been through, I could work out a better way to help him past it.

I nibbled half-heartedly at the chicken wing to keep up appearances, then asked, "Can you tell me more about the whole Sophia thing? I mean, not the details of her death but what Connor went through."

Harper blew out a breath. "Crap. I guess I did offer." She squared her shoulders. "It was horrible. He was devastated over it and almost destroyed himself and his company trying to hunt down her killer. He stopped sleeping, Maria could barely convince him to eat, and he pulled so much of his security team off their normal duties to help him search that he lost a bunch of big clients."

"Oh." It was hard to imagine the strong, self-assured, and seemingly invincible man I knew broken. I felt like an insensitive oaf, and my heart ached all over again for him.

"After watching him spiral for months, me, Mom, Maria, and a few guys from his company held an intervention. Amazingly, he pulled himself together. Started looking after himself. Got his company up and running again. And stopped searching . . . I think he had to quit cold turkey, or he wouldn't have been able to quit at all."

I let out a shuddery breath, not unlike Harper's a moment ago. "Wow."

Harper's next words flipped my world on its axis again. "After that, his already overprotective nature got even more over the top, and he hasn't really dated anyone since, until you."

Until me.

He'd taken a chance on me. The same way I'd chosen to risk my heart with him after a long dry period following my divorce. Mae had told me the first time I met her that he hadn't brought a girl home in ages, but I'd figured she was mostly jesting. I'd had no idea what a big deal it was. Sure, I'd been honored he'd opened up to me, dropped some of his walls, but not even that had I understood the significance of.

My chicken lay forgotten. The grease congealing against the cardboard. I no longer had it in me to keep up appearances.

It was all I could do to keep from crying.

"Look," Harper said, "I don't know the details of your falling out, and he's frustratingly controlling and overprotective as a brother, so I can hardly imagine how annoying he must be as a boyfriend. But . . . if you could work it out, well, I think you're good for him. And underneath the annoying, I think he's a pretty amazing person. The best kind."

"Thank you." I managed to squeeze the words past the lump in my throat. It meant a lot that she thought I was good for him. For all their differences, she knew her brother well. And loved him deeply.

Like I did.

I had some serious contemplation to do.

Harper grabbed my hand and pressed it in her callused palm. "No problem."

We drove without speaking for a while. Was it selfish to pursue Connor? To force him to face the scars left behind by that tragedy? I didn't know. I was pretty sure part of him wished I would slink out of his life, never to be seen again. But that was his fear talking. Fear of something that would probably never happen. Surely that wasn't a good reason to throw away our relationship?

Harper seemed to want me to push. To help him through it. If I could. So had Mae until I'd told her about Rick. And they'd both witnessed every stage of the Sophia ordeal.

I spoke without thinking. "You don't happen to have a photo of her, do you?"

Harper looked at me with pity in her eyes. "Yeah . . . You don't want to see that."

Oh. Right then.

She kindly changed the subject. "So, there might be one positive side to this whole Teddy fiasco. I'm ready to admit I need to rethink my dating strategy."

"Are you serious? That's great."

"Yeah, I figure maybe I'll look for a nice guy with good qualities irrespective of the car he drives, and I'll start buying lottery tickets in the hopes I might be able to afford my own cool car someday."

"Sounds sensible." Well, not so much the lottery ticket part, but it was a big step in the right direction.

She screwed up her face in mock exasperation. "Ugh, you're such a spoilsport. I don't want to be sensible. I just want to find someone nice. So I was wondering, do you think you could set me up with that doctor friend of yours?"

She was talking about Levi, a Taste Society doctor and friend of mine she'd glimpsed when he'd come to give antidotes to six human-trafficking victims I'd been fighting to save. Harper had been there to save me, a feat she'd accomplished very handily with the help of a giant wrench.

I studied her. "You know he drives a medical van, right?"

Her shoulders wilted a little. "I know."

"Okay. I'll scope him out for you."

Despite the risks involved in dealing with Harper's violent ex and her scary driving, she dropped me back to my apartment in one piece, and I finally had some time to myself.

The problem was, I no longer wanted it. I wanted to be with Connor.

But as enlightening as my conversation with Harper had been about what Connor had gone through, it hadn't given me any bright ideas on how to persuade him I was worth the risk of going through that again. So rather than do anything about my own love life, I texted Levi and arranged to meet up the next day, then went to bed to catch up on some sleep.

CONNOR

I spent a few hours at the office before noticing my presence was putting everyone on edge. My team knew me well enough to sense my bad mood whether I showed it or not.

Seeing as team morale was critical to efficiency, and none of them were responsible for my ill temper, I left for the seclusion of my home office. I had enough reports to review to swallow all my time between now and next week, so it was better to have fewer interruptions anyway.

When I'd first started dating Izzy, a number of my employees had commented good-naturedly on my improved mood. Since the breakup, only Nick had been bold enough to ask if something was wrong.

Yes. Best to be alone right now.

The dog, who still didn't have a name, raced up to me, nails *slipping and sliding and scratching against the timber floor-boards. She wriggled with enthusiasm, pressing herself against my legs and leaving a fresh coating of fur all over them. At this rate, I'd never be free of fur again. Even after I'd rehomed her.*

Mom was in the kitchen, and I could tell she wanted to talk as soon as I saw her face. She was about to be disappointed.

She set aside whatever she'd been heating on the stove. "I've been thinking about why you and Izzy broke up."

"Then please stop."

She crossed her arms. "No. This is serious. And you will hear me out, Connor Emmett Stiles."

Every now and then Mom channeled the authority of a drill sergeant. This was one of those times.

I leaned against the counter in resignation.

"You know how important it is to me that you don't let your life be adversely shaped by your father's passing, and I know what happened with Sophia was incredibly painful, but I think you're making a mistake. One you may deeply regret."

"Mom—"

"I'm not finished. Now I'm sure you haven't told me the full story, but it seems to me that you broke up with Izzy for some of the same qualities you admired her for in the first place. Because she's good-hearted, selfless, and prepared to stand up for what's right. Those are excellent qualities to have in a partner. You know that as well as I do. And if you reject her because of the risk those qualities bring, where does that leave you? Are you going to marry someone who's too self-centered or weak-minded to put themselves in danger? We both know that would

be a terrible match for you, and you've never been attracted to that sort of person anyway. I'm worried if you can't move past this, if you allow your fear to make this decision, you're going to end up alone."

"Then I'll end up alone," I said. "Now if you'll excuse me, I have work that needs doing."

I strode to my home office and shut the door with enough finality to ensure Mom didn't follow. Then noticed the dog had snuck in with me. If I opened the door to kick her out, Mom might take it as an invitation to continue her lecture.

I sank into my ergonomic chair and turned on the computer. The dog settled down on my feet—something she'd taken to doing whenever I was home.

Oh well, my pants were already covered in fur anyway.

I stared at the login screen for much longer than it warranted. Damn Mom and her unwanted wisdom.

The monitor went to sleep.

Instead of waking it up, I pulled out the ziplock bag Izzy had given me and passed one of the smelly treats to the dog.

8

I WOKE UP TO A KNOCK on the door. My bedroom door rather than the front, which was rare. A moment later, my housemate Oliver slipped inside carrying a tray.

Like me, Oliver called LA home thanks to a broken relationship. But I'd moved here to get away from my ex, whereas Oliver had followed his girlfriend over only for it to end in an acting career for her and a lot of resentment for him.

He said he stayed for the weather. Which made sense given the dreary climate in England. Especially since he loved wearing novelty T-shirts so much, and it was almost always sweater weather in the UK.

Meow trotted in after him, leaped onto the bed, and sniffed my face delicately in greeting. While she was happy enough to nap with me when he was out, she spent her nights with him.

Her favorite person had come to a halt a few feet away. He looked like he'd just gotten out of bed himself, with his feet bare, jaw unshaved, and dark blond hair scruffier than usual.

His posh British accent, however, was as impeccable as always. "Morning, Iz. Etta mentioned you'd had a bad day yesterday, and I know this has been a rough week for you, so I thought you could use a little TLC."

I shuffled my way into an almost-upright position and rubbed sleep from my eyes as if it might help me understand what was happening. "Huh?"

"I present to you, breakfast in bed!"

Oliver came closer and lowered the tray with a flourish so I could see its contents. Meow looked too.

There was a Pop-Tart, a piece of buttered toast, a bowl of cereal, a cup of tea, and a bottle of beer.

"I wasn't sure what you'd be in the mood for, and I'm no cook, so I thought I'd give you a range of options."

His efforts—which most primary school children could've replicated or one-upped—brought a smile to my lips. "You shouldn't have."

Oliver's lips quirked too. "You mean I *really* shouldn't have, right? Sorry, I feel bad about subjecting you to my terrible culinary efforts after all the times you've whipped up gastronomic delights for me. But I was hoping the thought might count for something or that it would make you laugh at me if nothing else."

I laughed and assured him, "The thought definitely counts." Then I stopped petting Meow for a second to select the cup of tea and Pop-Tart from the tray. "This is perfect, thanks." I should've gone with the toast, but he was right. This week *had* been rough, and at least I hadn't gone for the beer. Not that I could imagine stomaching beer for breakfast. Gross.

Oliver shook his head. "You know things are bad when you consider *this* pathetic offering perfect, but I'm glad you like it." He pointed at the beer. "Are you going to drink that?"

"Nope." I patted the bed. "Sit down and tell me a funny story or something."

"Okay." He sat down by my feet and took a swig of his beer. "Once upon a time there was this girl who was sad for some reason, but she wouldn't tell anyone what was wrong. So her friend served her breakfast in bed dosed with truth serum—"

I experienced a moment's panic when in my sleep-addled state I thought he was serious, and my brain strove to identify the substance in the mouthful of Pop-Tart I'd been chewing. Then I realized that one, there was no known truth serum that worked reliably outside of fiction, and two, if there was, it wouldn't be available or even heard of in Oliver's world.

"—and she told him what was wrong, and they figured out a way to fix it and then everyone was happy. Also, three guys walk into a bar. The fourth one ducks. That's the funny bit of the story."

I was automatically formulating a response to divert his attention when I realized that Oliver was pretty much the sole person that I might actually be able to talk to about this. Unlike Etta, Mae, and Harper, he was far enough removed from Connor that he didn't have any emotional stakes and wouldn't judge me for supposedly dating someone so soon after I'd broken up with Connor, only to change my mind not long afterward.

Meow purred encouragingly from where she'd stolen the warm patch on my pillow, so I took a deep breath and let an edited version of events spill out. How after going on a couple of dates with Rick I'd realized how much I wanted Connor back, except Connor was refusing to even talk to me about it. How I had so much to explain and apologize for and promise to do better, but none of it was going to have any effect if I couldn't get him to listen. And I was stuck for fresh ideas on what to do about it.

"So why not write to him?" Oliver asked. "In an email, or a letter if you're feeling old-school."

It was an excellent point. One I probably would've come up with eventually now that I'd slept and recovered from the conversation on the stair landing, but still. "That's actually a good idea."

"Hey, no need to sound so surprised. As a bartender I'm a fount of relational wisdom, you know. I hear more sob stories than most psychologists on a weekly basis, and it's impossible not to pick a few things up."

"Like write a letter if your partner's not talking to you?"

"Sure. Or like, funnily enough, going to a pub and spilling your guts to a random bartender doesn't work as well as communicating with your partner about it."

I chowed down the last piece of my Pop-Tart, put the remainder of my tea on my nightstand, then slid forward and gave Oliver a hug. "Thanks, Oliver. You're the best housemate a girl could wish for."

He blushed. "Of course, Iz. You know I'd do anything for you. Well, almost anything."

It was only when he stood up to leave that I realized his T-shirt said:

PEOPLE DISAPPOINT. PIZZA IS ETERNAL.

I didn't want to think too hard on the fact that this was whom I was taking relationship advice from . . .

———

GALVANIZED BY THE POSITIVE START to my day, I bounced out of bed determined to make the most of it. I used my time in the shower to mull over what I would say to Connor, then sat down to write. After two hours, I'd written a thousand words and discarded 917 of them.

This was going to be harder than I thought.

Deciding a mental break would do me good, I got up to swing by the supermarket for ingredients and make a new batch of dog treats. Between Etta's dog Dudley, Levi's dogs Waffles and Syrup, and now Connor's new dog, they were going to be in hot demand.

Thinking Dudley might like to accompany me on my walk to the shops (seeing as I was buying things for him after all), I planned to pop in on Etta before I left. But when I walked past her window and saw her and Mae huddled together, I chickened out. I wasn't ready to experience the combined force of the pair of them again.

I did still walk at least, enjoying the sunshine on my face and pretending it would make up for the Pop-Tart breakfast. I was supposed to be thinking further on Connor's letter, but I found myself pondering what Etta and Mae were up to instead.

They'd been spending a lot of time together since Mae had come down from San Bernardino County for a visit, and it was always disconcerting when the two of them started scheming. When they'd first met, they'd "joked" about opening a PI business, except I was no longer convinced it was a joke. Etta had recently returned from visiting Mae with a fancy new camera she claimed was for a newly acquired interest in bird watching. I thought it was more likely she was using it for her long-held interest in people watching. And with Etta's thirst for adventure and shooting things, Mae's PI background, their combined intelligence, and a bunch of time on their hands, they were the epitome of a dangerous duo.

But they weren't my problem to solve right now. If they had landed a private investigation gig, the pair of them could take care of themselves. It was the people they were investigating I'd be worried for. Or if they were plotting something to cheer Connor up, I'd effectively eliminated myself as a player on the board by telling them about Rick.

Dammit. It had crossed my mind more than once after his death that if I'd kept my mouth shut that night, they would never have found out about our supposed relationship. But it's not as if I could've predicted what was coming, and the damage was already done.

Half an hour later, I was back in my apartment ready to cook up some doggy drool-worthy treats. While I sliced meat and prepared the other ingredients, my thoughts returned to what I should say to Connor. I needed to apologize for not taking his concerns for my safety more seriously. I hadn't realized how deep his wounds ran. But I also needed to lay out my side of things and try to convince him—using the cold hard logic that he loved so much—why he shouldn't let this issue keep us apart. I'd use that same logic to go through all the ways I'd been thinking we could work together to fix this and reach an agreement we were both happy with. Chances were we'd have to compromise, but that's how relationships worked.

This letter idea was growing on me. It gave me a chance to formulate the most rational and compelling argument possible without letting my emotions get in the way. Something I'd risk doing if we were talking it over in person. Connor thrived on rational and compelling . . .

I caught myself about to taste Syrup's special "cookie"

mixture and gave more of my attention over to the baking after that. Most dogs liked dehydrated meat. Syrup liked broccoli. I'd been experimenting, trying to come up with something she enjoyed even more as part of my effort to win the shy dog over.

I was getting Syrup's special treats out of the oven when Etta let herself through the door. Her eyes went straight to the tray I was holding.

"*Savory* cookies? Wow, things must be worse than I thought. Wanna talk about it?"

"The cookies are for the dogs," I said, avoiding her other question. "These are cheese and broccoli with bacon grease. And I'm dehydrating a bunch more slivers of chicken, beef, and lamb heart too."

I'd found an old dehydrator on Craigslist for twenty bucks and hadn't been able to resist buying it, but I'd quickly learned to avoid liver if I didn't want to stink out the house. While Dudley had been happy enough to eat the treats I made for my two-legged friends, I'd wanted to offer him a more healthy alternative.

Etta picked up one of the cookies and sniffed it. "It doesn't smell half-bad, actually."

"I wouldn't recommend it. I put some liver powder in there too."

She placed it back on the tray hastily. "Well that's awful sweet of you, and Dudley appreciates your efforts, but don't think I didn't notice you avoiding my other question."

I suppressed a groan. Etta was harder to divert than

a bloodhound on a deer trail. You might be able to convince a bloodhound to give up the chase if you had a tasty enough treat. Etta wasn't so easily swayed. "Thanks, but I don't want to talk about it."

She opened her mouth to protest, so I jumped in quickly. "And I'm feeling better after a solid night's sleep anyway."

Imagining trying to divert Etta from the trail by offering her cookies reminded me of the ones I'd seen on Hunt's desk. I finished transferring the dog treats to a cooling rack and decided to have some fun. "Are you enjoying the chocolate-chip-and-salted-caramel cookies I made you?"

"Oh yes, they were scrumptious."

I raised an eyebrow. "What do you mean *were*? I made you a double batch."

"So you did, dear. But you know, Mae has been over a lot this week," Etta covered smoothly.

"Didn't she only arrive two days ago?" *Gosh, was it really only two days ago?*

"Well yes, but we had a lot to catch up on. I was actually hoping you could bake me some more cookies today? Except with pecans instead of chocolate chips this time."

"But salted caramel and chocolate chips are your favorite."

Etta found the four-pack of jelly donuts I'd bought in a weak moment at the store and fished one out for herself. "That's true, but I like to change things up sometimes, and I've had a hankering for pecans lately."

I couldn't hold my game face any longer and smirked. "You mean Hunt has a hankering for pecans lately. I saw my cookies on his desk. He told me you made them for him."

She froze, donut halfway to her mouth. "You didn't rat me out, did you?"

Etta had been acting differently since dating Hunt. Instead of the neighbor who picked through lovers like an assortment of chocolates, the parade of men to her apartment had stopped. Instead of oversharing details of relational encounters, she rarely spoke about Hunt at all. My theory was she was embarrassed—not just about going steady but that she was dating a man almost her own age. She would certainly be embarrassed if I'd ratted her out. I suspected my irrepressible friend was in love.

I laughed and swatted her arm. "Of course not. Your secret's safe with me. Any other special requests now I know what's going on?"

Etta beamed and resumed eating. "Well," she said between mouthfuls, "it'd be wonderful if you could have them ready early this afternoon. I have something I need to sweeten him up for."

"Consider it done."

"Thanks, dear. Your mother raised you right."

Trying to get Etta to talk about her past had become a game of sorts. I jumped on the opening she'd given me. "Speaking of mothers, how is it that yours never taught you how to bake?"

"Oh, it wasn't for want of trying on her part. Now have you seen your pesky housemate about the place? I wanted to ask him something."

I had to hand it to her. Etta was good at answering questions without really answering them. "Oliver's in his room."

Having promised to make Hunt's cookies in a hurry, I washed the mixing bowl and baking trays twice (the last thing I needed was Hunt getting food poisoning), then assembled the ingredients for the salted-caramel-and-pecan cookies. It was a recipe I'd made so many times by now, with the exception of the pecans anyway, that my thoughts drifted to the letter while I worked.

Meow rubbed herself against my ankles, and I fed her some of the scraps of fresh meat I'd saved with her in mind. "See?" I told her. "There are benefits to having dogs around."

She licked her lips and stared at me haughtily.

Etta reappeared just as I was slipping the tray of cookie dough into the oven, which made me realize how much time had passed. "What were you two talking about for so long?"

She scraped her finger around the mixing bowl I'd yet to wash again. "Nosiness isn't a becoming trait, you know."

I snorted. "Said the pot to the kettle."

Her finger carried its loot into her mouth and came out clean. "Why, would you look at the time? I need to skedaddle, but I'll pop back for those cookies soon. Thanks again, dear." She kissed me on the cheek and, true to her word, skedaddled from the apartment.

That piqued my curiosity. Besides, it was nearing midafternoon, so I slapped together some sandwiches and knocked on Oliver's door. "Hey, I made us some sand-wiches for a late lunch."

"I don't feel like eating," he called out, sounding glum.

What? Oliver always felt like eating, especially when he was feeling down. "I hope you're decent because I'm coming in."

He was the picture of gloomy in bed. Back slumped against the headboard. Chin tucked far enough that his hair had flopped into his eyes. He was staring blankly at his laptop and couldn't have looked any more depressed if his ex walked up to the bar and ordered a Bitch Slap cocktail.

"What's wrong?"

He shook his head instead of answering.

I tried again. "What did Etta want to talk to you about?"

"Nothing I want to talk about a second time," he mumbled.

Oh boy. "Do you need me to tell you a funny story about a boy who was sad and whose friend dosed him with truth serum to convince him to talk and helped him figure out a solution and then everyone lived happily ever after?"

His lips tugged upward just a bit. "No, I'm good. But thanks."

I eyed his T-shirt again. "Want me to order pizza?"

He didn't say no immediately, so I made the decision on his behalf.

"I'm ordering pizza."

I called the pizza place and turned the cookies around, pondering the oddity of both Etta and Oliver refusing to tell me what they'd discussed. What would those two talk about that they couldn't let me in on?

Then I received a phone call that shoved all thoughts of *that* mystery from my head.

9

WITH MERE MINUTES BEFORE Connor arrived, I raced to transform my home hairdo, clothes, and lack of makeup into a professional ensemble, hoping my hair didn't smell too noticeably of lamb heart and broccoli. Then I tapped on Oliver's door again.

"Sorry, something's come up, and I need to head out, but there's a pizza with your name on it that'll be here soon, so make sure to answer the door when someone knocks. And when we both have some spare time, I'm taking you to see that movie you've been raving about. The one with those, um, cat alien thingies, okay?"

Meow had trailed in after me, wondering if there were any more treats, so I picked her up and placed her on the bed with Oliver. "I'm going to make you a deal," I bargained with her. "Look after Oliver while I'm gone, and I'll ply you with treats when I get home."

Leaving Oliver with Meow on his lap and at least a half smile on his face, I snatched the cookies out of the oven and texted Etta to let her know the special order was cooling on the kitchen counter and she was welcome to come over and help herself since I had to run out.

I also reminded her to be certain to get the ones with pecans rather than broccoli in them.

Then I rushed downstairs to meet Connor, who was picking me up on his way to the police station. I wasn't sure what was going on; all he'd told me was that there'd been developments on the case and Hunt wanted us there immediately.

In the seconds between spotting Connor's black SUV and opening the door to get in, my nerves jangled like keys in a jogger's pocket. I'd spent much of the morning thinking over all the reasons we should be together, but I doubted he'd been doing the same. And we hadn't left things in a good place. Would it be awkward today?

I reminded myself to focus on the job, to compartmentalize. That's what Connor would do—without an ounce of trouble, no doubt. Somewhat reassured, I slid onto the tan leather seat and offered a cautious smile. "So maybe I boasted too soon about my efficiency in closing the case yesterday."

"Yes," Connor said.

My chest tightened. Was his monosyllabic response

Connor being his typical self? Or was it heavy with meaning?

After the longest pause in the history of the world, he added, "My ego is duly soothed."

His tone was as dry as the California desert, but for Connor it was downright playful. And for him to even make an attempt at humor was significant. My next breath came easier.

"Excellent. Then perhaps you and your ego could fill me in on what's happened? What has Hunt told you?"

"That someone has come forward and is claiming we've got the wrong guy."

Shock swept through me. "What? Who? Why?"

I sensed Connor's amusement in his slight shift of tone. "That's what we're going to the station to find out."

"Right. Thank you for sharing your insight with your humble lead investigator."

"You're welcome."

We drove in silence for a minute while I grasped for something else to say, then resolved to keep quiet. I didn't want to broach any of the relationship topics I'd been mulling over; I'd save them for the letter. The atmosphere in the car was comfortable—amazingly so considering our last conversation. I wouldn't risk disrupting it.

"The dog has a name now," Connor volunteered.

My hopeful heart leaped. He genuinely seemed to be working at reaching out. Maybe he *had* been thinking about the same things as me. "Do tell."

"I want to make it clear that I had no part in this decision. Mom and Maria had been pushing me to choose a name, but I refused, so they took matters into their own hands."

"Well, now I *really* want to know."

"Petal." He announced the name with all the enthusiasm a teenager would muster for the word "homework."

"Oh, that's a . . . cute name."

"Yes, if she were an old lady's dog, it would be perfect. I'm sure they chose it primarily to embarrass me."

I wouldn't put it past the pair of them. Although being older ladies themselves, maybe they just liked it. "Embarrass you how?"

"You know, if I take her for a walk and have to call out her name, or when I'm trying to find her a new home and telling people about her."

"Serves you right for refusing to choose a name. In my experience, going against the wishes of your elders never ends well. Count yourself lucky they didn't call her Barbie or Fluffy Wuffy Ruff Puff."

"Or Schnookums?" Connor suggested. It was the term of endearment I'd chosen for him early on in our acquaintance just to annoy him. It had worked.

Now he shrugged. "Her name will be someone else's problem soon enough." Another minute passed. "She loves those treats you gave me by the way."

Imagining Connor being persuaded by Petal's beseeching puppy-dog eyes into giving her treats made me smile. I couldn't wait to meet her.

When Connor began to speak again, my hopes rose further. He rarely offered so much in the way of unprompted personal conversation.

"I've been wanting to say . . . I mean, maybe it's obvious, but you're welcome to continue hanging out with Harper and Mom without any awkwardness on my part. They're on your side anyway."

Oh. The sentiment was sweet, but the words punctured my ballooning optimism. He was extending an olive branch. But it wasn't the kind of thing you needed to say to someone you were planning to get back together with. And what did he mean they were on my side? Harper might be hoping we'd work it out, but that was because she didn't know about Richard Knightley yet. Mae mustn't have mentioned to Connor that she'd given up on me after learning about my "new boyfriend."

Realizing I needed to say something, I cast around urgently for a response that wouldn't reveal his words had had the opposite effect on my feelings than he'd intended.

"Thank you. I saw Harper last night, actually." Crap, I hadn't been planning to mention that.

Connor was blissfully unaware of the trouble he was causing me. "I'm glad. She doesn't have many girlfriends who are good for more than a fun night out. What did you get up to?"

Double crap. "Oh, you know. Had some girl time. Talked about boys." I tried to keep any odd inflections out of my voice, as if we'd just met for a meal rather than confronting her angry, violent ex. To be fair, we *had* talked about boys, and since we were both girls, you could feasibly classify it as girl time.

I was saved from having to dig myself in any deeper by our arrival at the 27th Street Community Police Station. Time to focus on the case that apparently wasn't over after all. Yep, I was sure I'd be able to compartmentalize.

We found Hunt at his desk where I noticed there were three fewer cookies than yesterday. No wonder Etta needed more already.

He was not in a good mood. Actually, I wasn't sure I'd ever seen him in a good mood. He skipped the niceties and went straight to scowling. "I knew having a guy voluntarily confess to double homicide on a high-publicity case was far too convenient."

Hmm, how come he hadn't mentioned it to us then?

He pushed back from his desk. "The second guy suspiciously coming forward to volunteer information is in the box. You may as well watch while I speak to him."

I'd learned "the box" was cop lingo for the interview room. He led us to the same one where we'd spent so many hours yesterday.

"You don't trust today's volunteer," Connor observed. "Any reasons for that?"

Hunt ran his fingers over his mustache. "This guy makes my whiskers itch." And with that informative explanation, he stepped into the interrogation room. Connor and I entered the adjacent viewing room—or viewing closet as

I'd overheard an officer affectionately call it—and looked through the one-way glass.

The stark walls and run-down furniture were the same, but the man waiting on the uncomfortable chair was nothing like yesterday's interview subject. Damon Wood was as black and handsome as Stanley Cox was white and shabby. Wood was in his midthirties, with short-cropped hair, intense eyes, and a body in excellent shape, the latter made clear by a close-fitting T-shirt.

Hunt explained that he'd be recording their session and switched on the recorder.

Damon sized up the device and shook his head. "You know you can get much better audio recorders than that, right? Better quality sound. Better microphone configuration. More playback options. Automatic backup in case of SD card failure or corruption—"

"That's fantastic"—Hunt interrupted—"but you said you had information relevant to the Isaac Anand and Richard Knightley case. Let's stick to that, shall we?"

Damon shrugged. "Suit yourself." He leaned forward. "I obtained a copy of Mr. Cox's confession—"

"How?"

"That's not important. What you need—"

"How did you obtain the confession, Mr. Wood?"

"Will you just listen? There are bigger things at stake here—"

"Then answer my question so we can move on."

Damon let out a beleaguered sigh. "If this is how you

run your investigations, like a dog seizing a bone without noticing the dinosaur skeleton it's attached to, there's no wonder you need my help. You need to learn to prioritize."

Hunt was unmoved. "How did you get a copy of the confession?"

It was hard to tell from our vantage point, but it appeared the pair of them had a staring contest.

Hunt must've won, or Damon merely concluded that Hunt would never hear what he had to say if he didn't answer this question. He dropped his gaze. "Hypothetically let's just say the police department should hire better tech experts to make their systems harder to hack. Although I can understand it must be hard to attract the best of the best when you have limited funding and are situated next door to Silicon Beach and Silicon Valley where a tech-savvy teenager can turn millionaire overnight with the right start-up."

This time Hunt did react. A flush crept up his face. "Are you confessing to hacking the LAPD database?"

"No. I'm not confessing to anything. I'm trying to tell you that the murderer of Isaac Anand and that other dead guy is still out there, and the man in your cells is just a patsy. But if you're not going to listen, I'll go elsewhere. Since I walked in here as a concerned citizen looking to *help* you with this case, you can't keep me here."

Hunt leaned back in his chair. "Actually, I can now you've given me reasonable cause to suspect you of a cybercrime. And this inferior recorder here picked all that up."

Damon facepalmed. "Well, frack me. No wonder you guys never catch anyone."

I shifted to get more comfortable. This questioning session was going to take a while. Hunt did the same, keeping quiet to see what his interview subject would say next.

"The point I've been trying to make since I first walked into this station at least three-quarters of an hour ago is that I read the confession and Stanley Cox's method all checks out except for one noticeable omission."

"What's that?"

Now that Damon was able to talk on his preferred subject, some of his frustration leaked away. "He needed a hardwired connection to the system to do any of it. Isaac wasn't stupid. You couldn't touch his AI system without being in the house on a specific computer or having a hacking device connected directly to it. Since I doubt the murderer was on the premises at the time—I mean, even you guys should've been able to figure that out—I'm guessing you're looking for a hacking-purposed microcomputer that would be about the size of a double adaptor or a large dongle. Probably plugged into the back of one of Isaac's computers where it would be out of sight and connected via an Ethernet or USB port."

If what Damon was saying was true, it did seem like a strange thing for Stanley to leave out of his confession. But did the police know about it already and have an explanation, or was this news to Hunt too?

Hunt gave no indication either way. "What's your interest in this case, Mr. Wood?"

"Let's see. How about not letting someone get away with double murder?"

"I'm sure you're a true saint, but let's not waste any more of each other's time than we have to." Hunt sounded bored. "What prompted you to *obtain*"—he put steel into the word—"a copy of the confession?"

Damon smiled. "Let me give you a brief lesson on the reality of the tech industry. I'll try to keep it simple. I mean, no offense, but your average beat cop is to us what the Amish people are to you."

Funny how when someone said "no offense," what followed was almost always offensive.

"The frontier of technological development is both cutting edge and cutthroat. It advances so rapidly that regulations can't be made fast enough, let alone methods to enforce them. Stealing. Espionage. Using malware to hinder the competition. You name it. This kind of stuff is going on all the time. In most cases, we don't bother to call you in because you wouldn't understand the finer points of what's happening anyway."

Hunt yawned to demonstrate his lack of interest. "That doesn't answer why you're so invested in this particular case."

"My point is, I spend a lot of my time keeping track of those shady dealings, and I don't normally involve the LAPD except for an occasional anonymous tip that you guys tend to ignore. But this one involves murder, so I foolishly thought you'd be interested in my game-changing expertise. Hell, I even thought you might be appreciative."

"So you're the self-appointed cyber police?"

Damon smiled wider. "Something like that."

"Did you know Isaac personally?"

"Yeah, I did."

"Is that why you're here?"

The smile fell off Damon's face. "No. I'm here so you arrest the right damn person for this! How many times do I have to tell you? I feel like I'm teaching my ninety-year-old grandmother how to send an email, except this time she forgot to put her hearing aid in."

Hunt remained calm and quiet. "Did you know Richard personally?"

"No."

"What was your relationship with Isaac?"

"A casual friend."

"Do you have any theories on who might want him dead?"

Damon massaged his neck. "Finally you're getting to the important questions. I don't know anything concrete, but I heard rumors that he achieved some big breakthrough recently. He was respected in his field, so those kinds of rumors attract attention. Some of it can be bad attention."

"Be explicit, Mr. Wood."

"Someone might've murdered him to steal his breakthrough and keep it secret."

"Any ideas on who that someone might be?"

"As I said, I don't know anything concrete, but when one

of your guys is feeling motivated enough to do something proactive on the case, tell them to look at Tony Callahan."

"Who's Tony Callahan?"

"I'll let you Google him yourself. I've got better things to do with my afternoon, and I know you'll be verifying everything I say, so as you said earlier, Officer, let's not waste each other's time any more than we have to."

Hunt stood up. "That's Commander to you, and we're not finished yet. Are you going to sit tight for a little longer, or do I need to formally arrest you on suspicion?"

Damon rolled his eyes and slouched down into his chair. "Of course I'd love to stay." He gestured at the grubby walls and the table chipped and worn from countless hours of interrogations. "The decor in here is so nice after all. I really like what you've done with the place."

10

WE MET HUNT IN THE HALLWAY, where he accosted the first officer he saw. "I need Stanley Cox in the second interrogation room. Now. And see if Officer Mendez is around to talk tech with a witness on the Anand-Knightley case."

Connor waited for the policeman to scurry away before saying, "I assume that means we didn't know about the killer needing a hard-wired connection?"

Hunt frowned. "The tech team was still working on identifying the origin of the hack, and the job's priority status was downgraded after Cox's confession, so Wood could be right. Mendez will be able to confirm either way. Then I can arrest the bastard for hacking our system."

Connor nodded but said, "He only admitted to doing it hypothetically. I'd ask you to reconsider."

"Why?"

"I'm sure you figured out he knows more than he's letting on. If we arrest him, he'll clam up and be cut off from his network, so we won't learn any more. If we let him go and keep tabs on him, he might lead us to something he's trying to hide."

"And if he commits a crime after we let him go?"

"Then you'll have more evidence than you have on him now. If this guy is as tech smart as he seems to think, he won't have left any hard evidence for you to find with a warrant, and his one line about hypothetically hacking the police database isn't going to be enough to make the charge stick."

Officer Mendez—a policewoman I recognized from the crime scene as the person who'd been talking to the AI security system—strode toward us, and Hunt grunted. "I'll think about it."

He gave Mendez a rundown of Damon Wood's claims and asked her to delve into the tech details of it. Then he went to the second interrogation room where Stanley Cox was now waiting.

Stanley didn't look too worse for wear after one night in jail, but then he hadn't been in good shape to begin with. His clothes were still shabby and rumpled, and he had neither lost weight nor gained hair.

Unless you counted the gray stubble on his jaw anyway.

Hunt took one of the two empty chairs. "Mr. Cox, I hope you're enjoying your stay at our fine establishment."

"Free room and board with food and company included, what's not to like?"

After my own jail experience—spending a night on a hard, narrow bed with a cellmate who snored like a malfunctioning jet engine and threatened to kill me for my breakfast grits—I could think of a few things not to like.

Hunt's mind was elsewhere. "Give me the details of how you hacked into Isaac Anand's security system. We know what you did when you were in there, but how'd you get in?"

"I've already confessed to the double murder. What do the details matter?"

Hunt's expression hardened. "You've been very cooperative so far. Don't stop now."

"That's exactly it. I *have* been very cooperative. I spent over three hours yesterday answering your endless questions, and I don't want to do it again."

Oh dear. As if Hunt wasn't in a bad enough mood after discovering this high-profile case was no longer resolved. Now his second interview subject was giving him as much attitude as the first.

Worse, Stanley's reluctance to talk gave credence to Damon's claims.

"Then answer the question and you can get back to your cell."

Stanley frowned. "I don't appreciate your tone."

"Don't mess with me, Cox. I'm not in the mood."

"Since I'm about to go to prison for the rest of my life, I don't see how that's my problem."

Hunt banged his fist on the table, making Cox and me jump. "Answer the damn question. How did you hack into Anand's security system?"

"I'm not saying another word until I have an attorney present."

"It's a bit late to start being close-mouthed now. We have your full confession on tape."

"I know. But while we're waiting for an attorney to be appointed to me, I can at least return to my cell for a while. You interrupted a fascinating conversation with my cellmate."

Hunt stood up, his posture rigid. "We'll get you an attorney, but you'll be waiting right here for however long it takes them to bother showing up. I'll tell them not to hurry."

Connor and I returned to the hallway to meet Hunt, though with the mood he was in, I was reluctant to put myself in his path.

A hapless detective didn't have the same intel. "Hey, is one of these interrogation rooms going to be free soon?"

Hunt's neck turned a splotchy red. "Give me a few more minutes."

The detective put his observation skills to good use and hurried away.

Hunt swore. "I'm sure as shit not letting Cox go back to his cell, so we'll have to get rid of Wood."

Mendez exited the other interrogation room and joined us. "He knows what he's talking about," she reported. "I'm going to see if I can find a microcomputer now."

"Do you have any more questions for him?"

"No. If his theory's correct and I find the hacking device, our team can take it from there."

"Great," Hunt said in a tone that implied otherwise. He strode into where Damon was sitting. "You're free to go, Mr. Wood. I'll walk you out."

I guess he didn't want Damon left unsupervised in the police station after learning about those hacking-purposed microcomputer thingies.

Connor and I tagged along behind them. There didn't seem to be much point in all three of us waiting for Stanley's requested attorney, and they were heading for the exit. That meant we were close enough to overhear Damon's last words to Hunt.

"By the way, you should take my advice on those recorders more seriously. SD cards can be corrupted with a powerful and rapid enough shift in the magnetic field, hypothetically speaking." He delivered a final cocky grin, then stepped out the station doors.

"What's that supposed to mean?" Hunt muttered.

Connor came up beside him and crossed his arms. "I suspect that means your memory card isn't going to work when you try to download that interview later."

Hunt's mustache bristled dangerously. "Then I'll add tampering with evidence and destroying police property to the bastard's charges. You better hope you're right that he'll do more good than harm walking free."

Oh boy. Hunt had reached a new level of annoyance

now. If he hadn't been standing between me and the exit, I would've fled after Damon.

Connor must have been thinking along the same lines. "In the interests of doing good, there doesn't seem to be much point in Izzy and me waiting around while you grill Cox. We'll touch base later."

We left Hunt fuming in the doorway.

———

CONNOR AND I CROSSED the police parking lot and climbed into his SUV. The LAPD would dig into Tony Callahan—the man Damon Wood had named as a possible suspect—as well as Damon himself. Hopefully, their history and recent activities would paint a picture that helped us piece this whole thing together.

But Damon wasn't stupid and must know his coming forward under the circumstances would cast him under suspicion, so I wasn't optimistic we'd find anything incriminating about him. Besides, if he could so easily obtain confidential police files, he could probably delete any criminal history from the system and perhaps put in false records for Tony Callahan too. It was eye-opening and pretty scary to wrap my head around. What so-called facts could be trusted in a case like this?

But that was a problem we'd face farther down the track. We needed a solid suspect first.

Connor was looking at me expectantly. "Are you still

wanting to take lead when Hunt's not nearby?"

Did I? The case seemed a whole lot more complicated than it did yesterday. But my reasoning hadn't changed. "Yep, just give me a minute to figure out the next step."

I said the words confidently as if I knew what I was doing. Then experienced a moment of panic when my brain gave me nothing to corroborate my assertion. What were the key points of what we'd learned today, and what were their implications? I was hyperaware of Connor waiting for instructions, the engine idling. I blocked it out.

If Damon's information was correct and Cox hadn't just left that part of his confession out by chance rather than design, then what? What did it mean? Most likely, that Cox was either a patsy paid to confess to a crime he didn't commit as Damon claimed, or he had an accomplice he was protecting.

I didn't know where to start on the patsy thing, and only one accomplice sprang to mind.

"Let's pay Patty Wilkinson another visit," I said.

On the drive there, I fleshed out my theory.

"What if Patty Wilkinson found out that Isaac was going to somehow ensure Rick won both trials? It would destroy everything she'd worked for. None of the victims would get their money, and her public awareness campaign would be discredited, ruined beyond resuscitation. But if the scammer was killed?" I drummed my fingers on the armrest while I thought it through. "Most of the press around his murder would mention the class action lawsuit, even more so if he's murdered by one of his alleged victims. And by taking out Isaac too, they might avoid losing the trial altogether."

Connor nodded. "It's a solid hypothesis. Where does Cox fit into this? What's their relationship?"

"He'd have to be an accomplice. Patty doesn't have the tech skills to pull off the murder, but she *is* charismatic and persuasive. She knew Cox was depressed, desperate. Maybe she convinced him it was necessary. That his sacrifice would be worthwhile and she'd remain on the outside as a spokesperson to work the media the right way. Plus she had far more money left than he did. Who knows? She could've promised to take care of his wife as part of their bargain."

"Good. Let's see how she reacts to the news that Cox might not have done it alone and learn what she has to say for herself."

We parked outside Patty Wilkinson's house. The tangerine paint and the sweet fragrance of the flowering jasmine that climbed the latticework seemed less charming today.

She made overly strong tea again and sat us down in the same formal dining room.

"I had no idea Stanley would do something like this if that's why you're here. If I'd known, I would've tried to talk him out of it, force him to join in with more of our support sessions."

I pretended to take a sip of tea from my dainty teacup and stayed quiet to see what else she'd volunteer.

"I feel like I failed him, you know? Let him down by not

realizing how desperate he was. I mean, I knew he kept to himself more than the others, but I thought that was just his personality rather than a cry for help. Not everyone wants to be pushed into joining a community. Especially after what happened with his wife, being rejected that way. He didn't want to be told it wasn't his fault, not yet. Wasn't ready for it. But if I'd known . . ."

She trailed off. Her eyes glassy. It was a hell of an act if that's what it was.

I waited a little longer before prompting, "Tell us more about Stanley and his interactions with the group."

"Why are you asking? The paper said he confessed, didn't he?"

Oh yes, she was sharp. It made it all the more scary she'd been conned out of her money. I'd looked up some of the statistics she'd rattled off after the first interview, and it was all true. These types of scams were far more widespread and sophisticated than the general public knew, and most of the victims weren't people clueless about technology and whose mental faculties had been worn down by age. They were smart, savvy retirees in prime mental health.

I laid my first card on the table and watched carefully for her reaction. "We have a source who's claiming Mr. Cox confessed to the crime to protect someone else."

Her eyes widened, her head went back, and she took a quick intake of breath. Shock. But was it shock at the idea he might not have done it? Or shock we'd found that out?

"Really? Who?"

"That's one of the reasons we're here. We're trying to find out."

"What did Stanley say about it?"

Another shrewd question. Should I lead her on to think he might betray her, or admit he wasn't talking?

"I'm afraid I can't disclose any further details. Can you please tell us about Stanley and his time within your group?"

"Gracious. I don't know. As I said, Stanley kept himself at a distance. He wasn't rude or anything—I mean he was quite helpful, actually. Despite being a private man, he made the sacrifice of sharing his story with a journalist to raise the profile of our case and spread awareness. I asked him to since he'd worked with computers most of his life, and that would make it clear to everyone that smart, tech-savvy people can be suckered in just as easily as the rest of us. And his computer skills came in handy for our little group too."

She took a mouthful of her tea and set the cup on its saucer while she gathered her thoughts.

"A bunch of us had used Skype before, for talking to kids and grandkids interstate and that sort of stuff, but Stanley helped us set it up for our support sessions. Made it so we could do a big conference call across the country. He was very patient with me, and from what I heard everyone else too, when he was talking them through it, like our own personal tech support. But even after going to all that effort, he didn't join in the sessions often. He said it was hard for him to get computer access, but I invited him to come over and share mine, and he didn't take me up on it. I thought he just needed some space."

"Was there anyone he took a liking to? Anyone he might want to protect?"

Patty rubbed the back of her hand absentmindedly as she thought over my question. Or pretended to.

"Honestly, not that I can think of. I mean, I think beneath the anger he loved his wife and I could imagine he might do it for *her*, but there's no way she'd be behind the murder. She's pinned the blame firmly on Stanley, and she's not in California anyway."

I agreed. From everything I knew, the wife was a long shot.

"What about for money?" I asked.

The unconscious hand rubbing froze. "Money? As in confess to murder for a payout? Wow." Her hands fell apart. "I hate to admit it, but I think that's possible. I mean, he's old enough that he couldn't be hoping to enjoy a windfall himself after being convicted of a double homicide . . . But maybe to set things up for his wife . . . Oh, wow . . ."

Time to lay my other card on the table. "There's one other thing, Mrs. Wilkinson. Stanley claims that he killed Isaac Anand—the second victim—because Isaac was going to rig the lawsuits to ensure Richard won. Had you heard anything like that?"

I could see the exact moment it occurred to her that this piece of information gave her a solid motive where she had none before.

"No, no I hadn't heard anything like that." She met my gaze squarely. "I can see you're not sure whether to believe me, but it's the truth. Besides, I can't imagine how that would be possible. I'm sure our attorney Mr. Dimond would've told you we didn't have a lot of strong evidence, so there's nothing critical to make disappear, and I can't see how they could hope to throw off an entire jury. Or two entire juries. There are all sorts of measures put in place to prevent that sort of thing."

I nodded but didn't move to agree or reassure her. "Thank you for your time, Mrs. Wilkinson."

We left Patty and her teacups, not knowing much more than when we arrived. She was likable, and she'd made some good points. Especially that it was difficult to imagine *how* Isaac could've rigged the criminal trial or the class action case to ensure Rick got off.

But Rick had struck me as overly confident about it when he was alive. At the time, I'd assumed it was arrogance since it was one character trait he'd had in abundance.

Then again, Patty being so likable and persuasive was exactly why she might've managed to convince Cox to mastermind the murder and then take the fall for it.

How could we determine which scenario was true? I supposed we could talk to a bunch of the other lawsuit plaintiffs and get their views on both Patty and Stanley. But that seemed like it could take an awful lot of time for very little return. Especially when Patty was only one of our suspects. Stanley's wife might be worth interviewing at some point as well to find out if Stanley had sent her any money, but that was a shot in the dark too.

Given it was almost six o' clock, Connor and I agreed it could wait until tomorrow. By then we'd have more information on Damon Wood and the man he'd named, Tony Callahan, and could choose the most promising lead. The case wasn't urgent—it didn't seem likely the killer would strike again anytime soon. And if I hurried, I could still make it to my prearranged catch-up with Levi.

———

CONNOR RETURNED me to my apartment building but did not escape unscathed.

Before I'd even gotten out of the car, Etta was trotting down the stairs and waving. She arrived at the curb moments later, a little breathless. "Connor, I was hoping you'd drop by. I have a favor to ask."

I paused. No way was I going to miss this conversation.

"I'm not sure whether you knew this, but my niece is arriving tonight—she's coming over from London to star in a new TV series. I'm certain I would have mentioned her to you."

No, she most *certainly* hadn't. I'd never heard Etta mention any of her family except for her dearly departed husband and mother.

Etta went on without giving Connor a chance to respond. "Anyway, she's going to be a private investigator in this TV series, and she's super excited, as you can imagine. But she's a studious girl, so she wants to make sure she portrays the job right."

Uh-oh.

"So I told her I knew someone who was a professional PI, and I'd ask to see if you wouldn't mind her tagging along—just for a couple of days. I know you're busy." Etta's spiel came to a stop, and she caught Connor with a hopeful smile.

I struggled to avoid smiling myself. Connor was never going to agree to this.

His face betrayed none of his feelings on the matter. "I'm sure Mom would love to show your niece the ropes. Why not have her do it? She might be offended you didn't ask."

Etta shook her head. "I asked Mae first, but she said she came down here for a holiday and she's shown enough wannabe PIs the ropes over the years. Told me it's high time you took a turn."

What? That didn't sound like Mae. What were these two up to?

"I see." This time Connor looked pained. "Well, I suppose I'd be okay with it, but I'm collaborating with the LAPD on the current case, so I had better run it by Hunt first."

Now I was even more confused. Since when did Connor ask Hunt for permission? Was he turning over a new cooperative leaf?

Mr. Cooperative slipped his phone out of his pocket. "I'll call him now."

As he dialed the number and put the call on speaker, I finally realized what he was up to. Hunt would *never* say yes to a civilian tagging along on a case, and Connor knew it. The sly fox was passing the buck.

Hunt's gruff voice answered for all of us to hear. "Solved the case yet?"

I'd forgotten about the bad mood we'd left him in. If there'd been a chance in a blue moon before, it was now a complete impossibility.

"No," Connor said. "But I was wondering whether it would be okay to let an up-and-coming actress tag along with me for the next few days? She wants to learn how PIs work."

I held my breath and waited for the penny to drop.

"You do what you want, Stiles. I'm not your father."

Connor didn't quite manage to hide his shock.

Neither did I. Not that anyone was watching.

Then, with a sinking feeling, I remembered that special batch of cookies Etta had requested. To sweeten Hunt up for something, she'd said.

Maybe I wouldn't mention that to Connor.

11

I RUSHED UPSTAIRS to feed Meow and change into something more casual for my matchmaking visit with Levi. The apartment was quiet, and the smell of bacon and broccoli cookies as well as dehydrated meat hung in the air. Probably because the dehydrator was still running and the cookies still spread over the kitchen counter where I'd placed them to cool. Lucky Meow wasn't a fan of broccoli. The dishes were on the counter too. The only differences from when I'd left were that Etta had taken Hunt's cookies, and Oliver was gone—he was working a late shift tonight. I hoped he was feeling less mopey.

Meow trotted to greet me, tail high. I picked her up and carried her around while I retrieved the treats from the dehydrator and wire racks, then placed them in takeout containers I'd purchased from the shop earlier today for this purpose. It took me twice as long with one arm occupied holding her warm weight against my chest, but her purring made it worth it.

Unfortunately, that was the upper limit of my skills. "I'm afraid I'm not talented enough to operate the can opener one-handed," I apologized as I put her down.

She forgave me when she spotted the magical utensil that made her dinner appear. I fished a tin from the cupboard and opened it without reading the label. A move I regretted when the all-too-familiar scent wafted up to me. *Ugh! Minced cod.* It was the variety I'd been forced to taste months ago, and I still couldn't feed it to her without the ghost of the flavor coating my tongue and tickling my gag reflex. Trying not to breathe, I spooned it into her dish and retreated to my bedroom. There I discarded my black work pants for jeans, my shirt for a sweater, and my low slingback heels for trainers.

A minute later, I was heading out the door, a couple of takeout containers tucked in my bag, promising Meow I'd be home for a cuddle when her breath smelled less like minced cod.

Levi's house was an inviting white A-frame, set on a large block in Van Nuys in the San Fernando Valley. A wisp of smoke drifted up from the sturdy stone chimney in preparation for the encroaching evening cold.

Not that it was really that cold, but Angelenos were delicate that way. It would be getting down to forty-eight degrees, and I think I'd heard a weather reporter refer to it as "freezing."

Forty-eight degrees was just about swimming weather in other parts of the world.

I crossed the pretty garden, admiring the last of the winter blooms and wondering what Levi had in store for spring. I'd visited a few times since he'd offered the hand of friendship. Sometimes I'd bring Dudley over and we'd all walk together. Other times we'd sit on his back porch and make each other laugh. It was nice to have a friend who knew the truth about my job, and Connor was plenty confident in his own attraction to not be threatened by it.

This time though, I had a mission. A date for Harper. And the quickest way to any pet lover's heart—or in this case, preparing that heart for another woman—was through winning over their pets.

Pity Connor wasn't head over heels for his newest houseguest yet.

I rang the doorbell, and Levi appeared in the doorway. With his angelic face, wicked dimples, and molten chocolate eyes framed with lashes so long that even blinking seemed flirty, it was no wonder Harper was interested. Now I needed to find out whether that interest might be mutual.

I held up the plastic takeout containers. "I come bearing gifts."

"For me?"

"Of course not. You know I'm just here to see Syrup and

Waffles." His two giant rescue dogs were sniffing and shuffling behind him, waiting for their turn to say hi.

Levi grinned easily. "Well, I won't hold that against you." He stepped aside so I could greet them. "Did you want to enjoy the last bit of daylight on the back porch?"

"Love to. Especially if there's a cup of tea on offer." My tummy rumbled, and I realized I hadn't had dinner yet. "And a snack if you have anything."

"Seems only fair since you keep my dogs in snacks."

I followed him to the kitchen, and Syrup and Waffles followed the containers. Unless I held them over my head, they were convenient sniffing height for the pair of them.

"Can I see if Syrup likes my new cookie experiment? I made broccoli and bacon grease ones this time."

Levi placed the kettle on the gas burner. "Go for it. If she doesn't eat them, I might."

"Now I'm concerned about that snack I asked for."

"Oh, dog kibble isn't good enough for you? You should've warned me you were fussy."

I was tempted to throw the cookie I was holding at his head, but I placed it in front of Syrup instead. She was a shy, fawn-colored Great Dane cross and didn't trust me enough to eat out of my hand yet. Waffles, a smaller but braver Scottish deerhound mix, shoved forward too. "Don't worry, boy, I haven't forgotten about you." I handed him a couple of slivers of dehydrated chicken. He tossed them down without chewing, and by the time I looked over at Syrup, her cookie was gone as well. I grinned and selected some more treats for them. "You're out of luck, Levi. Syrup likes her cookies just fine."

Waffles got lamb heart this time, and Syrup danced with impatience as I put her second cookie on the floor. It disappeared as if by magic.

Levi was still occupied with our tea, so I turned back to the imploring eyes of the dogs. "All right, last round, guys. Then you'll have to beg Levi instead." I selected beef for Waffles, not that I was convinced he kept them in his mouth long enough to taste the difference, and offered the cookie to Syrup, palm up. Why not? It was worth a try.

She stepped forward somewhat cautiously, then shoved her nose into my hand and gobbled the cookie, leaving slobber in its wake. A hefty amount of slobber. I was too thrilled to care.

I washed my hands, then put the lids on the containers and placed them on top of the fridge—one of the few surfaces high enough to be out of the dogs' reach—before the four of us went outside. Levi and I sank into the padded swing seat while Syrup and Waffles trotted out to do a sniff patrol of the yard. We sat in silence for a minute, enjoying the serenity, the tea, and the snacks. He'd rummaged up roasted macadamias, cracked pepper chickpeas, and a spicy dip with slices of celery and carrot—all of which were much better than dog kibble.

Levi shifted on the swing cushion. "Look, I'm really sorry about bringing up the human-trafficking doctor stuff with Connor. I assumed he knew—"

"No, it's not your fault. He *should've* known because I should've told him. I only have myself to blame."

"Well shit. I'm still sorry. I feel terrible . . . Is, um, everything okay between you?"

"I'm working on it being okay between us."

He banged his head into his hand. "Oh no."

"No really, it's fine. We'll be fine. I have a plan."

Okay, a plan I wasn't superconfident in, but I was confident I'd persist until Connor took me back.

Or shot me for my relentless pursuit.

"Good. I'm glad. And look, I've known Connor for years now, and I can guess at why he's having a hard time digesting the doctor thing. I've worked through some similar baggage from my Army days . . . So anyway, if you wanted me to try talking to him . . ." He left it open-ended. A question.

"Thank you." It was an incredibly sweet and gracious offer. Levi had been both of those things unfailingly toward me the whole time I'd known him. "I'll let you know if I need backup."

"Deal," he agreed.

"I did have an agenda for coming today though."

"Oh hell, don't tell me you need more syringes."

"No!" *Thank goodness.* The last agenda I'd come to him with was one I hoped to never repeat. "I was wondering, for the sake of a friend, if you were interested in dating right now?"

His teeth flashed in the weakening light of dusk. "I'm intrigued. Tell me about her."

"Well, she's smart, funny, and gorgeous in that tall, athletic way. Works as a mechanic, which tells you something about her confidence in coloring outside the lines of normal, and she has a thing for fast, flashy cars. Likes to have fun. But above all, she values her family more than anything."

I knew family was important to Levi too. As was having someone he could laugh with.

"What's the catch? Is she allergic to dogs or something?"

"Nope, she loves dogs."

His teeth flashed again. "In that case, I'm absolutely interested in dating right now."

"Good."

The hounds in question padded over to the swing seat and demanded attention. I'd have to give Harper some of my special treats. But I still had a final hurdle to navigate with Levi first.

"Um, there is *one* thing I should warn you about."

Levi rubbed Syrup's ears, making her groan with pleasure. "I *knew* there had to be a catch. Hit me with it."

"She's Connor's sister."

Waffles chose that moment to hop into the gap between Levi and me—a gap that was most definitely not Waffle-sized—sending the swing seat rocking madly and our tea sloshing in our mugs.

We both shuffled aside to make more room, and Levi looked at me over Waffles's scruffy fur. "That might be worse than the dog allergy."

"But she's nothing like him!" I protested.

I didn't know what it meant that I was saying that about the man I loved like it was a benefit.

Levi smirked as if the same thought crossed his mind. "Okay . . . Does this mean I would've seen her about the place?"

"Well, you saw her handiwork once. Remember the human trafficker who'd been knocked out by a wrench?"

"Not something I'm likely to forget."

"That was her. She sped to my rescue straight from her garage and grabbed the first weapon she had handy."

Levi put down his mug. There might not have been much tea left after Waffles's efforts. Plus it freed up his hands to pet both dogs. "Wait. You want me to ask out a girl who knocked a murderous human trafficker unconscious with a giant wrench and who also happens to be Connor's sister? Are you sure this isn't payback for letting it slip with Connor? Because that combination makes me kind of nervous."

I leaned over Waffles and punched Levi half-heartedly in the shoulder. "I'm sure. She's great, I promise. And you aren't trying to tell me a war veteran is scared of a girl with a wrench?"

"First, I was a doctor, not a soldier. Second, it was a really big wrench. And third, well yes, a little."

I laughed. "Then it sounds like the ideal foundation for a wonderful relationship. Here's her number." I texted him the contact details. "Ask her out already."

He threw up his hands in mock defeat. "I'll do as I'm told, but only because I'm kind of scared of you too."

We passed a pleasant half hour chatting about nothing in particular, and I left with a light heart, feeling like I'd done a good deed.

But returning home to my empty apartment after an evening of playing matchmaker emphasized my own loss. I missed Connor.

I picked up Meow and sat down to write.

CONNOR

The house was quiet. Mom was asleep, Petal presumably tucked in with her since she hadn't come to greet me. And Maria had gone home for the day, back to her doting husband Armando.

But that was just it—Maria would always return to him. The most life-threatening thing about being my housekeeper was tripping over the vacuum cleaner or the dog who'd taken to stalking it.

Being a Shade was a whole other matter. And being danger-prone Isobel Avery was even worse. I didn't know a single other Shade who'd gotten into as many scrapes as she had, and she'd only been doing it for six months. Despite what Mom thought, I hadn't made the decision to break it off with her lightly. It was the logical action to take.

I strolled down the hallway and tried to find pleasure in

the perfect order. Everything was spotless. Clearly, Maria's last job of the day had been to tackle the relentless invasion of dog hair. Izzy hadn't been here to throw her clothes on the floor or leave a spatter of toothpaste in the sink. It was nice.

But it wasn't as nice as having her warm body and warmer smile waiting for me.

The front door banged shut as I changed my plans for the evening and headed to the shooting range.

I blamed it on the wind.

12

THE NEXT MORNING DAWNED too soon. I'd stayed up late agonizing over every last word in my letter, and now I had to decide how to deliver it to Connor.

Should I just hand it over in the car? Except we'd agreed to keep the case and our personal lives separate, and he'd respond better to what I'd written if he could read it in private and have time to process it first.

No, I'd give it to him after we'd wrapped up our work for the day.

Decision made, I enjoyed a slice of cold pizza for breakfast, although the fact that Oliver had left any reignited my worries over his strange turn of mood yesterday. Not that dramatic changes of mood were unusual for Oliver. One minute he could be in a full-blown rant about his monarch and the next laughing wholeheartedly at Meow chasing a cockroach. But that was just it—when he was down about something, I could usually snap him out of it with a good meal or a joke or change of topic. Plus I'd never known him to lose his appetite over anything. Last time he'd gotten gastro, he *still* ate my share of the leftovers from dinner the night before.

But despite my concern for Oliver, I had a self-defense lesson to get to, a double homicide case to unravel, and the man I loved to win back. Not to mention that Etta and Mae were up to who knows what, and whatever happened with Harper and Levi would rest partly on my shoulders.

So with Oliver fast asleep after his late shift, I had no choice but to leave that mystery unsolved. For now.

I rushed out the door, spent an hour running through self-defense situations with Nick, then hurried home to my apartment to meet Connor. Once again, he didn't look a whole lot more rested than I did. What was keeping him from sleep? Work overload? His mother's machinations? Or . . . Petal's snoring? The thought made me snort aloud, drawing his eyes to mine.

"Sorry," I said. "A bug flew up my nose."

Yeah, sure, that was a believable explanation.

"Let's hope that's the worst thing that happens today," Connor said, and with those ominous words, he handed me the research the police had done on Damon Wood and Tony Callahan. Lucky he handed me a coffee too.

"Thanks." I got to work familiarizing myself with them.

Connor pulled the car to a stop when I was a few pages in. I looked up and saw we were outside a Best Western hotel. "Who are we meeting here?"

"Adeline—Etta's niece." Connor didn't sound happy about it. In fact, if I didn't know better, I might've thought he blamed *me* for finding himself in this mess.

I suppose I had introduced him to Etta. But since he was always lecturing me about standing up for myself and saying no to her, I wasn't sure how she'd contrived to not only persuade him to allow her niece to tag along but go out of his way to pick her up too.

He hadn't brought a coffee for Adeline, however—just me—and I felt strangely flattered.

But I didn't let it stop me from teasing him.

"You know, I used to think you were so strong and in control of every situation, but it turns out you're just a pushover like me."

He turned a dubious gaze my way. "What are you talking about?"

"Let's see, Etta said jump yesterday, and you asked how high?"

Connor's mask slipped enough that his forehead creased in displeasure. "I can't believe Hunt said yes to that request. *He's* the pushover in this situation."

I didn't say anything. I didn't need to. I simply pasted a knowing smirk on my face and left it at that.

Five minutes went by. I used the wait to continue reading the files, but I could sense Connor's growing frustration next to me. "What time is she meeting us here?"

"Eight thirty."

I checked. Adeline was late. Connor didn't appreciate people being late.

Another five minutes passed.

Oh dear, Adeline was not getting off to a strong start here.

Finally I spotted movement out of the corner of my eye, and a curvy brunette in a short white dress and floral four-inch heels came up to the rolled-down window.

Guess she hadn't heard it was the cold season here in Los Angeles.

"Hi, you must be Connor Stiles, and Isobel, was it?" she asked in a charming British accent. "I hope I didn't keep you waiting long."

Connor wasn't charmed. "You did. Fifteen minutes in fact."

"Oh. Sorry. My agent called, and we had to go through the terms of my contract, which is still under negotiation—"

"We're working on a double homicide case, Ms. Thorne. Tomorrow be on time or take your own car."

Knowing what it was like being on the receiving end of Connor's disapproval, I leaned across the center console to catch her attention. "Don't take it personally. He's this grumpy with everyone."

She flashed me a grateful smile. "Thanks."

"But I'm still leaving you behind if you're late again."

"Yes, sir!" She swung herself into the car and bent forward

to murmur in my ear. "If I'd known he was so good-looking, I would've told my agent to sod off."

That was when I noticed exactly how attractive Adeline Thorne was and began second-guessing my kindness.

But that was silly, right? I was a bigger person than that. Maybe.

Regardless, I hoped her agent would have something even more enticing for her tomorrow.

———

BY THE TIME WE'D ARRIVED at our new suspect's company headquarters in Ocean Park, we'd caught Adeline up to speed on the basics of the case. She'd proven to be a quick learner. In some ways, that is. Not so much on the how-to-not-irritate-Connor front.

She shimmied out of the SUV and whistled at the generously proportioned three-story building. From the ground, you could just make out the rooftop garden, which must have had views to the beach. "He *owns* this? What's the policy on dating suspects?"

Connor ignored her.

"Sheesh, I was kidding. Is there some rule against private investigators having a sense of humor?"

I joined in out of sympathy. "Oh, Connor has a sense of humor. It's just buried *deep, deep* down."

Connor said nothing.

We crossed the road toward the exorbitantly expensive

building, and I hoped the secrets inside it would be easier to unearth than Connor's sense of humor.

Tony Callahan, the man Damon Wood had fingered for the double murder, wasn't quite in the league of Bill Gates and Steve Jobs, but he wasn't so far off from where I was standing. Of course, we were less interested in how rich and successful he was than in how many people he might've killed in pursuit of that success.

Officer Mendez had found the microcomputer Damon had assured us we'd find, and Stanley Cox had continued to be uncooperative in explaining how it got there.

So Stanley was covering for someone.

And if it wasn't his partner in crime, it was someone who'd paid him to confess to a double homicide he didn't commit.

On the basis of Tony Callahan's background report, he might just be that someone.

We entered the three-story building through a set of silent sliding doors, and a minute later a pretty receptionist was leading us through the inner labyrinth. It was obvious the place had been fitted out by a professional interior designer. The warmth of exposed timber ceilings contrasted with the sleek cool of polished concrete floors, and the effect combined with expert lighting, artfully placed furniture pieces, and thriving indoor potted trees was both impressive and inviting.

I was also impressed that Adeline effortlessly kept pace in her four-inch ankle breakers as we were guided to Tony Callahan's private office.

His receptionist (who might've been chosen as a complementary accessory to the interior design) tapped on his door. Our person of interest opened it.

Seeing us all there must've made Tony wonder how *interested* we were. "Wow, three of you. What's the occasion?"

Connor ignored the question. "I'm Connor Stiles, a consultant with the LAPD, this is my colleague, Isobel Avery, and this is Adeline Thorne, who's, er . . . basically our student intern."

Adeline stiffened in my peripheral vision, less than pleased at this introduction. That would teach her to irritate Connor.

Tony's gaze brushed over us. "Well, it's a pleasure to make your acquaintance. All of you." Despite the words, his attention settled on Connor. Adeline probably didn't like that much either. "Come and take a seat."

Tony's private office shared the design theme with the rest of the building, right down to the potted tree in the corner. Since there were only two visitor chairs, the receptionist came back wheeling a third, and we sat down.

Connor slipped his spiral-bound notepad out of his pocket, and Adeline, seeing this, reached into her dainty floral clutch (which matched her shoes, I realized belatedly) and retrieved a slim leather journal. Was she going to mimic everything Connor did?

She opened it and waited for something noteworthy to happen. I switched my attention to the man we were here to see but not before noticing that his desk was especially large—as if he were competing with Lyle. Had I missed the memo on desk size being the new compensation commodity?

Tony himself was in his late forties, with a prominent nose, shaggy eyebrows, and well-cared-for olive skin that made him look younger. He was stocky without being overweight and had a full head of immaculately greased hair. I had an inkling he was rather proud of it.

I willed Connor's attention my way, not sure if he'd want to ask the questions in front of Adeline, but he gave me a nod, so I jumped in. "Thank you for speaking with us, Mr. Callahan. We'll try not to take up too much of your time—"

"I'd appreciate that."

Right. "Allow me to get straight to the point then. A source suggested you had a lot to gain from Isaac Anand's death—"

"Let me guess. Was your source Damon Wood?" Tony was so sure of the guess that he didn't wait for affirmation. "Fine, we might as well get comfortable while I go through the whole damn story again." He mumbled something about "the relationship that just keeps on giving" and took a swig of water from the expensive-looking bottle on his desk.

"Story?"

"Did Damon mention when he was sticking you on my trail that we were romantically involved once? No? I didn't think so."

Darn, why wasn't that in the report?

Adeline scribbled furiously in her notebook. A pointless exercise since the LAPD would seize it as part of the nondisclosure agreement she'd signed.

Tony continued. "Three years ago, for about five months, we were together. It ended badly, and he's been flinging around accusations about me to anyone who'll listen ever since. A textbook scorned lover."

I allowed doubt to show on my face. "That seems extreme."

"Yes," Tony agreed, overlooking my doubt. "Damon is highly intelligent when it comes to tech, but his emotional intelligence is another matter. When I hired him, I didn't care about that. When I fell for him, I didn't care either. But when it ended—"

"Wait, he was your employee?" *That* had been in the file, but Mr. Callahan obviously liked to have the upper hand, so I'd give it to him and see what he'd volunteer.

"Yes. I know it goes against conventional propriety to have a boss and employee sleeping together, but it happens all the time. So long as it's between two consenting adults, in most cases, there's no harm done."

Adeline made eyes at Connor.

"But?" I asked, struggling to focus.

"But Damon doesn't have the maturity of most adults."

It seemed Tony had tired of the subject.

Adeline returned to her energetic note-taking. She didn't seem tired at all.

When the receptionist had wheeled in a third chair for

us, I'd been closest and so had sat down on that one. Unlike the sleek aluminum creations Adeline and Connor were occupying, mine was a high-end office chair.

Which meant it could swivel.

I swiveled so Adeline was out of my peripheral vision. "Well, as a result of Mr. Wood's suggestion, we did some research. And we noticed that when stocks in Isaac Anand's company plummeted after the announcement of his death by a possible AI malfunction, you purchased every one of them you could get your hands on at an excellent price. Which gives you a controlling interest with Mr. Anand no longer around."

I left Rick out of it. With zero connections between him and Tony, if Mr. Callahan was behind this, Rick was collateral damage.

"Sure, I saw an opportunity and took advantage of it. Nothing wrong with that."

"It was convenient for you that the method of murder cast serious doubts on the worth of Mr. Anand's research and intellectual property assets. A risk you didn't mind taking in buying up all his stocks."

"Was that a question?"

"No, just an observation."

Tony clasped his hands together, unperturbed by our conversation. "Observe away, Ms. Avery. I spend a lot of my time monitoring the leading minds of the tech industry. Truth be told it's what I do best. Most of my employees are far smarter than me when it comes to technology. My strength is in assembling talent, assessing the industry, and steering the two in a lucrative direction."

He waved a hand at his luxurious office as if it proved his innocence.

"Naturally, I'd been watching Mr. Anand, and the rumors of his breakthrough were enough to entice me to take that risk. Not that it was much of a risk. I have a history of rewarding my investors very well, so those stock prices should rebound quickly with it coming under my parent company."

"I see," I said.

His calm explanation seemed entirely reasonable. So why did he make my skin crawl? I looked at Connor, seeing if he wanted to jump in with any questions. I was out.

Tony used the opportunity to put forth his own agenda. "In the interest of rewarding my investors, I must say I hope the LAPD is protecting the intellectual property assets on Mr. Anand's computers that were seized. Any idea when I can expect to have access to them?"

I stood up. "I'm sure they'll be released to you as soon as Isaac Anand's murder is solved."

"WHAT DID YOU THINK?" I asked as the three of us walked to the car.

I wasn't directing the question at Adeline, but she was quick to share her opinion. "Seems reasonable to me. I know this one girl who found out her longtime partner was cheating on her, so she convinced him that they'd both get each other's names tattooed over their hearts for their anniversary and got him to go first. When his was done, she broke up with him right there in the tattoo parlor and left her spite forever burned into his chest. What this Damon Wood guy did sounds pretty tame after that." She pulled a section of wavy hair over her shoulder and primped it. "Plus Tony's got this great sexy, sophisticated vibe going on. It's a pity he's gay."

"He might be bisexual," Connor pointed out. Was he trying to deflect Adeline's attention away from himself?

She flicked her hair behind her. "No way. He didn't look at me once."

Well, at least she'd kept quiet during the interview. But if that was the sum of her conclusions, what had she been writing in that journal?

I nudged Connor, hoping for a more useful point of view.

"I don't trust him any more than I trust Damon Wood, but he's appearing to cooperate and we don't have anything on him yet to push further. I say we pay Wood a visit. Tell him he'll need to give us more if he wants to see Callahan go down for this. He might be more helpful with that motivation."

I was pleased I'd been thinking along the same lines. "Let's do it."

Damon Wood worked half an hour away in an ugly,

squat building in Downtown LA, a stone's throw from a piñata store and a place advertising adult massages. The interior wasn't much better than the exterior. Threadbare carpet, fluorescent lighting, and three guys sharing a room the size of Tony's office. Tony's office smelled a lot better too, but the computers here seemed equally top-end.

I couldn't believe Damon had complained about the decor of the interrogation room.

His two colleagues stared at Adeline like elementary school kids at a magic show, and I was forced to admit there might be some merit to her gauge of Tony's sexual orientation.

Of course, that wasn't what we were here to investigate.

The report the LAPD had compiled on Damon Wood had revealed very little. Maybe suspiciously little. He'd worked here for the past two years, paid his (insignificant) taxes, had a good credit score, a crappy car, and an expensive internet plan. He rented a one-bedroom unit in Crenshaw not far from here, and his single apparent splurge outside his tech-related gear was a gym membership. One he actually used based on his physique.

Once again Connor did the introductions—conveniently implying without explicitly stating that I was associated with the LAPD too—and Damon led us to an adjacent meeting room. It had better carpet and plain but new furniture. I wondered if the big screen on the wall meant they preferred to have meetings via video calls to prevent prospective clients from seeing their locale.

Damon sat at the head of the table, so I took the second seat down and angled away from Adeline again to help me stay focused. "We did as you suggested and spoke with Tony Callahan."

Damon arched a dark brow. "Let me guess, he claimed it was all just a personal vendetta because we used to be lovers." It wasn't a question.

Behind me, I could hear Adeline taking notes. It was easy to distinguish the difference between her wild scribbling and Connor's quick, precise strokes as he jotted select information in shorthand. What had she even heard that was worth writing down this early in the interview?

I arched an eyebrow back at Damon. "It seems you two have danced this dance before. Why didn't you tell us?"

"Because I wanted you to investigate him without the instant prejudice our history brings."

That seemed reasonable too. An accusation against an ex-lover was instantly suspect, and Hunt had already been refusing to take him seriously.

"Is there any truth to it?" I asked.

"No. I mean, yes, we were lovers, but his shady activities were the *reason* we broke up, not something I invented afterward out of some kind of personal mission to ruin his life. I assume you noticed his company has benefited greatly from Isaac Anand's death?"

"Yes, but it's hardly solid evidence he had his hand in the double homicide."

"No shit, Sherlock."

Adeline snickered, then coughed in a poor attempt to cover it.

Damon ignored her. "He's a smart, successful businessman. He's not about to leave a trail of incriminating evidence for you to follow straight to his door, and he's rich enough to pay others to do the dirty work for him. Take Stanley Cox, for example. Owning up to a double homicide he didn't commit. Doesn't even know all the details of how it was committed. I've been thinking about that apparent oversight. I don't suppose you've found the device, have you? Maybe it'll link to Tony somehow. But no, if that were the case he would've paid off a dirty cop or something to retrieve it by now . . ."

Damon spoke fast, more to himself than to me. I waited until he'd wound it down before steering him back to his version of their relationship story. "What kind of shady activities did you witness while you were together?"

He rubbed his jaw. "You have to understand I was naive and head over heels in love. I let a lot of odd things pass by without questioning them too closely because I wanted to believe the best of my new boyfriend."

"What kinds of things?"

"Well, first it was the little stuff. Like he was a very private man, never shared anything with me about his family or childhood or past, and he took a lot of phone calls in another room, many of them at odd hours in the middle of the night. That was all explainable enough though. I figured he'd had a hard childhood, wasn't close to his family if he had one, and was a successful businessman with international contacts. But then there was this one time I found a bag of cash lying around the house. I mean hundreds of thousands of dollars. Who needs that much cash for anything but illicit activities? Even then I didn't think about it too hard." He glared at me as if I was somehow to blame for this oversight.

I nodded sympathetically. "Sure. So what *did* make you think about it?"

He shifted his glare to the table. "The breaking point was when he stole intellectual property from a friend I went to college with. There was this big contract coming up in vehicle fleet tracking and management. Tony had a team working on a tender for it, but they weren't going to be able to achieve everything the company was after. I mentioned in passing that my friend had specialized in vehicle fleet management systems for years and made a few big advances, not thinking anything of it. Then a few days before contract submissions closed, I hear from my friend that there was a break-in at her office. I didn't put two and two together until Tony took me out to dinner to celebrate landing the contract."

Interesting. That painted Callahan's "observation" and "talent-finding" in a different light.

Damon was still talking, lost in the story now. "I questioned him about it, and he claimed his project team had had a breakthrough, but the timing was way too convenient, and when I asked one of the guys on the team, he looked uncomfortable even while he confirmed what Tony had said. I mean, I know this industry is moving fast and a lot of people employ gray hat activities that push the ethical boundaries a bit—but to steal the life's work of a little company just to fatten his own wallet? We broke up soon after."

Wow.

Damon's eyes refocused on me. "Then the bastard fired me and ruined my reputation in the industry, ensuring I'd never get another decent job. Exactly who is *he* accusing of pursuing a personal vendetta?"

13

"I SUPPOSE WE'LL HAVE TO PAY another visit to Tony Callahan," I said, feeling like the ball in a game of Ping-Pong. We were back in the SUV after finishing up with Damon. "How are we supposed to figure this out when all we have are conflicting versions of events and only one man's word against the other's to go by?"

Connor answered before Adeline this time. Probably because she was busy admiring the piñata she'd insisted on buying for some party tonight.

"This is a game to them. So we keep applying pressure until it stops being fun. I just wish the bastards had the decency to work closer together."

Adeline put the colorful dinosaur down and spoke up from the backseat. "Are you sure applying pressure is the right approach? I mean, you're not getting very far with them, and I was watching YouTube videos last night, and they said the best method of interrogation is actually to establish rapport, make them feel like you understand them and that kind of thing. I could give it a go if it'd help. I'm great at getting people to like me."

Connor and I shared a look and politely declined.

Half a long hour of politeness later, we were back in Ocean Park. Tony Callahan was not pleased to see our group again. Not even the oh-so-likable Adeline. But he allowed us into his office anyway.

The poor receptionist had taken the extra chair away since we'd left and so had to fetch it back. I nabbed it for myself, figuring it would be more comfortable than the aluminum ones and had the swivel capability to boot.

Since Connor had suggested we apply pressure, I didn't bother with small talk. "Damon Wood told us you stole intellectual property from a friend of his. That that's why you broke up."

Tony let out a long-suffering sigh. "Did he tell you about my Japanese sex cushion too?"

What? Eww. "No."

Adeline scribbled in her notebook.

"Oh good. He must have finally stopped spreading that rumor." Callahan leaned back in his chair, folded his arms, and made direct eye contact with me. The unspoken yet clear-as-day message was that he couldn't care less. That I was wasting his time.

I smiled pleasantly and gave him my own unspoken message: suck it up, princess. Aloud, I said, "We've confirmed the timing of your breakup coincided with landing the vehicle fleet management contract."

The corners of Tony's mouth turned down, reacting to my unspoken words rather than the spoken ones. "So what the hell does that prove? That he can spin a good lie? He was upset, he fixated on the break-in, and he either realized it was a great story that would be impossible to wholly refute or was deluded enough to convince himself it was true. Regardless, it doesn't make his claims any less false."

Tony's denial didn't prove Damon's claims any *more* false either. But he wasn't going to acknowledge that, so I stuck to the facts. "Then you fired him and blackballed him out of the industry." The long drive between their offices had been handy for checking up on their stories.

"Is that another observation, Ms. Avery?" His arms slipped apart in irritation before he remembered himself and returned to his *I couldn't care less* pose. "Yes, after Damon started spreading accusations about me, I fired him. I'm a businessman, and you can't have someone casting aspersions on you in your own company."

If Callahan's scowl was anything to go by, the memory still pissed him off.

"He didn't stop there either. He made so much noise there was an investigation into it—an investigation which turned up nothing, I'd like to point out—so after that, I made some phone calls to warn other companies about him. I'm not a saint. I had to do something to prevent him gaining credibility with which to continue his vendetta. But I've always told him that if he'll just publicly retract all this and personally apologize, I'll make sure he gets a job worthy of his skills."

Despite Callahan's denial of sainthood, he seemed pleased by his own generosity.

"I'm not a monster either," he said, allowing his arms to fall to his sides, more relaxed now that he'd had a chance to vindicate himself. "I just couldn't waste any more time dealing with the fallout of Damon's smear campaign. He's lucky I haven't sued him."

"Why haven't you?"

Lines re-emerged on his forehead. Perhaps realizing I wasn't as convinced as he wanted me to be.

"Because I've got better things to do, and no one except fresh, unsuspecting blood pays any attention to him anyway." He sat up straight. "Speaking of having better things to do, are we done here?"

"Yes, Mr. Callahan. For now."

Hopefully, he'd take the hint and allow the poor receptionist to leave the extra chair here.

SEEING AS HUNT HAD INFLICTED Adeline upon us, we figured we'd return the favor by swinging past the police station. Plus we were getting nowhere fast talking to

Tony Callahan and Damon Wood. We needed to up the pressure, and for that we needed ammunition. Our hope was that Hunt had fared better working on the hacking device angle.

I was curious to see what Adeline would make of her aunt's boyfriend. And vice versa too. It might be fun to see Hunt on his best behavior. But when Connor brusquely introduced them, Hunt gave a half nod of acknowledgment, Adeline returned it, and that was that.

Perhaps I should've predicted their interaction—or the lack of it anyway. Adeline was proving, on the whole, to be self-absorbed, and Etta's cookie bribe could only push Hunt so far. Still, receiving a half nod of acknowledgment was miles better than my first interaction with the commander.

He gave us an update. "After confirming Anand's security system was hacked through the microcomputer Mendez found, we've been reviewing the surveillance footage outside his home to see who had opportunity to plug it into one of his computers. We only have thirty days of footage, but we're hoping our killer is on it."

"And?" Connor asked.

"We've found four individuals connected with the case, and two of them are dead. I have the relevant footage isolated if you want to see it."

We crowded around the computer monitor on Hunt's desk to watch people walking to and from Isaac Anand's front door. The video was in color and better quality than what your average security camera recorded but still low resolution.

The officer who'd gone through the surveillance hadn't bothered to isolate every time Isaac went out or returned home, so the first person we saw was Richard Knightley. It was two and a half weeks before his murder and strange to watch knowing how his life had ended. He crossed the lawn like he'd been there before, dressed smart casual in jeans and a shirt with a jacket slung over his arm and a pleased look on his face. Was that because he knew Isaac was going to help him win the trial? He left half an hour later, his step confident, unhurried.

Tony Callahan was the next to appear. A few days after Rick's visit. Tony was in a business suit, carrying a briefcase that could've easily fit the hacking microcomputer inside it. He didn't stay long. Within five minutes, he was striding back across the lawn, taking his briefcase with him.

What had he been doing there? And why hadn't he mentioned it to us? Five minutes was enough time to plant the microcomputer if Isaac had gone to the kitchen to grab drinks. Tricky but not impossible.

I glanced at the file names of the remaining surveillance video snippets. Stanley Cox and Patty Wilkinson weren't listed. So had they planted the device more than thirty days ago? Did they have an unidentified partner? Or were they innocent, with Stanley being a mere patsy as Damon wanted us to believe?

Thinking of the devil summoned him to the screen.

Damon Wood had visited Isaac one week before the murder. He was dressed in another fitted T-shirt and faded jeans and was carrying a black duffel bag. The zipper was partially open showing a splash of muted green.

"How much does a duffel bag of cash weigh?" I asked aloud.

Hunt didn't hesitate, making me wonder how often this question came up. "About twenty pounds depending on the size of the bag."

So nine kilos then, my mind converted. "Can you play that again?"

We watched Damon stride across the lawn to the door a second time. It was hard to tell, given he was a muscular guy, but the bag looked lighter to me.

Then again, Harper had made her toolbox with its collection of lethal wrenches seem like it weighed nothing, and she was half his size.

Adeline leaned over Hunt's shoulder, trying to get a better view. "Can't you zoom in on the image to see what's in the bag?"

Hunt snorted. "Not unless you're on TV. In the real world, you zoom in on a blurry image and you get an even more blurry image."

Somehow Adeline transformed the jibe into a positive affirmation. "Guess I'm in the right industry then."

I had to admire her easy confidence. Even if I did find it irritating.

Whatever was in the duffel bag, it appeared emptier

when Damon left three and a half hours later. What had he been doing with Isaac for so long? One thing was certain: he'd had ample opportunity to plant the microcomputer. But why on earth would he tell us about it if he'd been the person to do so?

The last snippet of footage was Rick on the night of the double homicide. He was still wearing the clothes we'd gone to dinner in. The realization made my stomach flip. He strode up to the door, expression eager. No way could he have known he was about to die.

So who had?

14

WE WERE BACK AT TONY CALLAHAN'S office twenty minutes later. I was as weary of seeing his face as he was of seeing mine.

While I didn't think the receptionist felt any differently, she did a better job of faking it. Even when she had to fetch the chair for the third time today.

I was tempted to just sit on Connor's lap. But instead, I waited until we were seated, and she'd shut the door behind her, before saying, "We know you visited Isaac Anand two weeks before his murder. What were you doing there?"

Tony took a moment to respond. I wondered if he was counting to ten under his breath. Or imagining shoving my wheeled chair straight out his office window. "Like I said, Ms. Avery, I observe the industry and collect talent.

I heard rumors Mr. Anand had made significant advances in the field of AI robotic communication and so made him an offer."

"What was the offer?"

"Well, I wasn't sure of the specifics of his breakthrough, so I told him I was interested in learning those specifics and that there were millions of dollars on the table if it was of use to me."

It said something about how long I'd been rubbing shoulders with the rich and famous that my eyes didn't boggle at his casual mention of *millions*. "What did he say?"

"No."

Bet that wasn't a word Tony heard often. But why had Isaac said no? Did he have his own plans for the break-through? Or—it hadn't occurred to me until now—but was it possible the entire breakthrough was a lie? A rumor Isaac had started to somehow disguise the lump sum Rick might pay him for rigging the court cases? It would explain why no one knew any details. I shelved the possibility for later and focused on Tony.

"How come you didn't tell us about your visit earlier?"

"Because you didn't ask."

"Is that why? Or is it because it makes Mr. Anand's sub-sequent death, which gave you the ability to buy a signifi-cant share in his company stocks, even more convenient for you?"

Tony glanced at the window, lending credence to my suspicion that he was fantasizing about shoving me out of it. "Convenient, yes. Evidence of foul play, no." He stood up. "I've been cooperating with you lot all day. If you're not going to arrest me, I'm done talking, and if you are, I'm still done."

Well, at least I'd pushed him past the point of this being a game.

"One more question, Mr. Callahan, then we'll let you get on with business. Why are you still *doing* business? Don't you have enough money?"

He frequently earned more cash from a single contract than Richard had managed to scam out of all his victims combined. Tony was only in his late forties, but he could've easily never worked another day of his life.

The man in question threw back his head and laughed. "My dear girl, *no one* has enough money. Now please kindly escort yourselves out so I can make some more."

With that terrible sentiment bouncing around my brain, we traveled to Tony Callahan's ex-boyfriend's office. An office which suggested Damon took a different view on the value of wealth—at least where that wealth went hand in hand with stealing from a friend.

But there was one subject the pair agreed on. They would've been happier to answer the door to Tom Cruise selling Scientology than our tiresome trio.

Nevertheless, Damon led us into their company meeting room. His colleagues had no such sentiments about our presence and swiveled in their chairs to watch Adeline pass by.

At least one of them must've eaten their lunch in the meeting room because it smelled like fried onion instead of stale body odor and the cheap formaldehyde-treated furniture. We all took the same seats as the first time, and resignedly I raised my mental hackles and psyched myself up for the conversation.

It was exhausting being the hard-ass asking the questions. Something I'd never appreciated when Connor was doing it.

"Why were you at Isaac Anand's home a week before his murder? Carrying a duffel bag that was a whole lot emptier when you left three and a half hours later, we noticed. Seems you had plenty of time to plant that hacking device you told us about."

Damon's hackles were already raised. "Unbelievable. I hand you the keys to your case, and you think I did it. Check your records. You'll find the DEA received an anonymous tip that day leading to the seizure of four hundred pounds of cocaine being shipped into the Los Angeles/ Long Beach Seaport. That was our doing."

"What do you mean?"

"Ever heard of a group called Vigilance?"

"No."

"That's because you're not supposed to have heard of them. We're an anonymous, global community of hackers who do what we can to prevent or expose major criminal operations foolish enough to leave clues online."

"What does Vigilance get out of it?"

He studied me for a second and let out a harsh laugh. "What happened to make you so cynical? You look so sweet and innocent."

I smiled—or perhaps bared my teeth. "I have an asshole ex-lover in my past too."

There, Adeline, how was that for rapport building?

I could hear her scribbling in her journal again.

Damon seemed pleased with my revelation. Maybe because I'd inadvertently called Tony an asshole.

"What we get out of it varies depending on the individual. Most Vigilance members have normal lives with ordinary day jobs. Maybe they have a social conscience and want to be part of something bigger or better or more exciting. Maybe they've been victimized and want to be empowered instead. Maybe they're trying to atone for something. Hell, I don't know."

"What do you get out of it?"

He crossed an ankle over his knee. "None of your business."

Right then. "So you and Isaac were both part of this . . . Vigilance group?"

Damon sighed. "Yes. Member anonymity is a big deal, and I wouldn't normally reveal someone's affiliation, but Isaac's dead, so I guess it won't hurt him now."

"What was his motivation?"

"The subject never came up. Some people can take someone's good intentions at face value and not be so suspicious of every damn thing."

Subtle. "If anonymity is such a big deal, how did you guys meet?"

"We both worked enough local angles that we started to recognize each other's online aliases. Every now and then a job comes along that's a particularly difficult hack, one that takes multiple people to pull off. You can link together online, but it's easier to coordinate in person, so Isaac and I would team up sometimes."

That didn't fit with the picture I'd built of the man who'd been working with Rick. "If Isaac was so interested in justice, how come he was helping the likes of the scammer Richard Knightley?"

"He wasn't."

"How do you know?"

"Because he'd never do that. He was one of the good guys. That's why I'm trying to make sure you solve his murder!"

That was the most genuine emotion I'd seen from Damon—a break from his usual veneer of superior contempt. "Why would Stanley Cox say he was then? You read the confession."

"How would I know? I'm an expert on computers—not people. You're supposed to be the detective here."

I ignored the false assumption behind that statement. "Why didn't you point out the inconsistency when you came into the station?"

"Because Cox was lying! I thought I'd made that clear, and it seemed pretty inconsequential compared to lying about a *double homicide*. If you took everything else he said at face value after that, I guess I overestimated your intelligence."

Lovely. "And the contents of the duffel bag?"

"I brought snacks. You know, energy drinks. Chips. Pretzels. Twinkies. Do you need to see the damn receipt?"

"Do you have it?"

His hands jerked upward in frustration then returned to his lap. "No. Do you have your receipt from the last time you bought food?"

Yes, because I never cleaned out my bag. But no need to mention that. "The duffel bag was partially unzipped, and we could see a muted green color inside. None of the snacks you mentioned fit the bill." Not that I'd memorized the packaging of every variety of snack food, but the ones I could think of were all bright, bold colors.

Damon frowned, trying to remember—or invent a plausible lie. "It must've been the wasabi peas. Isaac loved them."

I thought back to the footage. The green could've been wasabi peas. A duffel bag of snack foods would've been lighter than the nine kilos of cash too, so he might even be telling the truth. "Okay. Thanks again for your time, Mr. Wood."

He pushed to his feet. "Ugh. Just solve the case already. Then I can do the polite thing and tell you you're welcome and actually mean it."

Connor, Adeline, and I let ourselves out—an easy feat since this was the fifth time that day we'd interviewed one of the embittered ex-lovers.

"Gosh," Adeline said. "I thought it was only actors that had to repeat the same scenes over and over." She pushed a strand of glossy hair behind one ear. "Are you sure you're doing this right?"

DAMON'S STORY CHECKED OUT. Or at least the timing of it did. Four hundred pounds of cocaine had been seized after an anonymous tip that day. It was possible he'd anticipated we'd find the footage and concocted the whole Vigilance spiel in preparation, but I was beginning to believe him.

That left a discrepancy in the case. Maybe an important one.

"The relationship between Isaac and Rick is bugging me. Damon is adamant that Isaac wouldn't be helping him, but then what possible reason could Stanley have for claiming he was?"

Adeline straightened in the backseat and declared with great solemnity, "Somebody's lying." She waited for a beat before adding, "Was that good? I think that was good."

It took me a moment to cotton on that she'd said it like the final line of a high drama TV show before cutting to commercial. Apparently, she'd gotten bored observing and had moved on to practicing her lines.

It *had* actually been pretty good. Not helpful, but good. I didn't feel charitable enough to say so though.

Thankfully, Connor prevented me from having to analyze that further by answering my original question.

"We know Cox is hiding something. Maybe he's trying to protect a partner who planted the microcomputer in Isaac's house. Or maybe he wasn't involved in the crime at all and doesn't know how the microcomputer got there. But that doesn't mean he's lying about what Rick and Isaac were up to. Most of the details of his confession were correct, and even good guys have a price."

"So Damon might be wrong," I mused. "In which case, I guess Patty Wilkinson would be our top suspect given her affiliation with Stanley and the fact that it gives her motive to kill them both. A motive that no one else seems to have. But if Damon is right, and Isaac *wasn't* helping Richard, what would someone like Callahan get out of claiming he was?"

"A willing patsy," Connor said. "Cox might not have agreed to confess if he knew Isaac was innocent. That the murders weren't about justice or vengeance—just acquiring some tech breakthrough he didn't care about."

Geez. That was cold. But strategic. Like Callahan. But would he have planned it all out in advance, killing Rick so he could pay one of the scam victims to confess and tie up the story in a neat little bow? Or had it been a happy accident that Rick was killed along with Isaac and quick thinking on the murderer's part to acquire a patsy out of Rick's dirty laundry? And if it was the former, how the heck would the murderer have known about Isaac and Rick's meetings?

I had a lot of questions and very few answers.

But I had an idea for where we could find some. "With so much hinging on whether Isaac was helping Richard or not, why don't we do some digging into Mr. Anand's character?"

I saw Adeline's nose wrinkle in the rearview mirror. "Digging? Is that code for just talking to more people? Not even suspects this time? Because my phone reminded me I have a nail appointment this afternoon I need to get to."

Connor kept his expression bland as he said, "Good. The first step to any successful investigation is to have trust-worthy hands."

I managed to contain my snort. Barely.

Before Adeline left, Connor informed her she'd need to leave her notebook with us as part of her nondisclosure agreement.

"But there's nothing about the case in it," she said.

What? Then what had she been writing all those times?

Connor held out his hand. "Let's see."

She rolled her eyes but dug it out of her clutch and gave it to him.

Inside were impressively drawn sketches of everyone. On the first page, Tony was sliding down a pile of money, prominent nose first.

The level of detail she'd squeezed into such a tiny space was astounding.

I shot Adeline an incredulous look.

"What? It helps me concentrate."

On the next page, Damon was swinging a baseball bat at a piñata of Tony's head. The left side of Piñata Tony's jaw had already been caved in and was spilling out candy.

Next, Connor was posed on a wingback chair, straight-backed, grim-faced, and for some reason—shirtless.

Given Adeline had never seen him shirtless, it was remarkably accurate. Damn how I missed his chest, his embrace.

Ahem.

And on the following page, I was . . .

Oh, I wasn't in there at all.

Right.

Connor returned the notebook to Adeline without a word. She tucked it into her clutch, grabbed her dino-saur piñata, and took her leave without bothering to thank Connor for allowing her to shadow him. Or sketch him shirtless for that matter.

She did, however, promise to see us tomorrow.

Lucky us.

15

FIFTEEN MINUTES LATER, Connor and I were en route to Alhambra in the San Gabriel Valley. He broke the comfortable silence. "At least one worthwhile thing came out of our monotonous morning."

Did he mean uncovering the discrepancy over whether Isaac was helping Rick? Or was it that he could now check off "having an artist sketch me shirtless" from his bucket list?

"What's that?"

"It freed us of Etta's niece."

I grinned. "Maybe we'll have to interview more boring suspects first thing tomorrow then."

A smile tugged at Connor's lips. "Maybe we will."

It was silly perhaps, but after discovering Adeline would

be joining us, I'd been worried that rather than the case bringing Connor and me together, it might push us farther apart. Not that Connor was the type to latch on to the nearest pretty thing—Harper's revelations made that clearer than ever. But what if he and Etta's niece had gotten along really well? Learning about Sophia and how different she was to me raised the uncomfortable question of whether I truly was a good fit for Connor, and Adeline might have made me question that even more.

But instead, it had been reassuring to witness their obvious disconnect. Connor's complete lack of interest despite her generous assets had been reassuring too. And it had highlighted some of the reasons we did suit each other. We cared about justice and doing a job well and could be stronger in both those pursuits when we teamed up. Family was important to us. If I did manage to win Connor back before our Australia trip and he met my parents, I knew he'd try (at least by his standards) to make a positive impression, the same as I'd tried with his family. We might go about things in different ways, but the life values—the big stuff—we shared.

And we made each other laugh. Well, smile in Connor's case. When you pared it down like that, it was a solid foundation for a relationship.

Connor stopped the car in front of an old red-brick home mostly hidden by well-watered trees and shrubs. The street the house was on wasn't a particularly nice one, but the flourishing garden brightened it. We walked up the concrete driveway onto the postage-stamp-sized porch. Up close, it was obvious the building had been meticulously maintained, from the condition of the mortar to the new roller shutters on each window.

Isaac Anand's parents had died when he was young, leaving him with one living relative in the United States. He had more distant relatives in India, but he'd never traveled there in his thirty-one years on earth, so it was his grandmother who we'd come to see. Connor knocked on the freshly painted door.

The woman who opened it was built like a tree in harsh country. Short and stout and a little bent, but made to last, having weathered some of the harshest conditions life could throw at her.

But her resilience didn't lessen her grief or pain. It just changed the way she dealt with it.

She listened quietly while Connor introduced us, then asked, "Have you got news for me about my grandson's case?" Her accent was strong, but her English was perfect.

And her question, with its mixture of hope that we might have news and hopelessness because nothing would bring her grandson back, hit me like a bucket of ice water.

Knowing what a jerk Rick was had rendered me partly immune to Lyle's grief, but now the tragedy of the crime penetrated. This brave woman had left her birth country of India and everything she knew behind for a shot at a better life, a better future for her family. Yet the land of opportunity had turned out to be a land of tragedy, and in its soil, she'd buried her husband, her only child, and would now be burying her grandson too.

Isaac, who had been little more than a vague, hazy figure in my mind the past few days, flashed into high definition. And remembering his body sprawled on the carpet left me sick with regret.

"I'm afraid not yet, Mrs. Anand," I said, fixing my eyes on her searching brown ones in an attempt to drown out the image of her grandson. "But we're so sorry for your loss and are doing everything we can to find who's responsible."

She dropped her gaze and shrugged. "It would not do him any good anyway."

I got the impression she said so to be polite rather than meaning the sentiment. How could she mean it? How could anyone find peace when a loved one's killer was roaming free?

Yet Connor had, I remembered. At least enough to get on with his life.

Until I'd come along and blown things up.

I swallowed hard and focused on Mrs. Anand. "We're still trying to get a more comprehensive picture of why he might have been . . . targeted. May we come in?"

"Yes, please do."

I hoped our efforts would be enough to find the person responsible, to go some way toward helping her find peace.

Inside the house, the complex patterns and bold hues of India sat alongside several framed posters of Elvis and a retro diner booth seat. There was also a large flat-screen TV with surround sound in the living room that I suspected Isaac might've had something to do with.

Mrs. Anand had us sit down and offered us homemade chai tea, but I declined, not wanting to put her through the trouble. When she had lowered herself into a red armchair too, I asked, "An acquaintance of his said Isaac was part of a secret online group. Do you know anything about that?"

"Online? Ever since I bought him his first computer, that is where he spent most of his time. Yes, I believe he was part of a group. I am not sure how it worked exactly, but it was for a noble purpose he told me. Maybe a charity or something like that? Except I think he said they stopped bad things from happening. Sorry, he did tell me about it, but I never really understood."

"That's okay, anything you can remember is helpful. Did you ever meet any of his friends from this group? Or hear of anything specific he was working on?"

"No, no, it was all online." She said it as if "online" was as inaccessible to her as the planet Jupiter. Maybe it was.

"This is a strange question, but did Isaac have a fondness for wasabi peas?"

Her face creased in a heartbreaking smile. "He loved them. Used to be disappointed when people gave him candy instead at Halloween."

So Damon hadn't been lying about that. "Do you know anything about his current projects? There were rumors of a breakthrough of some kind."

She shook her head helplessly. "He did not tell me much

about his work; he knew I could not understand it. But he was very excited . . . about a month ago maybe? He said he was creating something that would make his parents and me proud."

His dead parents, she meant. How could it be that some families were pummeled by such tragedy?

"Did he give you any hints?" I asked.

"No. He wanted to surprise me, and I have all the patience in the world for that boy." Her eyes didn't tear up, but her hand shook as she touched the beads around her neck. "Had, I mean."

It was an effort to keep my mind on the questions. "Do you have any idea what his relationship might've been with the other victim?"

The network of lines on her face deepened into a frown, and she straightened in her armchair. "You mean Richard Knightley? When you people asked me the first time, I could not remember where I had heard the name. But I saw him on the nightly news and realized why it was familiar. That horrible man stole millions from people. I have no idea what my dear boy would be doing with the likes of him."

"Then I'm sorry to ask, but is there any possibility he might have been working with him, maybe helping to clear Richard's name?"

"No. Not a chance." She met our gazes. Read the doubt in them. Her hand went up to touch the beads around her neck again—a gift from Isaac?—and she took a deep breath. "Let me tell you a story." She paused as if gathering strength to tell it. "You may or may not know that Isaac's parents were killed in a terrible situation. Some good-for-nothing thieves tried to rob a Best Buy store, and when they got caught in the act, they took hostages. They killed four people. Including both Isaac's parents"—her face momentarily crumpled—"and my only son."

The break in her composure was almost the undoing of mine. It was stupid that I was so little impacted by the death of a stranger until it was made personal in this woman's grief. But I suppose if we felt the loss of every injustice in the world, we would crumple under the weight of them.

I had no idea how Mrs. Anand hadn't done so under the weight of hers alone.

She went on. "My husband died of a heart attack the year before, and so that is how I found myself trying to raise a six-year-old when I was almost sixty myself. Let me tell you, sixty is too old to raise a child single-handedly. We were okay for money thanks to my son's life insurance, but the young have an energy only they possess, and I was exhausted trying to keep up."

In some backward corner of my brain, it struck me that I often felt the same way about Etta.

"Truth be told, I was relieved when Isaac took to computing. It slowed him down a little. But I am getting off track. The point is, I had no energy left for anything else like gardening, or maintenance, or even shopping sometimes, and that is where my dear neighbor Burt came to our rescue time and time again. He did everything my husband would have been doing. And he was like a father figure to Isaac. Those two would spend hours tinkering in Burt's work shed, repairing things or making bits and pieces for around the house, and who knows what else? Isaac loved and appreciated Burt more than most kids love and appreciate their real fathers."

Her hands were steady again. "All this is to say that when Burt was tricked by one of those telephone scams, not as bad as some but bad enough that he would have had to sell the house if he wanted to keep food on the table . . . Well, Isaac heard about this and said Burt had been there for him through everything, and he was going to return the favor. But we both knew Burt would not accept a handout. He is far too proud for that. The man would not go to a doctor for help if he was dying. So, my wonderful boy came up with a plan."

A ghost of the proud smile she would've beamed at Isaac flitted across her face.

"Isaac still would visit once a month to tinker in Burt's work shed. It was an excuse to keep him company and help with the gardening. But anyway, Burt keeps all sorts of things in that shed, so after the scam, Isaac chose this random old bowl he kept his screws in and said, 'You know, I think this might be antique Indian pottery. Do you have any idea how much that stuff sells for? Me either. But I have a friend who can value it for us. How about I take it to him and see what he says?'"

She was becoming more animated in the retelling now,

remembering the good that had happened before the loss. I could almost imagine the bright, shrewd, and kind grand-mother she would've been to Isaac growing up.

"Burt had no need for the silly thing, and so he agreed Isaac could take it. My dear boy brought him back an envelope full of money, claiming he sold it for forty-five thousand dollars. Burt insisted on giving him a finder's fee, but Isaac had planned for that as well and chosen the pretend value accordingly. So he took a cut of the money, which kept Burt and his pride happy, and old Burt is still my neighbor to this day. Which is why you must see, someone who would go to all that trouble for a victim of one of those scams would not help that Richard boy. No way. Not a chance."

And wouldn't you know it? I believed her. Which meant Cox was lying. Or had been lied to himself.

We needed to find out why.

———

HUNT WASN'T AT THE STATION. An apologetic police officer gave us the reason.

"He's taking a very, very late lunch with his lady friend. I swear I hadn't seen the man do anything but eat at his desk in twenty years, and now he seems to take a lunch hour every other day. It's as if he doesn't have thirty unsolved cases breathing down his neck. But at least he's less of a grump when he comes back."

"We need to talk to Stanley Cox again," Connor told him.

The officer grimaced. "Hunt hates being interrupted at these lunches of his. But you're the consultant working the case with him, right? I'll grab Cox for you, and you can go ahead without him."

Which is how I found *myself* in the interrogation room five minutes later, face-to-face with the man claiming the double homicide as his own handiwork.

Stanley looked much like he had when he walked into the station and confessed. Not just because he was wearing the same clothes—well, except for his belt and shoelaces, which must have been taken from him. I hoped his underwear at least had been washed or changed too. Regardless, his second night in jail hadn't seemed to faze him any more than the first, and Hunt's questioning about the microcomputer had left him unaffected.

I wanted ours to be more successful.

Connor introduced us both and explained we had a few more questions for him, but Stanley's eyes were stuck on me.

Neither Connor nor I had expected the recognition in them.

"I've seen you somewhere before . . . Wait, you're the girl from the video! You were out to dinner with that scumbag before he died, and you took down the poor old man with the steak knife."

Crap. Not an auspicious start to questioning an uncooperative subject. If I denied it, he'd clam up and refuse to talk. So I had to come up with an explanation that would satisfy him fast.

"You're right," I said. "I was there, and I stopped the old man from losing his freedom on top of the money he'd already lost. Ever wonder why Richard didn't press charges? I talked him out of it. Something I couldn't have done if the man had actually attacked."

"Uh-huh, and who are you to have that kind of sway with the bastard?" He straightened as another thought occurred to him. "And what are you doing investigating this case? Did Knightley's rich daddy set this up?"

This was going from bad to worse. How could I turn it around?

In a stroke of inspiration, I realized my poor acting skills might just save me. When Connor had shown me the recording, I'd noticed I hadn't hidden my dirty looks toward Rick as well as I'd thought.

I searched for the video on my phone and showed it to Stanley. "I can't disclose my reason for being there, Mr. Cox, but I can tell you that it's not what it seemed. I share similar sentiments toward Richard Knightley as you." *Well, except for the murder part.* I tapped the screen as the footage showed my disgusted expression. "Does that look like someone who's on Richard's side?"

Stanley peered at it, chewed the inside of his stubbled cheek, then said, "Okay, I'll bite. What do you want to know?"

I left the phone in front of him, a reminder of our

mutual ground, and leaned back. "Tell me why you wanted Isaac Anand dead again?"

"The same reason I gave you the first time. Anand was helping Knightley rig the court cases. Plus the AI security system made for a convenient opportunity to take them both out."

"That's why we're here," I said. "Because we've established that Mr. Anand wasn't helping Knightley."

"Oh come on, I'm not an idiot. It's impossible to prove a negative."

"I have it on very good authority he wasn't helping Knightley."

Stanley huffed. "And I have it on good authority he was."

"Whose?" I asked.

He blanched, realizing he'd given something—tiny, but still something—away. Cox had been *told* Isaac was helping Richard. What did that mean?

Knowing he wasn't going to be tripped so easily into revealing new information again, I tried another tack.

"Well, if you won't share your source, let me tell you about Isaac Anand and why I believe he couldn't have been helping Knightley."

I recounted the whole tale that Isaac's grandmother had told us, letting my emotion color the story.

Stanley remained quiet throughout and was staring at the table by the time I'd finished.

"Mr. Cox, we've come across two holes in your confession now, and we're only going to keep finding more. First there's the microcomputer you neglected to mention and are refusing to explain how you got into Isaac Anand's house. And now we have compelling testimony that there's no way Anand could've been helping Knightley the way you claimed."

Stanley swallowed but didn't look up or speak.

"I don't know who you're protecting, but I suggest you think long and hard about whether they're worthy of it. If you've been paid to confess, the holes in your story mean no one's going to be convinced, so you're not going to get whatever you were promised. And if you did it for someone you cared about, well, we've just established they're lying to you . . . and if they're lying to you about this, what else are they lying to you about?"

It wasn't a question I expected an answer to. Not yet. So I continued on with my closing argument, the memory of Mrs. Anand and her quiet strength in the wake of so much tragedy spurring me on.

"You might think Knightley deserved what he got—he destroyed your family after all—but today Isaac Anand's grandmother is mourning the loss of the grandson she raised from the age of six. After burying her only child twenty-five years prior. Think about that as you sleep on your jail bunk tonight."

16

HUNT FOUND US mere minutes after Cox had been led back to his cell. Which meant I'd been mere minutes away from having my big closing argument ruined by the commander dragging me out of the interrogation room and throwing me into a cell next to Stanley's.

It was one thing to begrudgingly allow me to tag along with Connor, but civilians did *not* ask the questions.

However, since he'd missed all that, Hunt gave Connor a nod, ignored me, and made no mention of Etta's missing niece. Instead, he said, "The tech team has finally cracked some of the encrypted files on Mr. Anand's computer. You're going to want to see this."

He led us up a flight of stairs to the second floor I'd never been on. To my disappointment, it was furbished decidedly similarly to the first floor, except with dark brown carpet instead of tiles. The ceiling might have been a handspan higher as well. We walked down a corridor of closed doors and stopped at one that had POLICE COMMANDER W. HUNT in the cheap plastic nameplate. Hunt pulled a key from his utility belt and unlocked it.

The office within was small, cramped, and dusty as if it hadn't been used in a while but offered a privacy his desk in the open office didn't. He woke the computer—which was sleek, modern, and out of place, so I assumed it must have belonged to Isaac—and pointed at its screen. "What do you make of this?"

The image in question was an engineer's drawing of some kind of robot. It had a combination of wheels and legs, some sort of rectangular object mounted on its back, and a canister type thing attached to a . . . Was that a syringe? I checked the scale of the drawing and realized this robot taking up the size of the computer monitor was actually the size of a housefly.

My stomach dropped.

"What's it for?" I had to force the question out. Could it be designed for something innocent like administering medicines to save a nurse doing it? But then why make it so small?

Hunt folded his arms. "Good question. The tech team told me microrobotics is a field of almost limitless potential, most of it still untapped. But when I noticed the syringe, I pretended it was a classified military project and confiscated it. I didn't want them thinking too hard about the applications for obvious reasons—and who knows what else the decryption will uncover? It's going to take hours or even days to finish decrypting everything, but they said it's on autopilot now and shouldn't need anyone from the tech department looking at it again."

Connor straightened from where he'd been bent over the desk. "Depending on this thing's capabilities, it has dozens of potential uses. Spyware. Assassinations. Medicinal—"

"And the professional poisoner's wet dream," Hunt finished.

After six months of being a Shade, my mind had leaped to the same place as Hunt's, and I was terrified at the implications.

But Connor only nodded. "You're right. The Taste Society will need to be informed about this."

Hunt grunted. I got the feeling it wasn't his main concern, but I was too caught up in my own concerns to speculate further.

This kind of technology could revolutionize the poison industry. It would render Shades ineffective. Powerless. And as vulnerable as any untrained person without the genetic mutation. Which in turn would leave *everyone* defenseless against poison as a method of murder and sabotage. The robots would be widely available and almost impossible to trace back to their owners or operators, making them the ideal tool for the perfect crime. It would be a living nightmare.

"Not quite," Connor corrected, and I realized I'd been thinking aloud. "As soon as this device became available on any scale, tech would be designed to protect against it. The only way to gain a true edge would be to keep it secret and restricted to a select few."

That was somewhat reassuring. But all the same, I wondered what the world might've been like if we'd spent more time pursuing mutual well-being instead of new ways to kill. "What the hell was compassionate Isaac doing developing something like this? And how would it make his parents and grandma proud the way he claimed?"

Connor shrugged. "It'd have other potential uses too. Imagine sending these robots into dangerous or rural locations to provide medicine to those that need it. A modified version might be able to administer vaccinations in developing countries. And in developed countries, it could be useful in catastrophes where the infrastructure can't cope with the number of victims, like if there was an infectious outbreak or a biological attack, the robots could allow health professionals to remotely assist without risk of contamination."

Wow. It wasn't often Connor saw the positive possibilities before I did, but he was right. The miniature injecty robot thingy could be used as easily for good as bad. But what had it been intended for? And what did it mean for the case?

I caught myself chewing a fingernail and stopped. "Okay. But if this tech is what Isaac was killed for, our murderer was most likely interested in its darker uses rather than those altruistic ones. And if secrecy is critical to its effectiveness as a weapon, then that certainly increases the motive for murder a whole lot." My thoughts ran into another roadblock. "Except why would anyone think Rick knew about the injecty robot thing?"

OUR DISCUSSION OF the implications of Isaac's invention was cut short. Connor had a meeting he needed to get to, and Hunt wasn't about to humor me without him present.

We were hustling our way out of the police station when we ran into—almost but not quite literally—Lyle Knightley just outside. The lines on his distinguished face appeared deeper than a week ago, and I discovered that the upwelling of sympathy I felt for Mrs. Anand overflowed to him. Even if he had blamed me for his son's death.

"I was hoping to catch you here," he said. "Please accept my apology for my behavior the other day. It was a . . . difficult time."

Despite the fact that I was the one he'd been accusing and threatening, he directed the words to Connor. He knew who was in charge and was in professional negotiator mode.

Connor stared at him, unmoved, and I had a good idea about how this conversation was going to go down.

"Please. I need to know what's happening with my son's

case. The papers are full of contradictory information. Have you caught the person responsible or not?"

"We're not at liberty to share details of the ongoing investigation," Connor said.

"Ongoing? That means you haven't caught him, doesn't it? But didn't someone confess?"

Connor's lips compressed into a flat line.

Lyle must have understood it was all the answer he was going to get.

"Come on, man. We're talking about my only son here. Surely you can tell me something . . ."

It was strange to feel pity for a man like Lyle Knightley, but pity was what I was feeling. I shot Connor a pleading look, but he didn't see it.

"No, Mr. Knightley, we can't. Now if you'll excuse—"

"Please, Ms. Avery." Lyle must've caught the look I'd sent Connor and switched targets. "You know how much my son meant to me."

Crap.

But no matter what my empathy prodded me to do, Connor had entrusted me with taking lead on the case. I needed to stick to the rules.

Ugh. Who knew being a hard-ass was so much work?

"We're doing everything we can to make sure the right person goes to prison for this, but I can't tell you anything other than what you've seen in the media."

Lyle's demeanor changed, hardened. He stepped closer. Not a threat but a definite power play. "Don't give me that garbage. You're not a member of the LAPD. You're working for me!"

Connor placed a hand on Lyle's arm in warning. "We're partnering with the LAPD, and we're following their protocols."

"My son has been killed, and you're talking about protocols?"

"Certainly, Mr. Knightley. Because no one, no matter how sympathetic, rich, or powerful, is above the rules."

Lyle jerked away from Connor's hand and spoke through gritted teeth. "I've heard enough. You're just like every other disloyal lowlife out there who sees the Knightley family weakened and uses it to your advantage. Well, take it from me, the Knightley name still has some bite left, and you can be sure your boss will be hearing about this."

Had he been a less polished man, he might have spat his fury at our feet, but instead, he glared at us each in turn, then spun on his heel and stalked away.

Connor checked his watch. "Now I'm late." He resumed his fast pace toward the car, and I scuttled to keep up. "I have to get to this meeting, but the Taste Society needs to hear about Isaac Anand's invention immediately in case there are prototypes already out there. Are you okay to give the details to your handler?"

"Sure."

"Good. Make it clear it's too classified to speak about over the phone."

"Got it." I paused outside his SUV. "Did you want me to catch an Uber to save you dropping me home?"

"No. Your apartment is mostly on the way."

I scrambled into my seat, clipped my seat belt on, and called Jim, waiting for him to answer with, "State your ID" like he always did.

Instead, he said, "Don't identify yourself or anyone else. With the high-tech complications of this case, your employer doesn't want anything conveyed over the phone."

"Wait, you know who I am *before* I even give you my ID number? Why make me say it then? Do you have any idea how long it took me to memorize?"

He ignored my question completely. No surprise there. "Why did you call? And try answering that without giving me any explicit details."

"Um, I have important . . . news that, uh, my colleague suggested our employer should know immediately."

Man, conveying information without specifics was hard. I was not cut out to be a spy.

"Are you *sure* it's important?"

He asked the question the way my Aunt Alice used to ask if I was sure I needed the toilet twenty minutes into a road trip.

"Yes."

Jim sighed. "Then I know I'm going to regret this, but meet me at the Thirsty Pig at eight o'clock tonight. I'll find you."

He hung up.

Any irritation I might've had about him not bothering to check whether the time and location suited me was overruled by my curiosity to meet the man the Taste Society had assigned as my handler. He seemed to have been chosen for his complete inability to connect. Don't want secret colleagues to get too chummy, I guess.

That reminded me. The view out the window showed we were nearing my apartment, and I glanced over at Connor. On the topic of secret colleagues getting too chummy . . . I needed to give him that letter.

I dug through my bag to find it and kept it hidden until the car was idling at the curb. Then I all but threw it at him.

"Read this when you have a spare minute tonight. It's not about robots or anything, but it's important too."

———————

SINCE THE POINT OF MEETING in a singles bar was to avoid attracting attention, I figured I'd better dress right for the occasion. Somehow I didn't think Jim would appreciate my efforts. But I had given up trying to impress him and lowered my once-lofty goal to merely keeping his irritation to a minimum (I'd adopted a similar strategy with Hunt). Or, if I was feeling less cooperative, seeing how many pencils I could get him to snap.

What I hadn't wagered on was other patrons of the singles bar appreciating my efforts. The Thirsty Pig was the kind of establishment that was popular for cheap drinks rather than the decor. Come to think of it, the place smelled similar to how I'd imagine an alcoholic pig would smell too.

I found an empty table close to the entrance so I'd be easy to spot and hadn't even warmed up the seat before a guy with slicked-back hair and a Dodgers T-shirt strutted up to me.

"Can I buy you a drink?"

Seeing as I had no idea what Jim looked like, I hedged my bets. "That depends. Are you Jim?"

He lowered his voice to a sexy drawl. "Do you want me to be?"

Oh boy. "Sorry, I bat for the other team."

His eyes widened. "You mean the Australia team? I thought you had an accent. But that's great! I love baseball! My buddy and I were just debating this morning who's the best hitter of all time. Who's got your vote?"

"Um . . ." It took three minutes to convince him I knew nothing about the game. He shuffled off looking like I'd ruined his night, and another man walked up to me. This one was tall, dark, and . . . wearing a dress. There was no way Jim was in touch enough with his feminine side to don a delicate pink Prada knockoff, so I shook my head. "Sorry, I'm meeting someone here."

He leaned close, giving me a front-row view to his beautifully waxed chest, and said, "Oh no, honey, you're not my type. I just came over to let you know that your top's inside out."

I glanced down and saw the telltale seam I'd failed to notice. *Dammit.* "Oh, thanks."

He gave me a toothy smile. "No problem, hon. Those of us wearing high heels and pantyhose have to look out for each other."

Okay, my heels weren't high and I'd forgone the pantyhose, but I appreciated his point all the same. I slipped into the bathroom to correct my wardrobe malfunction and returned to my perch. Where the heck was Jim?

Watching the eligible crowd prowl or prance around depending on their inclinations deepened my need to win Connor back. If I didn't, I'd be forced to join the adult dating scene. Not appealing to a girl who'd prefer to spend her evenings curled up in bed with a fur-friend for company. On the flip side, I guessed that made me prime material for becoming a spinster cat lady. Except maybe I'd collect dogs *and* cats. Hmm . . .

Thankfully, my musings were interrupted by the approach of a third man. "Isobel," he said—no seductive vibes with this one—"I'm Jim."

Given his strict adherence to the Taste Society's no-names policy, it was strange to hear that sentence come out of his mouth. I studied the man in front of me in open curiosity.

For six months, I'd known him only as a voice at the other end of the phone. A rather grumpy voice. There was something in our limited conversations that made me think he'd seen what life had to offer him and wasn't impressed.

That he was fed up, but not motivated enough to change his cards nor depressed enough to give up altogether. And so it was that I'd always imagined Jim as your run-of-the-mill father of two point five children working a soul-sucking job because that's what you had to do and quitting was for the weak.

My mind had painted him with a well-lined face, ordinary brown eyes with dark pouches under them, two days of stubble out of convenience rather than fashion, and clothes that were serviceable but nothing special.

Jim met every one of my expectations.

Having said that, he was more attractive than I'd credited him for. His haircut was more interesting too—clipped shorter on the sides but a few inches long on top. That hair was unkempt now, but if he scrubbed himself up and changed his attire and attitude, it'd be like one of those high-school-loser-to-hottie transformations. Except with more wrinkles and less makeup.

Jim didn't show the same interest in assessing me before saying, "I'll grab a drink to blend in, and then you can tell me what was so important."

"Sure."

I watched him push his way through to the bar and decided I kind of liked him. He reminded me of the gruff uncle or family friend that had no idea how to show affection but had a soft heart underneath. Except I wasn't sure about the soft heart thing with Jim . . .

I *was* sure he didn't feel any such regard for me.

He plonked the beer down and looked me over as if I were a towering pile of paperwork that needed doing.

"Want me to check your drink?" I offered.

The lines on his forehead furrowed. "You think I'm stupid enough to get it spiked? Or are you just trying to drink for free?"

"Trying to stop you from dying, actually, but now I can't remember why I was going to the trouble."

He lifted his beer in salute. "That's the spirit. Let's keep this short, eh?"

I was glad I hadn't come to this singles bar tonight looking for love.

"Is life really that bad?" I asked.

"Course not. I got this way because it's so fun."

Right then. Whatever else he'd done with his time on this earth, he'd mastered the art of sarcasm.

I caught him up on everything that had happened, including the incredible tech discovery, expecting him to be shocked or surprised or *something*.

But no, his expression was bored, bored, bored. Bored like I'd just told him a superlong story about how hard it was to find the right shade of nail polish to suit every role and appearance an actress would be starring in—a tale Adeline had blessed us with earlier in the day.

Jim put his beer down. "Great. I'll pass it on."

"Great? It's not great. It could *kill* people, Jim. Surely even you care about that."

"Even me, hey? Nice to know what you really think."

"I didn't mean it like that—"

"Sure you didn't. Just remember this moment the next time you're asking me for a favor."

As if this guy would ever move an inch out of his way on my behalf. "I try very hard not to ask you any favors. I'm aware you don't appreciate them much."

"Try harder then."

What a thoughtful suggestion. "You know, I think I'd prefer to stick to phone conversations in the future."

He didn't bat an eyelid. "Well, hallelujah for that."

We stared at each other for a minute, then I got to my feet. "Right, if that's all you need from me, I have a cat to cuddle."

Jim didn't smirk or seem amused. He just looked bored.

If I ever saw that man animated, I'd be convinced he'd been poisoned. Or I had.

I drove home and collapsed into bed, too exhausted to worry about Connor's reaction to the letter.

CONNOR

It had been bad enough when I hadn't seen her for days. Like a gaping hole in my life. I hadn't realized exactly how large a space she'd carved out for herself.

But at least holes were silent.

Seeing her every day. The face that had been plaguing my thoughts. The lips I knew so intimately—how they looked in each situation—when she was amused, determined, or flushed with pleasure. The familiar curves I'd explored every inch of. The hope in her eyes when she looked at me. It was too much.

The letter was good. Logical. Rational. A compelling argument for all the reasons we should be together. She argued so persuasively for how we could make it work that, for a minute, I could almost believe it. Envisage it the way she could. Her words dredged up hope like a desperate man scrapes up mud from the bottom of a dry well.

I wished it could be enough to sustain me. But I knew better. I wasn't strong enough. Wasn't brave enough to risk confronting hell again. And I was sick of thinking this over and over every night only to come to the same conclusion.

Seeking calm, I found my favorite Handel concerto and turned it up loud.

Petal started howling.

I wasn't so far away from it myself.

17

"DID YOU OPEN THE LETTER I gave you?" I asked Connor on our way to the police station.

"Yes."

"Did you *read* it?"

"Yes."

Well, that was the first hurdle cleared. "Okay then. Would you like to share your thoughts?"

"No."

Aaaand we fell flat on our face at the second hurdle. Hmm. This conversation wasn't going the way I'd planned. The letter I'd labored over had to have evoked *some* thoughts and feelings in him. But how could I get him to discuss them?

Connor gave me plenty of silence to think it over.

Our vicinity to the police station made up my mind. I would let him get away with avoiding the topic—temporarily.

But tonight, when we'd finished for the day? I vowed I was going to force him to speak with me. No matter what it took. Because we were never going to be able to resolve this if he didn't.

For now though, I tried to lighten the mood. "All right. We'll talk about it later, but you're not allowed to claim your dog ate my letter and you've forgotten what it said."

"She's not my dog."

That wasn't the agreement I was seeking. "So you keep saying, but I noticed you didn't ask Hunt or Adeline if they know anyone looking for a canine companion."

"Maybe I asked when you weren't around."

"Uh-huh. Or maybe Petal is winning you over."

"No comment."

"You can refuse to comment all you like, but it's not going to change the inevitable happy ending."

I hoped he realized Petal wasn't the only happy ending I was referring to.

He refused to comment on that too.

Police Commander Hunt was in a similarly fine mood.

"Morning," I said.

He grunted.

Sheesh, what was with my life and being surrounded by grouchy, monosyllabic men? First Jim, then Connor, now Hunt. You'd think they were the only ones who had problems.

Even Oliver seemed to have caught a dose of the malady.

My musing made me glad to see Adeline walk through the doors, if for no other reason than to have a person around who knew how to smile. But then she opened her mouth, and I realized grouchy men might not be the worst company to keep.

"Good morning, fellow sleuths! Please tell me you had a breakthrough yesterday and we're doing something more exciting today. I need to experience a wide range of activities for my education, after all." She waved her hands in front of our noses as if she hadn't just prioritized her acting education above a double homicide investigation and added, "By the way, what do you think of this nail polish shade? Does it say 'serious but sexy' to you?"

If I said no, would she leave to get them redone?

I was saved from my ethical dilemma by a uniformed officer's arrival. "Commander," the officer said, giving the rest of us a polite nod, "Stanley Cox is saying he's ready to talk."

It turned out that Stanley Cox wasn't just ready to talk, he was ready to talk to me. A problem since as far as Hunt was aware, I'd never interviewed Stanley, so he shouldn't know of my existence, let alone my unofficial involvement in the case. Judging by the weird bulgy muscles in Hunt's jaw, he wasn't happy about it. But he wasn't pigheaded enough to let that get in the way of a crucial witness wanting to open up.

As I reached the door to the interrogation room, the

bristles of his mustache loomed in my peripheral vision. "You and I will be discussing this later."

"Looking forward to it," I lied, wishing he didn't still have the power to make my legs quake.

It wasn't my fault. If Hunt had pretended to be nicer, maybe Stanley would've been happy to talk to *him*.

The commander insisted on joining me inside, which left Connor and Adeline in the observation room. Adeline had smiled at the arrangement. Connor had frowned, perhaps not wanting to be the object of any further sketches. But I'd already pushed my luck with Hunt as far as it'd go, so I kept my peace.

Stanley looked worse for wear today, as if he'd aged years overnight. The wire frames did nothing to hide the puffiness and discoloration under his eyes, and even his hairline seemed to have receded farther in defeat. I felt a spike of pity for him. Which was silly when my intention had been to make him lose sleep over the whole situation.

Maybe Hunt and I could do a niceness transplant.

Stanley started speaking, and my inane thoughts skidded to a stop. "On Wednesday morning, I received a phone call from an unknown number. Not that my phone had any credit mind you, but I could still take incoming calls. The voice on the other end was digitally distorted, sounded male, but with tech these days it could've easily been a woman. Anyway, they told me they had some good news for me. That they knew I could do with some. That the son of a bitch Richard Knightley was dead, and that they'd killed him for what he'd done to so many lives like mine."

Stanley recounted the tale as if the words were ingrained forever in his mind, as if he'd replayed them to himself a thousand times. Maybe he had.

I listened in shock. Damon Wood was right. Stanley was just a patsy.

"The person said they were wondering if I might be interested, since they knew I was racked with guilt over ruining my wife's last years on this godforsaken planet, in claiming the murder as my own in return for a generous amount of cash. They explained how they'd done what they needed to do but were worried now about the flow-on effects to their family. And they knew the damage had already been done in mine but that this might be an arrangement that could benefit both of us. I could redeem myself, be seen as a hero to all the victims out there that knew the way I did the lawsuits weren't going to go anywhere. On top of that, they'd give me half a million dollars to do whatever I wanted with. Maybe give it to my wife. Maybe make my time in prison easier. They'd give me enough to do both."

Up until now, Stanley had been watching his hands, which were fidgeting on the table. But here he raised his eyes to meet mine.

"When I expressed my cautious interest, they told me they'd taken out a second guy as well. A guy by the name of Isaac Anand who'd been working with Knightley to make sure the cases against him would never succeed. And that I'd need to confess to his murder too."

He shrugged and looked away.

"Seeing as I'd been contemplating stepping in front of a bus the night before and ending my miserable existence, it seemed like a reasonable deal. And as they explained exactly how they'd done it, I kind of wished I'd come up with the plan myself. Except they didn't mention the microcomputer part. Guess I should've known the job would've required one, but still when you asked about it, I figured they'd left that detail out so as not to implicate themselves or whoever they got to plant it. Didn't change the deal we'd struck as far as I was concerned. But when you told me about Isaac and what his grandma had said, well, then I started wondering what else they'd left out or outright lied about. Were we even on the same side? What if Isaac really was a good guy? And what if his grandma hates me with the same hatred I held for Knightley?"

The edge of desperation in Stanley's voice in the last question spoke volumes. That was the crux of the issue for him. He'd spent so long despising Knightley and all the pain and destruction he was responsible for that the idea someone might feel the same way about him was horrifying.

Stanley shrugged again as if it could displace his shame. "So here we are."

"Thank you for your honesty," I said, meaning the words. It was gutsy of him to come clean. He was giving up all chance of his promised half a million, and he'd probably still face jail time for obstructing a police investigation. Plus

I was struggling to get my head around how someone could be so miserable that confessing to a double homicide they didn't commit seemed like a *reasonable deal*. The poor man.

Hunt was all business.

"Can you tell us any more about how the person spoke? Were their words cultured or rough? Did they use a lot of slang?"

"No, they sounded, I don't know, how a white-collar worker would speak rather than a kid from a bad neighborhood."

So, like any and every one of our current suspects then.

"How were they going to get you the money?"

"Well, toward the end of our conversation, after I'd agreed to the deal, they told me to go outside and pick up the cardboard box sitting by the door. That it was a 'good faith' deposit to prove they were trustworthy for the rest."

"What was in the box?"

"Fifty thousand dollars in cash. I assumed they'd get me the last four hundred and fifty in a similar fashion."

"Did you see who dropped it off?"

"No. But they put it there while we were talking, so I think someone else must have delivered it, or I would've heard their voice outside my door."

"Did you get the last four hundred and fifty thousand?"

"No. The agreement was I'd get it after I'd been convicted. Otherwise, I'd be able to take it and run."

"You know you're going to have to give us the fifty thousand, don't you?"

Stanley sagged so deep in his chair that he seemed in danger of spilling out of it. "I know." He fiddled with his cuffs and asked in a small voice, "What's going to happen to me now?"

18

THERE WERE TOO MANY people to comfortably squeeze around Hunt's desk, so he brought us into what must have been the briefing room. He flipped the whiteboard over so we couldn't read it, procured some paper from an old copier in the corner, and sat down at one of the tables. Connor, Adeline, and I pulled up seats to join him.

A ticking wall clock marked the passing time while we waited for Hunt to speak.

We were an odd group. Adeline was doing something on her phone—which could've been anything from googling more interrogation techniques to posting photos of her nails on social media. Hunt was massaging his neck like the occupants of the room pained him. And Connor was sitting economically still, as usual.

I hadn't missed the occasional glare Hunt had shot my way, letting me know my bawling out for talking to Stanley without permission was coming soon. Only Adeline's presence stopped it from happening now, which put me in the odd position of being grateful to her.

Hunt dropped his hand from his neck to the table with a thud. "Right. Let's review what we've learned from Stanley's confession this morning and"—he glanced meaningfully at Adeline, whose attention was still on her phone—"the tech we decrypted last night." That was another topic we couldn't delve into with Adeline present. "Then we'll figure out how that information affects each of our current suspects."

We all threw in our observations (most of Adeline's were of the unhelpful variety) and came up with a list.

- *The killer had sufficient funds to bribe Stanley*

- *The killer knew details of Stanley's personal loss as well as having some idea of his technical capabilities*

- *The killer was persuasive and used language suited to a white-collar worker*

- *The killer contacted Stanley about being a patsy only after the deaths occurred*

- *The killer claimed Isaac was helping Richard clear his name*

- *Stanley played no part in the crime*

- *The decrypted tech could be worth killing for—both to acquire it and keep it secret*

- *The murder method implies Isaac was definitely a target, whereas Richard's death may or may not have been intended. Therefore using Stanley as a patsy may have been planned in advance or a last-minute decision following Richard's accidental death*

That done, Hunt directed us to talk through the implications for each person of interest.

No one else jumped in, so I started with the woman who'd been my favorite suspect earlier on. "I think this pretty much rules out the class action lead plaintiff, Patty Wilkinson. Without Isaac helping Richard win the lawsuit, she has no reason to kill him. Plus even if she was misinformed about that, now our original theory that she partnered with Stanley has been disproven, the high-tech murder method doesn't fit. The woman still uses a paper address book for keeping track of her phone numbers for goodness' sake."

"Agreed," Connor said. "She would've struggled to get the money together too. Though I wouldn't dismiss her altogether. She could've partnered with other victims to both raise the funds and carry out the murder, then chosen Cox to take the fall for it for some reason. She's very dedicated to her public awareness cause, and her relationship with Cox means she'd know which buttons to push to convince him to confess."

Hunt was jotting down notes. "Who else?"

Connor answered. "Tony Callahan is still a possibility. He's smart, calculating, and prides himself on collecting the right technology advances at the right time. He also admitted to making an offer on Anand's breakthrough and being turned down. That said, he has no connection whatsoever to the Knightley scam case, which makes it less plausible he would've thought of buying off Stanley as a patsy—whether preplanned or after the fact."

Adeline looked up from her phone. "Actually, a quick Google search of 'Richard Knightley victims' brings up Stanley's personal story on the first page. So it wouldn't take a genius to put two and two together."

The article Patty had mentioned talking Stanley into, I remembered. I tried not to show my surprise that Adeline had contributed something helpful. She wasn't dumb by any stretch of the imagination. She just put most of her energy toward her own ends.

Hunt lifted his pen from the paper. "Is there any reason we can think of that would suggest Knightley might've known about the tech breakthrough and so was killed to keep it secret?"

I'd racked my brain over that and come up empty. "No. Not unless I'm missing something."

Hunt grunted. No doubt thinking it was more probable than not that I *was* missing something. "That leaves Stanley Cox, who has now ruled himself out entirely, and Damon Wood."

Connor shifted. "If Damon Wood is behind the double homicide, he's either the dumbest or smartest criminal I've ever met. Without his information, we may never have questioned Cox's confession or the idea that Anand might not have been helping Knightley. So either he's the killer playing a very, very long game and convincing us to trust him, or more likely, he's who he claims to be."

Which left us without a single strong suspect. A few possible ones, yes, but no solid leads despite all the new information we'd obtained. I voiced the next thought reluctantly. "There could be another entity we haven't even considered yet who was after Isaac's breakthrough. That kind of tech would be interesting to a lot of people."

Adeline drummed her "serious but sexy" nails on the table and summarized the situation for us. "So basically, you still don't know anything."

Ouch.

Hunt and Connor grunted in unison.

She missed our reactions and continued on blithely. "No wonder TV speeds this stuff up."

Hunt's mustache seemed to spring extra bristles. "You got something better to do?"

Maybe she noticed the bristles because her next words were more cautious. "Well, yeah, kinda."

Was that the tug of a smile under that mustache? "Feel free to leave then. The next step is above your clearance anyway, so you'll have to sit it out."

Adeline sighed. "Right." The nails drummed another

round before she fixed her pretty hazel eyes on Connor. "Do you think you could call me when something interesting's about to happen?"

"If there's an opportunity to," he said.

Adeline's faith in her own charms meant she interpreted his level of commitment differently to me. "Great!"

We watched her strut her way out of the room like an adoring fan had laid down a red carpet for this very moment and the paparazzi were waiting. I was fairly sure there wasn't an iota of regret between us.

Although I did wish I could steal some of her confidence.

And maybe that sketch of Connor she'd drawn too.

What had Etta been thinking forcing her niece's company on him? I couldn't believe she was trying to set them up. As much as she'd love to have Connor as a nephew-in-law, she was too smart to think they'd be compatible. But I also couldn't believe Mae would refuse to show Adeline the ropes.

So what was really going on?

Hunt pushed back from the table, reminding me that a far more important mystery required my attention.

"Let's see if those files have finished decrypting yet." He snatched up the sheet of paper he'd been writing on. "By the look of this, we'd better bloody hope there's something in them to give us a solid lead."

I jumped to my feet, not wanting to give him reason to pause and realize with Adeline out of the way he was free to yell at me.

Some people are bold and brave in the face of unjust punishment.

I prefer to put it off as long as possible.

———————

HUNT UNLOCKED the door, and we crowded into his office. He typed in a long password that, if he'd been the one to set it, was hopefully more complex than "password-password" or "IloveEttaHamilton," and a list of files and folders appeared on the screen. I peered over his shoulder.

Most of the file names were gobbledygook to me. I didn't even recognize half the file *types*. But there were a couple of folders that seemed more promising. One said *Presentation* and another said *Drugs Research*. Hunt must've been thinking along the same lines because he clicked on the Presentation folder.

Inside was a video file. He clicked on that too, and a window popped up showing a basic simulation of a square gray building. The unseen "camera" began circling around it, and Hunt turned up the volume so we could listen to the voice-over.

Armed criminals have invaded a commercial building and taken an unknown number of workers and customers hostage. Windows, entrances, and security cameras have been blocked off, eliminating visibility. The SWAT team arrives. Instead of going in blind and risking lives, they deploy a team of minia-ture robots, coordinated and initially transported by a larger, highly intelligent lead robot that is capable of carrying out the mission independently or liaising back and forth with the SWAT team.

The video showed a robot a bit larger than a smartphone, carting about a dozen tiny robots on its back.

The robots infiltrate the building through the air ducts, where the lead robot stays hidden and sends out specialized individual mini-robots. Several carry video cameras to set up a live visual feed of the area. Others carry microphones to relay intelligence to the SWAT team. Others carry chemical and biological sensors in case of a terror threat. And the smallest robots of all crawl down the walls and across the floors unnoticed toward the armed criminals.

The camera zoomed in on a familiar-looking robot, and I had a good idea of where this was going. But what was in the syringes?

Lightweight screens on their backs camouflage them on whatever surface they're crawling over, and they are light enough that the targets remain unaware when one climbs onto their shoes. After each armed assailant has an unnoticed passenger in place, the lead robot gives a command, and in sync, the smallest robots inject Xyloxium into their ankles. The syringes have an anesthetized tip so the criminals feel nothing until they are overwhelmed by the tranquilizer and collapse harmlessly to the floor.

Wow. I watched the simulated perpetrators fall within seconds of each other. Hostages huddled in the background. The way Isaac's parents must have been.

Xyloxium is instantaneous and nonlethal, and the dosage has been calculated for each assailant based on data the lead robot has gathered from the video cameras. The lead robot also calculates the risk of accidental fire to pick the optimum moment of attack. The SWAT team is alerted, and law enforcement is now able to safely apprehend the assailants and return the hostages to their loved ones.

The video ended, and the breath left my lungs with it. Seeing the heart of Isaac's project laid bare, hearing what must have been his voice explaining this almost miraculous invention—one that so clearly spoke of his own personal loss—packed an emotional punch. His final words *return the hostages to their loved ones* echoed in my brain and raised goosebumps on my arms.

It took me a minute of being rendered still and mute to realize no one else was saying anything either. Without a word, Hunt clicked out of the folder, then into the Drugs Research one. There were two files inside, both drug fact sheets.

The first was the sedative Xyloxium. No surprises there. I skimmed the information. Like Isaac had said in the voice-over, it was the incredible combination of instantaneous and nonlethal. Most tranquilizers took precious seconds or minutes to work and could kill at higher doses because they depressed a person's respiratory and cardiovascular systems. This one didn't. But the substance was strictly controlled and not available to anyone except certain government agencies and entities that met exacting criteria and clambered through an ocean of red tape.

That answered my question about why Isaac hadn't chosen the same sedative for his home security system.

I wouldn't put it past the rich and powerful to be able to get their hands on Xyloxium despite all that red tape. But since the sedative had to be injected rather than ingested, it wasn't in my Shade repertoire.

The second drug contained in the folder was harder to make sense of. Suadere, a substance that made people more agreeable, pliable, or easily persuaded. I recognized this one because it had been included in my training, but I had no idea why Isaac had taken an interest in it.

Hunt was skimming the Suadere fact sheet when an error message popped up.

File not found.

He closed it only to have another appear, and another, and another. "What the blazes is going on with this stupid machine?"

Connor stabbed a finger at the top left corner of the monitor where an Explorer window showed files disappearing one by one. "Something's wrong. Shut it down."

Hunt tried, but the mouse wouldn't respond.

Connor leaned over and pressed a few keys, cursed, then shut it down manually by holding down the power button. "I suspect we've just been hacked. Again."

"Impossible," Hunt growled. "My tech guys disconnected this computer from the shared networks and internet. It should be secure." He punched some numbers into his phone. "Mendez, get to my office on the second floor now, please."

My phone chose that moment to ring. "Harper, sorry but now isn't a good time."

"That's okay, I won't talk long. I just wanted to tell you I went out to dinner with Levi last night and it was ah-maz-ing! He was smart, funny, caring, a great listener. I mean, I couldn't bring myself to let him pick me up or drive me home in that van of his, but other than that . . ."

Mendez entered the already cramped room, and Hunt outlined what happened.

"Impossible," Mendez said, unconsciously echoing Hunt. "Unless—"

"Unless what?"

"Unless they managed to get some kind of hacking device inside this room. Hang on, I think there's a scan-ner in here somewhere." She rummaged through the desk drawers.

I interrupted Harper's ongoing monologue. "That's wonderful"—Hunt turned to glare at me—"but I really do need to go."

Mendez turned the scanner on and pointed it around the room. Despite this activity, Hunt didn't shift his gaze.

Not good.

Harper huffed in my ear. "Okay, okay, what's the hurry? Is something exciting going on?"

Mendez pointed the scanner at me, and the beeping sped up.

"Goodbye, Harper!" I said a little shrilly, hoping the advancing scanner was going to reach me and then continue on past.

Instead, Mendez followed the increasingly frantic beeps to my bag.

Crap.

19

I TRIED NOT TO BLUSH as the contents of my bag were laid out for all to see. Taser. Wallet. Mascara. Keys. Lip gloss. A couple of pens. Concealer. Pepper spray. Tissues. A few over-the-counter painkillers. Oh gosh, my spare pair of underwear. And now my feminine hygiene products. Even as a fellow woman, Mendez looked a bit awkward handling those. A collection of crumpled receipts and a copy of the letter I'd written to Connor. I sure hoped they wouldn't pry into that further. A few squashed muesli bars I kept in case of emergency. Never mind that technically you'd die of thirst first. There was also a single chopstick (like that would ever come in handy), an unused dog poop bag, a toy mouse I'd bought for Meow ages ago, and a tiny complimentary bottle of hot sauce I'd been given at a restaurant.

I really ought to clean out my bag more often.

The final item was a black rectangular thing about the size of my phone, and one I didn't recognize.

"This would do it," Mendez said.

Hunt chose that moment to get real close. "Care to explain, Avery?"

"I've never seen it before, and I have no idea how it got there. Or what it is, actually."

"You could at least come up with an original excuse."

Connor intervened on my behalf. "C'mon, Hunt. What could she possibly want with it?"

Hunt didn't budge, his mustache still inches from my face. "Mendez, see if you can get any clues off that device, will you? Digital or physical." When she'd left, Hunt sneered at me but answered Connor. "Oh, I doubt Avery had any use for it. But the bloody Taste Society is a whole other matter!"

Connor snorted. "Really? You're accusing us of stealing now? You're letting your personal feelings go too far this time, Commander."

Hunt turned on him, freeing me to breathe again. "The proof was right there on that desk!"

"Izzy is saying she didn't know it was in her bag. I believe her. You should too when your temper cools. The real question is who had motive and opportunity to plant it there?"

My growing relief nosedived. "Everyone," I squeezed out. "I've been there talking to every suspect we have with that bag on my shoulder. It wouldn't have been all that hard for one of them to slip it in there at some point."

The revelation fired Hunt up further. "This is exactly why we should never let civilians on a case! No professional would be lugging around a giant bag full of shit they don't need, unaware of its contents. It's the perfect place to plant a bug—or in this case a whole bloody microcomputer! What the hell even is that?" He stabbed a finger at the pink toy mouse.

The worst thing was—of all the occasions he'd accused or belittled me or questioned my competence—this time he was right.

"Sorry," I said. "I didn't think—"

"Damn straight you didn't."

Connor interjected again. "You're hardly one to talk. You allowed Adeline on this case without protest. Why? Because your *girlfriend* requested it? At least Izzy has a valid reason for being involved, and she's proven her worth more than once. This would be a very different conversation if Adeline's was the bag responsible. In fact, for all we know, hers has been tampered with too."

I doubted it. Adeline only carried around a stylish clutch and had changed it on both days to match her outfit. But I appreciated Connor's argument nevertheless.

Unfortunately, it didn't change the fact that someone had just stolen the incredible breakthrough that Isaac Anand had most likely died for. But that led me to another realization. One worth interrupting Connor and Hunt's continued bickering over. "Whoever did this probably *wasn't* the murderer."

"What?" they both said.

"The murderer had that hacking microcomputer connected to Isaac's computer for days, weeks, or even months. They could've stolen these files then. Which means a second party is most likely behind this."

Hunt cursed.

But at least it wasn't directed at me so much this time.

———————

HUNT WAS TOO DISGUSTED to discuss the case with me any further. The silver lining was that he was so mad about the hacking device planted in my bag that he seemed to have forgotten about the Stanley Cox thing.

But I was angry at myself about that hacking device as well. What if my ineptitude meant Isaac's amazing plans for his tech never came to fruition? Worse, what if whoever had stolen those plans used them for evil instead of good? I knew Connor would say it wasn't my fault. That it could've happened to anyone. But it wasn't true. It would never have happened to Connor or Hunt.

Connor and I went out for an early lunch to give Hunt a chance to cool off. Neither of us were particularly hungry—my appetite had been dulled by guilt, and Connor's hadn't developed yet—so we prioritized coffee over food and went to the Conservatory for Coffee, Tea & Cocoa. It was a quaint little place in Culver City that roasted their own coffee and baked their own pastries and did a darn fine job of both.

We ordered, grabbed a table outside, and ran over everything we knew about the case once more. The problem was, not only was whoever just stole the tech not likely to be the murderer, but it also begged the question that if Isaac *had* been killed for this tech the way we'd been leaning toward, why did the murderer leave the files on Anand's computer for someone else to find? Especially since the tech lost a lot of its effectiveness if it wasn't kept secret. Sure, the files had been heavily encrypted, but why not go the extra step and delete them altogether?

Which meant that with Stanley's second confession pretty much ruling out Patty Wilkinson and now the logic of killing Isaac for his technology breakthrough not adding up, none of our suspects seemed to fit.

I licked pastry flakes off my fingers and took the final sip of my short black. Then I dug a pen out of my bag—the bag that had gotten me into so much trouble—and found a clean section of my napkin on which to organize my thoughts.

None of our suspects were looking probable, so I pushed them all out of my head and focused on what was left at the most basic level.

Halfway down the left-hand side of the napkin, I wrote Isaac's name, and opposite that on the right, I wrote Richard's. At the top of the napkin in between their two names, I scribbled *hostage-rescue robots,* and after a minute, I added the persuasive drug *Suadere* down the bottom.

So we had this jerkface fraudster. We had a sweet do-gooder. Plus a groundbreaking microrobotics system that could be worth millions or even billions, but Isaac had been trying to use altruistically. And we had this drug that makes people easier to influence. How did all these fit together?

With the abundant media coverage, Isaac had to have known about Richard's fraud activity. In fact, I'd forgotten about the prosecution's list of alleged victims the LAPD had found on his computer that first day but that proved beyond a doubt he knew who Richard was. So why would Isaac have had anything to do with the scumbag?

He hadn't had any trouble kicking Tony out when he'd made him an offer he wasn't interested in. Yet by the phone and surveillance records, it appeared that Isaac had *invited* Rick into his house on at least two separate occasions. Why?

For that matter, since he wasn't helping Richard clear his name, why would Isaac have been interested in the lawsuits at all? Curiosity because of his beloved friend Burt? Something to do with his membership with Vigilance? But then wouldn't Damon have known about it?

I bit back a sigh. If Damon *had* known about a Vigilance project concerning Knightley, he wouldn't have seen fit to tell us about it. He was convinced Tony was behind the murder and equally convinced of everyone else's stupidity, so he would avoid giving us any other trails to follow. Besides, Knightley might be too small-time to bother with for the likes of Vigilance.

I stared at the napkin some more. The Suadere was another oddity I couldn't figure out. It would be useless in a hostage situation because it only made someone more malleable, not erased their will altogether. The hostage-takers might be persuaded to agree to less favorable terms, but they wouldn't just put their guns down and walk out with their hands held high. Injecting them with a sedative and rendering them harmless made a lot more sense and was what Isaac had designed the miniature robots to do. So why was he researching Suadere?

I was tempted to cross my eyes and stare at the napkin like one of those 3-D Magic Eye pictures. Maybe it would help me spot the true story hidden in the jumble . . . or maybe it wouldn't.

Only Connor's presence stopped me from trying.

Think, Izzy, think.

If we were right in believing Isaac had been the one to initiate contact with Richard, given that was what their phone records indicated, I needed to put myself in his shoes. What could he possibly want from someone like Richard Knightley?

That's when it struck me.

As a member of Vigilance and a close friend of some-body who'd been scammed by a similar setup, he'd want what anyone in that situation would. Justice for the victims.

I imagined Isaac spending long hours on his hostage-rescue project and seeing the news coverage about Knightley every time he turned on the TV. From what I'd gathered about Mrs. Anand's grandson, he would've wished he could rescue those victims as well.

What if his mind had combined those two subjects?

Not to use his robots to take out Richard. That wouldn't do the victims any good. But as Connor, Hunt, and I had quickly ascertained, you could put anything in that syringe.

I tapped the word *Suadere*. "Is it possible that Isaac was planning on using his new tech invention to convince Richard to give back his ill-gotten money to the victims somehow?"

There'd been plenty of public speculation that the lawsuits would fail and even if they didn't, that the victims wouldn't get their money anyway. So what if Isaac planned to circumvent the whole thing and get the money for them? That put his having the prosecution's list—which included the names of the victims and the amounts they'd lost—in an entirely different light. But how would he do it?

Connor shook his head. "The drug provides a significant nudge toward being agreeable, but it doesn't override someone's will altogether. And from what you've told me, Richard would never be persuaded to return the money. Plus the effects don't last longer than an hour, so unless he could get ahold of the money in that time—unlikely since he'd buried it as deep as he could for the lawsuit—it wouldn't be that simple."

Everything Connor said was true. There was a drug commonly known as Devil's Breath that turned people into biddable zombies with no will of their own, but Suadere was more subtle and a lot less dangerous. Devil's Breath could convince a person to do anything, including hand over every cent to their name, but they'd know they'd been drugged. Suadere could nudge someone into doing something without them ever realizing their brain had been tampered with.

Was that it?

"Okay, let's leave the victims out of it," I said. "How might Isaac persuade Rick to willingly give him millions of dollars?"

"Well, people hand over money to solve problems. I suppose Rick's biggest problem was the impending trial."

I thought about it. Rick had seemed pretty uncaring about the trial, but there was no doubt in my mind that he would've *loved* to have the jury proclaim him not guilty, to prove all the media stories wrong, and to walk away from his "creative business" practices without a single consequence. That was when I remembered that Stanley Cox wasn't the only one who'd claimed Isaac was going to help Rick clear his name. Lyle had said the same thing.

So why would Lyle be under that impression when it was evident Isaac would never help a scammer like Richard get away with his crimes?

Oh.

"What if Isaac was giving Richard a taste of his own

medicine by scamming him? He could've pretended he was somehow able to guarantee the outcome of both court cases and charged Rick a hefty fee for his services. A fee he was secretly planning on donating back to the victims. That would explain why Lyle thought they were working together to clear Rick's name even though we know Isaac would never do that. And if Isaac convinced Rick to hand over the money before the trial was over—probably with the aid of Suadere—Rick wouldn't realize he'd been conned until it was too late. Plus he could hardly tell anyone he'd paid Isaac to make his problem go away."

I'd caught Connor's interest. "If that was true and the Knightleys caught on to the scam, they'd both have a motive to kill Isaac. But then Richard's death makes no sense."

Yes, it was a strong motive to kill Isaac. And while Connor's second point was a good one, the pieces were clicking together in my brain thick and fast now, and I thought I could explain that too. Could explain all of it.

Why the people who knew Isaac swore it was impossible for him to be helping Richard, and yet Lyle and Stanley had told us that's what Isaac had been doing.

Why Isaac and Richard had been killed together, even though none of our suspects had a solid motive to kill *both* of them.

And why making any of our former suspects fit was like hammering a square peg into a round hole.

I realized I'd been doodling on my napkin in concentration. Oops. I dropped the pen and flipped the napkin over, hoping Connor hadn't noticed. My doodling skills were far less impressive than Adeline's. Mostly it was a lot of question marks, plus a pair of devil horns over the words *Richard Knightley.*

At least it wasn't love hearts.

Ahem. "Remember how Lyle said he was skeptical about Isaac's ability to clear Rick's name? Lyle told us he didn't know the details because Rick was mad at him for expressing that skepticism, but what if that was a lie? What if Lyle knew the details and was convinced Rick was being scammed? But Rick was stubbornly refusing to believe it?"

Connor raised a brow. "You're not suggesting Lyle would try to kill them both, are you?"

"No. He'd want to protect Richard and wouldn't take kindly to someone trying to cheat his son. It's no secret he's protective of the Knightley name either—he's said a few times how people are seeking to take advantage of their weakened position. I'm suggesting maybe Lyle felt like he needed to send a message. A powerful, lethal message about what happens to those who dare to mess with the Knightleys. Only Rick skipped out on their evening engagement and Lyle's plan went horribly wrong."

"Explain."

"At the time of the murder, Lyle had organized for Rick to be having drinks with him. Where he'd be safe. Except Rick got a phone call from Isaac, something that was exciting enough for him to drive straight over. I would guess Isaac wanted to secure the money before the trial began and

Rick could realize he'd been deceived. But regardless of the reason, Knightley Junior, being the selfish cad he was, blew off his dad without even telling him about it."

"So why didn't Lyle just call off the murder?"

"I'm betting Lyle wasn't able to do the hacking required himself, so he must've outsourced it. Maybe he couldn't get ahold of that third party in time to get them to reverse the coding changes they'd made to the AI. Remember how many phone calls he made to Rick that night? Too many for a father used to his son's unreliable ways."

Connor used his own napkin for its intended purpose. "Yes, that did strike me as over the top. And I thought Lyle's word choice was odd when he said his son 'wasn't supposed to die.' He'd also have the money and knowledge to make that offer to Cox. An offer that was only made after the murders. But he couldn't have planned to use one of the scam victims as a patsy beforehand if he believed his son would be safe with him, so it would've been quick thinking on the part of a grieving father."

A sudden breeze flipped my napkin over and blew it toward Connor. In my haste to snatch it back, I knocked over my glass of water. Dammit. That was probably more embarrassing than the doodles.

Lucky I had my napkin on hand to mop it up.

Connor donated his napkin to the cause and waited patiently.

I put the sodden, inky mess on my pastry plate. "Lyle didn't turn his millions into more millions by being thick-witted. Or emotional for that matter. He's smart and he's the one and only suspect we have that *all* the details make sense for. It must have been Lyle."

Connor stood up. Maybe to avoid the last of the water dripping off the table. "All right. Let's go tell Hunt we've identified his murderer for him. And that we don't have a single shred of evidence to prove it."

20

HUNT WAS ABOUT AS PLEASED as I'd imagined he'd be. Meaning I was pretty sure he was envisaging rummaging through my bag and finding something to break.

After putting our heads together and going over every possible angle we could think of for another hour, we were convinced it must have been Lyle. The problem was, none of us had any ideas how to get him convicted for it.

He may have pulled off the perfect crime. Or at least close enough to perfect that no jury would find him guilty.

The police had been unable to trace the microcomputer found in Isaac's home to anything at all. It was a common model, and while they'd confirmed the device had been used to make the changes to the AI security system, they hadn't found any identifying information on it.

Someone would've had to plant it there, but the micro-computer was free of fingerprints. The thirty days of surveillance footage was a dead end too since no one had conveniently carried the device in their hand on their way to Isaac's front door. Plus it could've been smuggled in prior to the thirty-day period we had coverage for.

With Richard's DNA on file, the police would be able to check for probable DNA matches with Lyle at the crime scene, but we weren't holding our breath. He'd probably convinced someone else to plant it for him, and even if he hadn't, his DNA in Isaac's house was hardly incriminating by itself. It's not like we would ever find a murder weapon with his prints on it.

Murder by machine, by a few simple code changes, was incredibly clean.

Between the voice distortion, burner phone, and unseen cash drop-off, Lyle had ensured that Stanley Cox would be useless in identifying the person who'd hired him.

The strongest link we had was that only Stanley, who'd been told what to say by the killer, and Lyle himself had claimed that Isaac was helping Richard. But if my theory about why Lyle had killed Isaac was correct, that part of Mr. Knightley's story hadn't been a lie.

Our best shot was finding someone Lyle had enlisted to help him pull it off. The mysterious hacker who'd changed the AI. The person who'd planted the microcomputer in Isaac's home. Perhaps someone he'd paid to make the cash drop-off to Stanley's door. But we had no leads on any of those fronts, and without a chance of getting a warrant to go through Lyle's house and computer, no way of acquiring them.

In short, proving Lyle's guilt might be impossible.

Connor suggested we call it a day so we could look at it with fresh eyes tomorrow. We'd all experienced how sometimes the brain worked better on a problem when you stopped focusing on it and did something else for a while.

Except in this case, I couldn't summon much hope of that happening. The subconscious was a powerful tool, but it couldn't conjure up evidence where there was none. There might be more than one way to skin a cat, but what do you do if you don't have a cat to start with?

Connor drove me home in silence, both of us worn out from rehashing the case every which way. It was only when he stopped the car that I recalled the vow I'd made this morning.

I needed to convince Connor to talk about our relationship.

What had he thought of the letter? What was he thinking about us? Surely he had to agree that we could make this work—so long as he wanted it to. I jumped off that train of thought before it pulled up to Sob-story Station. Of course he wanted to. He'd said he loved me a little over two weeks ago. Things didn't change that fast. And he'd made every effort to be kind and break the ice after our painful talk on the stair landing, hadn't warmed to Adeline in the slightest, had stood up for me against Hunt on numerous occasions, and brought me coffee each morning. Of course we were going to make this work.

Now I just had to convince him of that.

I cleared my throat. "Um." Off to a good start. "I need you to talk to me. Share your response to that letter."

He started to protest, but I interrupted.

"No. Look, I know you can't have anywhere else you have to be right now since we're taking an unexpected afternoon off. And I know this is hard for you to talk about. But I think we both want this to work if it possibly can. I recognize you have your doubts, but I believe we can figure this out. It's like a case though—we need to hash it out, talk about it from every angle to find the solution, and I'm refusing to let this go until we've at least tried. So if you want me to stop bugging you about this, the way to get that to happen is to talk it out with me. Now. Before you can come up with some excuse not to."

Connor expelled air from his nose. "You're not going to let this go, are you? I thought we'd agreed to keep our work and personal lives separate."

"We did. And we are. That's why I brought it up now we've finished for the day. Besides, it shouldn't come as a surprise I'm not giving up so easily. You once described me as the most impossible woman you've ever met."

His shoulders—those oh-so-strong shoulders—actually sank a fraction, and for a second, I thought I'd won.

"All right," he said. "When the case is over, we'll talk."

My mouth opened and shut like a fish. It was a brilliant

maneuver. One I couldn't find a comeback to that wouldn't jeopardize the concession he'd just made.

Fine. I'd wait till the damn case was closed. But if he thought he'd found a loophole because it was looking as if this case would never be resolved, he was going to be disappointed.

I wasn't going to let Lyle get away with taking Isaac from his grandmother. And now I had even more reason to see Lyle Knightley behind bars.

21

I WAS THROWING Meow's new pink mouse around the living room (new to her at least) when a fully formed plan walked itself into my mind. A plan to do the impossible, to trap Lyle into convicting himself.

The only problem? Connor would hate it.

I turned it over in my head, desperately hoping I could get someone else to do the dangerous part. The part that might just blow up everything I'd been working toward achieving with Connor. But as much as I wished otherwise, I was the best person for the job. Probably the only one able to convince Lyle the threat was real.

Hunt and Connor might've had opportunity to do what I'd be claiming, but I had the advantage of knowing Richard and Lyle before the crime had been committed.

And thanks to my attempted sabotage of the job interview, Lyle already thought of me as someone who was fame-hungry, uncaring, and amoral. The type of person who would do something like this.

On top of all that, if Lyle didn't go for option number one, I was the only individual on the case he'd perceive as weak enough to try option number two: attack.

God help me, I wished I could be more like Adeline in this moment. She'd have no problem choosing her personal interests over the well-being of others. But when I thought of that crappy old bowl Isaac Anand had pretended was worth forty-five thousand dollars and thought of the grandmother who'd lost both her only son and now the grandson she'd raised as her own too, I couldn't do it. Couldn't let Lyle get away with this if it was in my power to prevent.

Which meant I had to tell Connor the plan. I'd promised I wouldn't see anyone connected to the case without him, and I had to keep that promise at all costs if we were ever going to be able to work from a place of trust and equal footing.

Unfortunately, keeping the promise jeopardized the happy ending I was keeping it for.

I banged my head on the foot of the couch, apologized to Meow for bailing on our game, and picked up my phone.

This was a conversation that needed to be had face-to-face, so I asked Connor to meet me at a park by my house. A park he'd taken me to once when I'd been upset, not realizing my comfort came from food more than nature.

I was hoping he'd derive some calm from the greenery since it had been his instinct to take me there. I needed all the help I could get.

A short while later, I spotted his familiar striking figure and walked over to him. "I have good news and bad news."

"Then why do you look like you've been sentenced to life in the gym?"

"Um . . ."

"I'm not going to like this, am I?"

I wished again that Connor's worries could be eased by comfort food the way that mine and Oliver's and Hunt's— and well, almost everybody else's—could. Nature was wonderful and all, but this conversation needed a vista like the Grand Canyon to put into perspective.

A few leaves were not going to cut it.

"Maybe we should sit down," I suggested.

We found a park bench, and when we were seated, I took a deep breath and outlined the plan.

"No. It's too dangerous."

"That why I wanted you and Hunt there." I flashed him an encouraging smile.

Connor buried his face in his hands.

"Seriously, it's not that bad. I've been keeping up with my self-defense lessons—as you saw in that YouTube video—and I'll agree to absolutely any security measures you want. We can make this work."

His response was muffled by his fingers. "How about the security measure of not going in the first place?"

I tried for a chirpy and reasonable tone. "Any except that one. Unless you have an alternative plan—in which case, even that one!"

Connor looked up. "You don't have to do this. It's not even your job to do this. For heaven's sake, why do you need to do this?"

"Because Mrs. Anand has lost not only her husband and son but the grandson she raised as her own as well. She deserves justice."

"Deserves, yes. But it's not going to bring her grandson back, is it?"

I swallowed a lump in my throat, remembering Earnest. It was true, solving his murder hadn't brought him back. But I also remembered how much it meant to Mrs. Dunst that his killer was found. And how much would Connor have given to achieve that for Sophia? "I know. You're right, but—"

"Don't you get it? You could be killed getting this *justice*! Where's the justice in that? What about justice for me"— he cleared his throat—"I mean, the people who love you? Think about them before you run headlong into danger chasing this justice thing you value so dearly."

His words gave me pause, raising questions I didn't know the answers to. Was the risk—a small risk—to my life worth seeing Lyle go to prison for what he'd done? You could argue that he wasn't super likely to kill again, so what if I was risking my life just to give Mrs. Anand closure and see Lyle punished? Was that worth it?

I didn't know.

But what was the alternative? To turn a blind eye to any crime that didn't have immediate and fatal consequences? How many terrible things had been carried out and overlooked with justifications like that?

And where did that leave me? When I'd first come to LA, I'd been running from a bad situation, my life out of my control, shoved around by forces bigger and nastier than me. I'd felt powerless. Yet solving that first case with Connor, saving Dana's life, had shown me I didn't have to stay powerless. That we always have a choice. And I'd been getting stronger since then. I liked who I was becoming. For the most part anyway. So if I chose now to let this killer go free, would I be able to live with myself in the days and weeks to come? Besides, there was risk in *everything*. Life itself was a risk.

Even so, I was tempted to turn a blind eye just this once in the hopes of reconciling with Connor. The problem was, it wouldn't be just once. If we reconciled, we were sure to find ourselves back in this situation, and I wasn't okay with having his fears rule my decisions forevermore. So I had to explain, try to help him see things how I saw it. And pray that it wasn't going to be the final nail in the coffin of our relationship.

"I'm sorry," I told him. And I was. "I know you have damn good reasons to avoid loss at any cost, but life and death isn't something anyone has control over, and I don't want to make all my decisions as if it is. I could die tomorrow in a car accident—or shopping at Best Buy like Isaac's parents—or I could live until I'm a hundred and three. At the end of the day, the only thing I have control over is the choices I make in the hours allotted to me. And I want to stand up for what's right. The way you showed me. I'm going to talk to Lyle."

Connor stood up. "Then take Hunt along. Because this is exactly why I can't be with you."

22

I FOLLOWED LYLE KNIGHTLEY'S MAID down the corridor with heavy steps and an even heavier heart. I'd tossed and turned all night wondering if I was making a terrible mistake, but there didn't seem to be a right answer. It didn't stop me from having to choose though.

And Connor had made his choice too.

The maid announced me and held the door open so I could pass through.

This was the third time I'd entered Knightley Senior's office. The first time I'd been trying to convince him not to hire me. This time I was planning to make him forever regret the day he did.

"Ms. Avery. My maid tells me you have news about the case."

I smiled. "Something like that."

I let silence draw out for a moment, making him wait for it, making him start to wonder why I was sitting in front of him with this look on my face. I wanted him to feel uneasy, off-balance. In this discussion, I wanted him to know that I had the upper hand.

Then I plonked the microcomputer onto his oversized desk with a thud. "Mr. Knightley, you might remember when we first met I told you I didn't do this job for the money."

His eyes fixed on the microcomputer. "I remember."

"Great. Then you'll also remember the reason I do it is for the opportunity to rub shoulders with famous people."

He tore his eyes from the microcomputer and put on a neutral expression. "Sure."

"You told me working with your son might be my ticket to getting cozy with some of those celebrities. That I'd get an exclusive story they'd want to hear about." The day was ingrained in my memory since it was the last thing that happened before my relationship with Connor turned on its head. I made myself smile wider. "But I don't think you realized how right you were."

I stroked the microcomputer lightly to draw his attention back to it. "You see, I found this in one of Isaac Anand's computers when I was called out to the crime scene. I have this good friend who's an expert hacker, so I recognized it for what it was. The police hadn't clued in yet, so I thought to myself, hmm, if this baby leads to the murderer, I can either turn it in and be a hero, in which case I'll be famous. Or I can negotiate with the mastermind behind the whole thing and get so rich I won't even care about fame anymore."

Lyle frowned. "If that's from the crime scene, aren't you guilty of tampering with evidence and obstruction of justice?"

"Oh sure. That's why you're the only person I've told where it came from."

"I'm not certain what you're getting at, Ms. Avery."

"Well, I handed it over to my hacker friend, without giving him any context of where I got it, and asked him to find out whatever he could from it." My fictitious hacker friend had been inspired by my dealings with Damon Wood. "You can imagine my surprise when it led straight to you."

"That's impossible." Lyle was calm, but even his calmness told me I was on the right track. If he was truly innocent, he'd be livid.

I smiled some more. "That's what I thought at first too. I mean, surely you didn't *mean* to get your only son killed. Great piece of acting, by the way, blaming me for it and everything."

The muscles in Lyle's jaw indicated he clenched his teeth before catching himself. "You're insane. Is that the best theory you've got after four days of investigating my son's death? You said you were doing everything you could to find the *real* murderer."

I kept my voice bright and perky. "I did. It's just that

when I found him, I thought maybe you wouldn't want him caught after all."

"Why is that?"

"C'mon, Mr. Knightley, stop playing dumb. The way I see it is you can pay me to keep this between you and me, or I can hand this little microcomputer over to the police, and they'll eventually figure out the same thing my hacker friend did."

"Go ahead. This whole theory is ludicrous."

Well, crap.

I racked my brain for something else to say, but he'd called my bluff. Said he didn't care if I turned the micro-computer in to the police.

I'd been betting on him not being knowledgeable enough about hacking to be a hundred percent certain I was lying. And that the risk I was telling the truth would be sufficient to force him to act. To either pay me off or try to get rid of me. Either way, he'd incriminate himself.

But calling my bluff? What the hell was I supposed to do with that?

"Are you sure you don't want a minute to think about it?" I asked, buying myself some time.

His eyes flashed. In triumph maybe. The bastard was more used to negotiating than I was, and he was wiping the floor with me.

"I'm sure," he said.

I slipped the microcomputer back into my bag, moving slowly so I could replay our conversation in my head. The only genuine reactions I'd gotten from him were when he'd first recognized the microcomputer and when I'd brought up how he'd killed his own son.

"All right then. But before I go, can you level with me for a second? Was it an accident, or did you mean to kill him? Rick, I mean, or Richard, if you prefer."

His jaw muscle spasmed again. "I'm done with this conversation."

"I know there was a lot of friction between you. That you didn't always get along, but I thought, deep down, that you loved each other."

"Of course, that goes without saying."

"Yeah, that's why I figured it must've been an accident. I mean, that's why you'd arranged to meet with him the night he was killed, right? To keep him safe?"

"As I've told you, we were meeting for a nightcap before that idiotic trial started."

"Do you regret not letting him follow his dreams of owning racehorses now? Like maybe if you had, he would never have gotten all that bad publicity, never have dragged the Knightley name through the mud. Never have been killed accidentally at just twenty-four years old."

An angry flush was creeping up Lyle's neck. "Bitch. What do you know about parenting?"

"Well, I haven't had kids myself, but I know my parents never stomped on my dreams because they weren't fancy enough. Or you know, killed anyone. I'd call that setting a pretty bad example, wouldn't you?"

"You think you've got what it takes to be famous, Ms. Avery? You wouldn't last a second in the cutthroat world of the truly rich. All right, you might not fall victim to poison"—he gave me a thin-lipped smile—"but while your parents may never have stomped on you and your dreams, be assured that somebody would. You're weak. Easy to take advantage of. I'm almost tempted to give you the money just to watch you fall."

His lines about being weak and easy to take advantage of sparked an idea for a fresh angle to try. I gripped the desk like I'd been stunned. "Oh my gosh. All this time I thought it was an accident. But you actually did it on purpose, didn't you? To purge the Knightley name and keep it strong!"

The angry flush had reached his cheeks, turning them a mottled red. "No—"

"Yes, yes, I see it now. You're too smart to make such a basic mistake. To rely on Richard keeping his appointment when it was a matter of life or death—it's not as if he'd never stood you up before. Yes, I underestimated you."

I flashed him a smile as if I expected he'd be impressed by my cleverness, then hurried on before he could unclench his jaw enough to speak.

"You never intended to have drinks with Rick. That was just a way to make you look innocent, but you assumed he'd blow you off. Heck, you probably offered Isaac something to make sure of it."

Lyle gripped the edge of the desk. As I had a moment ago, except he was doing it in white-knuckled fury like it was all that kept him from pummeling me. "Get the hell out—"

I raised my voice over his. "You wanted him to die so the trial would get thrown out! You couldn't keep the Knightley name strong with a convicted criminal in the family. Nobody would respect you. So in brilliant, strategic, *cold blood*, you murdered your only—"

"Bullshit," he snarled. "It was an accident!"

Lyle realized he'd slipped up at the same moment I did. His eyes narrowed, and his mouth got so tight his lips disappeared.

"Like that was?" I asked sweetly. "Now we have my testimony to add to the evidence stacked against you. Also, this is probably the time to mention that the microcomputer I brought along today isn't the one I found at the crime scene. It's just the same model. The one that's going to send you to prison is in a safe place, and my hacker friend knows he's to turn it over to the police if anything happens to me." I leaned back and swung my feet onto the desk. There was enough distance between us that I wasn't afraid of him grabbing them. "So how much will you pay me to keep quiet?"

Rage simmered off him in waves, but Lyle was in control of himself again. His tone was mild and businesslike as he told me, "The problem with blackmail, Ms. Avery, is it's impossible to ever make it end unless you can take charge of the blackmail material. How can I do that in this situation?"

"Well, I'll give you the microcomputer once I have my money. No worries."

"I see," he said. "Would you mind getting that book for me, the one with the dark blue spine that's titled, *The Art of Negotiation*?"

"Um, sure." I wondered if he was only asking to get my feet off his desk, but I'd do whatever he wanted to keep him talking.

The more he incriminated himself, the better the case against him would hold up in court. Lyle would hire the best attorneys money could buy, and if we had just a single incriminating line or two, they'd twist his words so far around the jury would forget he was even the one to speak them.

I picked up the book he'd gestured to—it was more of a tome, actually, with a hard cover and the heft of one of those old giant encyclopedias—and carried it back to my seat. Unfortunately, I hadn't allowed for the desk's size.

As I'd observed the first time I'd entered his office, it was large enough for a woolly mammoth to shelter under, which meant when I put the book on it and slid it toward Lyle, I barely made it halfway—even squishing my chest flat against the timber to stretch as far as I could go. At least he had to be equally undignified in order to reach it from his side.

Both of us kept sober expressions and pretended we didn't look ridiculous.

He opened the cover, and I waited to hear what negotiation wisdom he would share with me. Was he trying to argue me down on price? A price I hadn't named yet?

"The thing is, Ms. Avery, I paid my dark web contact extremely well to make it untraceable, and I don't believe you." He flipped forward a few pages, revealing the middle of the book had been carved out, and scooped up a crude-looking handgun. "Which means we have a problem because *you* are now the one piece of evidence I need to get rid of."

Oh, this was bad. I raised my hands reflexively and squelched my sudden urge to pee. *The Art of Negotiation* indeed.

But I had my own move up my sleeve. "Has anyone ever told you how *squishy* your chairs are? They're very comfortable."

I'd chosen *squishy* as my safe word for old time's sake.

A shadow passed over Lyle's face before he masked his unease at my unorthodox reaction. "What?"

Hunt and Connor burst through the door. In socks. Because I'd warned them it would be impossible to walk unheard on the tiles otherwise.

Why didn't more movies portray gunfights in socks?

I swiveled to admire them, which turned out to be a mistake because the damn mammoth desk had lulled me into a false sense of security. Lyle's chair creaked behind me, and the next thing I knew the bastard had a fistful of my hair and was ordering me to my feet. I had no idea how he'd cleared that desk so fast, but since the hand in my hair was dragging me upward and a gun was nuzzling up to my spine, I didn't argue.

Crap.

"Put your guns down, gentleman." He sounded smug.

I had a front-row seat to Hunt and Connor's reactions. Hunt's mustache was on high alert like the scruff of a dog's neck or a cat's tail, and Connor . . . well, Connor's pained expression was a punch to the gut.

I'd thought after our conversation yesterday he would stay away, but when I'd rocked up to the rendezvous with Hunt's team this morning, he'd been there. Said he couldn't allow me to get hurt if he could help it.

And now his worst-case scenario of helplessly watching me die was closer than I'd been planning on letting it get.

Lucky I really had been keeping up with my self-defense training. And though Lyle might be a mastermind at planned murder—and apparently leaping or scrambling across massive desks too—he was less adept at sudden violent confrontations. Between holding my hair and the gun, the idiot had left my arms and body free.

I shut out thoughts of Connor and focused on the weapon at my back and the moves I'd run through hundreds of times.

Take a few seconds to prepare, Nick's patient voice advised. *If they wanted you dead, you'd never have felt the gun.*

I needed to know for sure which hand was holding the firearm. And I needed Lyle not to pull the trigger while I checked. "Please don't shoot," I pleaded, turning my head at the same time. It wasn't hard to sound scared.

The gun was still in his right hand.

I whipped around to the left. Hair ripped from my scalp, but I didn't hesitate. My right elbow smashed him in the throat while my other arm pinned his wrist holding the gun against my chest, nozzle pointing past my shoulder. My mind noted the sound of a trigger being pulled but no accompanying blast. A misfire? My body kept moving. I kneed him hard in his proud Knightley family jewels and used the distraction to wrench the gun from his grasp. The momentum came in handy for elbowing him in the face. I skipped backward, gun trained on him, putting distance between us.

His nose was trickling blood, but his hunched position suggested his groin pained him more.

Good.

Connor rushed in and, with a swift, brutal jab, turned the trickle into a flow. Then he grabbed Lyle's arm, spun him around, and pressured him to the floor. The speed of this maneuver sent droplets of blood arcing through the air to land on the desk that had betrayed me.

Trembling, I laid the gun down with great care and turned to see Hunt.

He was flat on his back on the tiles.

Oh no. Please no.

I rushed over to him. It hadn't been a misfire. I'd killed Hunt.

I searched for the blood. Maybe he was still alive. I had to stop the bleeding. But damned if I could find the blood-stain against his navy-blue shirt and pants. What a stupid color for a uniform where people might get shot! My mind skittered in panic even as my eyes roamed over Hunt's unmoving form. How the hell was I going to tell Etta?

"It was only a trank," Connor said from behind me, just as my gaze landed on a colorful cylinder lodged in Hunt's thigh. The dart, I realized. A trank dart.

Relief flooded through me. Then stopped.

The rise and fall of Hunt's chest, the sight of his droopy, sedated mustache—like a houseplant that had wilted under my brown thumb—imbued me with a new horror.

He was going to wake up.

Then he was going to kill me.

23

THREE UNIFORMS ENTERED the room. These guys were wearing shoes. I half expected them to shout at me to get away from Hunt's prone body since I was responsible for getting him shot, but while two rushed over to check on their commander, they barely glanced at me.

"He's only tranquilized," Connor repeated.

As if to punctuate his words, a guttural snore ripped through the taut silence.

One of the officers snickered.

I didn't share his amusement. If this got back to Hunt, he'd kill me twice.

Connor didn't crack a smile either, merely added, "First responders and a toxicology specialist are on their way."

Assured their commander was okay, two of the officers

went to relieve Connor of his burden. I made the mistake of glancing over.

Lyle's neat gray hair was sticking up in all directions, his black scholarly frames were skewed and cracked on his reddened nose, and his gaze was fixed on me with a look of pure, unadulterated hatred.

Just as well he was going to be locked up for a very long time.

As soon as Connor was free, he came and squatted on the floor beside me. My heart fluttered as he reached out and . . . switched off my audio transmitter. Oh.

"A Taste Society doctor will be here shortly. I called them first."

It made sense. Whoever came would be far better versed in sedatives and far better stocked in antidotes than your average paramedic. "Do you need me to ID the tranquilizer?" I asked, keeping my voice low and hoping I'd be able to do that much at least.

Connor yanked the dart out of Hunt's leg—making me realize it was probably similar to a bee's stinger, best removed to minimize the amount of poison that was released—and pointed to the side of the capsule where something was printed in tiny lettering. "No need. These are single-use Xyloxium darts."

The printed letters helpfully said: *Contains Xyloxium.* The instantaneous and nonlethal sedative Isaac had wanted to use in his microrobots.

"Aside from the label, you can tell by the color of the

liquid itself. See the neon-green staining? All batches are dyed before they leave the distillation factories to help authorities regulate its use. And these capsules can't be unscrewed and refilled like a normal trank dart."

I nodded, but I was wondering how in the world Lyle had gotten his hands on one of these. Perhaps I should just be grateful he had. Xyloxium meant Hunt had almost zero chances of complications.

By the time he'd rattled out another snore, his mustache quivering from the vibrations, Connor had stood up and Mendez had taken his place. She helped me remove my wire—which was a lot more complicated and old-school than the sleek watch I'd used for Taste Society business. But since she'd already pawed through my feminine hygiene products, having her hand up my shirt wasn't such a big step.

"Thanks," I said.

She'd been the one who'd helped me figure out what to say about the microcomputer. *We'll keep it simple*, she'd told me. *That way, if he knows more than you think, you won't say anything he knows is impossible, and if he doesn't know much, you'll keep him focused on the important part.*

She slapped me on the shoulder and glanced over where the other officers were leading Lyle away. "You did good." Then she looked down at Hunt's prone form. "Although I wouldn't hold your breath waiting for a thank-you from him."

I hid a wince. "Noted." Connor walked past, following

the officers who'd taken Lyle. "Um, I'm going outside to wait for the toxicology specialist to arrive."

Mendez grinned. "You worried Hunt might wake up?"

Maybe I hadn't done such a great job of hiding that wince. "Just need some fresh air," I lied.

She was still grinning as I withdrew to hurry after Connor.

I found him on the front terrace, watching the officers load Lyle into the police cruiser. His shoes were back on his feet. His spine was straight. And his mask was firmly in place.

I approached feeling hopeful. I mean, that had gone well, right? I'd shown him I was capable of rising to the challenge both mentally and physically. Okay, Hunt had been an unfortunate mishap, but from Connor's point of view, better him than me. It wasn't my fault self-defense training focused on protecting yourself without accounting for innocent bystanders.

Plus it was a positive sign that Connor had changed his mind at the last minute so he could be here to back me up. He cared enough not to trust my well-being to others. He cared enough to put himself through the high stress of being on the other side of that door, possibly unable to come through in time. He cared.

That suggested he was coming around to the idea that we could work this out.

"Thank you for being here today," I said.

He didn't respond. Not even a grunt. That made me feel less hopeful.

"Now that the case is resolved, when would it suit you to have that conversation?"

A white medical van pulled up to the curb—the van Harper had refused to be picked up in—while I waited for Connor to answer.

He let out a slow breath and without so much as looking at me said, "I can't keep doing this, Izzy. I just can't." Then he left me standing by myself on the terrace.

My eyes burned. Matching the stinging sensations on my scalp and elbow. I wasn't even sure what he was referring to. Having my back when I confronted the bad guys? Talking to me about our relationship? Our relationship full stop?

I swallowed the lump of misery in my throat. Connor was darn well going to talk to me whether he liked it or not. He'd given me his word. And I was sick of the sight of him walking away, avoiding the hard conversations.

For now though, I left my feelings behind as Connor had done me and jogged down to Levi. Someone needed to guide him to the patient.

"That was fast," I greeted him. It seemed like less than five minutes since Hunt had been shot.

Levi flashed his ready smile. "Nice to see you aren't the one needing medical attention for a change."

"Ah, nope. But it's kind of my fault that Hunt does."

His smile widened. "I might've heard." He was grabbing his gear as we spoke.

Change of subject time. "How'd your date with Harper go?"

He swung his bag over his shoulder and strode toward the house. "Great! Although she took a lot of pleasure in pointing out her hands were rougher than mine, and I have to admit she looks similar enough to Connor that I thought of him more times than I wanted to during a romantic dinner. But I was sufficiently terrified of her to ask for a second date."

He winked at me, and I laughed. "Good."

We entered the Knightley estate, and he lowered his voice. "But how are things with you and Connor?"

I sighed. "I might need to take you up on your offer of backup."

It was worth a try, right?

He nodded, his expression wholly serious for once. "Consider it done."

We reached Hunt's inert form. He looked strangely vulnerable lying on the floor in his socks. Two stern-faced officers were standing by, watching over him.

Levi checked his vitals, opening his eyelids, listening to his heart and lungs, and—after a quick question—rolling up his trouser leg to probe the puncture site. He spoke loud enough to include the officers in his findings. "The commander will have a hell of a bruise, but other than that, he should be back to normal in no time."

The officers visibly relaxed.

I was relieved too, despite knowing the chances of complications were almost nil.

Levi prepped the antidote. "This will wake him up

shortly." He glanced at me. "Since you're kind of responsible for getting him shot, maybe you should disappear before that happens."

"Good point." I bounced to my feet and hightailed it out of there. The sound of the officers chuckling trailed me down the hallway.

I DROVE HOME with a sackful of mixed feelings. I should've been feeling triumphant seeing as we'd pulled off the impossible and caught Isaac Anand's murderer at last. But I felt slimy from how I'd done it—twisting a knife into the wound of a grieving father. A murderer yes, but a grieving father all the same.

I was also acutely aware that Isaac's stolen tech, the tech I'd enabled to be stolen, was still missing. It seemed a poor way to repay the man who had poured so much of himself into altruistic projects; that the one closest to his heart would never see its legacy. And worse, would possibly be repurposed for killing instead of returning people home to their loved ones.

That unresolved blunder had also placed me on rocky ground with Hunt. And now with this morning's actions resulting in him being knocked out by a tranquilizer, I was exceedingly nervous about coming face-to-face with him again.

You'd think it wouldn't be that hard to avoid one person

in a city of four million, but with my penchant for getting into trouble and my neighbor dating him, a confrontation was inevitable. Perhaps with some effort and a pinch of luck, I might be able to steer clear of him until it was time to leave for Australia in two days' time. That would give him weeks to cool off. But that brought me to the thing that weighed heaviest on my mind.

Connor.

For the past two and a bit weeks, I'd been certain he'd come around. That it was only a matter of time and persuasion. But I was starting to lose that confidence. I'd tried almost everything I could think of, and with the trip I'd been so excited about just days away, things between us were looking grimmer than ever. Maybe it was time to examine the facts in front of me rather than what my heart wanted. To admit to the unpleasant possibility he'd been right all along. That maybe he *couldn't* overcome the demons of his past.

That maybe we were really finished.

But dammit, I wasn't going to give up until I'd forced him to talk to me. And there was no point torturing myself about what-ifs until then.

I stomped up the stairs to my apartment, hoping Oliver would be home to distract me with someone else's problems. But he was out again. It seemed of late that when he wasn't working at the Fox, he was drinking there.

At least it meant Meow was pleased to see me. I cuddled her for a while. But my mind kept returning to my troubles, so I reluctantly set her down to tackle the household tasks I'd been neglecting.

Even washing, scrubbing, and tidying were better than moping.

When the kitchen, living area, bathroom, floors, and my bedroom were clean, I stepped under the shower to clean myself. The water reignited the stinging on my scalp, so I wrapped a towel around me and gingerly approached the mirror. Time to inspect the damage.

The pain suggested clumps of hair had gone missing, but you couldn't tell it from the reflection. For the first time in almost thirty years, I was grateful for my unruly locks.

I left them wet and decided to while away some hours out on the stair landing. Sitting in the relatively fresh air where I could witness life continuing on as usual on the street below was good for the soul. I brought a book, a cup of tea, and three cookies out with me, all of which were also good for the soul. And today was definitely a three-cookie kind of day, so I didn't even feel guilty about it.

I'd been lounging on Etta's outdoor sofa for an hour or two, lost in the pages of my book, when Etta came out and sat beside me. The shift of the sofa cushion brought the painful flashback of when Connor had been the one sitting beside me. Just before he'd asked me out a few short but wonderful months ago.

Ugh. I forced myself into the present moment. I hadn't seen much of Etta lately. Partly on purpose, partly because I'd been so busy.

If Connor *wasn't* coming to Australia with me, I should invite her now to give her a chance to prepare. But I wasn't ready to give up on the trip I'd been looking forward to for over a month yet. Besides, Etta had no problem being spontaneous. Or so I justified it to myself.

I cycled through for a safe topic of conversation. "How's Adeline?" I asked.

Even that I felt guilty about. No one had called to invite her to the final confrontation with Lyle Knightley—the one part of the case she might've found exciting enough. But I was also kind of grateful she hadn't been there.

"Oh yes, she's enjoying Los Angeles. Apparently, you and Connor convinced her that the only type of detective she wants to be is the television kind. Thinks the real-life version is boring."

I wasn't surprised by the news. "I'm glad she's happy with her career choice then."

Etta eyeballed me. "Hmm."

What did *that* mean? Did she think we'd been boring on purpose? For goodness' sake, if Adeline had wanted adventure, she should've just hung out with her aunt.

Etta reached for the pocket where she normally kept her cigarettes and then stopped herself. She'd been trying to quit smoking for months now, for Dudley's health rather than her own. And while she'd managed to cut down a lot, she still snuck the not-so-occasional one when she thought nobody was looking.

It reassured me that the remarkable, adventurous,

smart-as-a-whip woman was still human.

"I've been thinking about *your* career choice again," she told me.

Oh no. Not again. She knew my job was classified and seemed to have adopted it as her mission to uncover the truth behind it.

Her first guess had been a honeytrap working alongside Connor's private investigation and security business for the rich. The next, an obsessed but clever closet groupie who'd found job roles that would get me close to the stars I so admired without ever letting them know about my all-consuming fixation.

Each time I'd played along in the hopes of encouraging her to stop digging. What would it be this round?

"You're a journalist," she said proudly. "One who takes on undercover roles to get close to the story. That's why you keeping rubbing shoulders with high-profile folk who then go on and get themselves in trouble. I couldn't figure out why you'd be hanging around the likes of Richard Knightley—pretending to admire him no less—until I saw you typing away on the computer for hours after he died."

Typing?

She was referring to my agonizing over that letter to Connor. A reminder that produced another painful pang. On the bright side, at least this hypothetical job wasn't humiliating.

But wait a minute. That must mean she'd never believed I was dating Richard. Did that also mean she'd never given up on me the way I'd feared? Before I could finish processing the implications, she continued.

"Although I don't see why you need to keep that so secret from your friends." Was that hurt in her tone? "It's not like I'd blow your cover, nor is it like I'm about to do anything newsworthy for you to surreptitiously report on."

"I don't know," I said. "Of all the people I count among my friends, I would say you're the *most* likely to do something worth writing about."

Her cheeks tinged with a delicate pink. "Oh." She sounded pleased.

I pressed my advantage while I had her on the back foot, seeking to move the conversation along before I got myself in more hot water. "Hey, you don't have any idea what's wrong with Oliver, do you? I've never seen him depressed for so long."

The day Oliver had gone from charming to mopey in a matter of hours, Etta's visit had directly coincided with the change.

Now she stretched out her toes to touch the stair railing, unconcerned. Maybe even amused. "Let's just say I wouldn't worry about that too much. I think he'll start to feel better very soon."

What the heck did *that* mean?

She didn't give me time to ponder it. "You'll never believe what Wendell told me this afternoon after he missed our lunch date."

Oh boy. Wendell was Police Commander Hunt.

I'd learned his first name after he and Etta had gone steady, but I'd never dared to call him by it.

"He said he was shot with a tranquilizer dart and knocked unconscious by someone I might know."

"It was an accident," I blurted in an eerie echo of Lyle Knightley's words. I cleared my throat. "But I'm sorry you missed your lunch date."

She chuckled and patted me on the knee. "Don't be. You shot the man and lived. I've got respect for that, girl. Now did you want to come for a walk with Dudley and me or not?"

Realizing how much I'd missed Etta's company, I jumped to my feet. "Absolutely."

She stood up too. "Then I'd better see if I can persuade that lazy hound to get off the couch."

CONNOR

I opened the front door to find Levi Reyes standing behind it. Adrenaline shot through my system.

"Did something happen to Isobel? Is she okay?"

I'd called in a favor and asked Reyes to wait around the block from Knightley's house today in case she got hurt—asked him not to mention the favor to her either. But she'd been fine when I'd left. What trouble could've found her this time?

Reyes gave a tight smile. "Now that's a complicated question. Can I come in?"

I let him inside before I'd finished interpreting his response and what it suggested he was really here for. Too late. I led him to the small sitting room, Petal dancing around our ankles, then poured us both drinks without bothering to ask if he wanted one.

If he didn't, I'd drink his too.

Levi helped himself to an armchair. "I know better than to tell another person how they should cope with loss. Anyone who's gone through hell and come out the other side with their shit mostly intact is doing well. Great even."

If it was someone else, I would've stopped listening and shown them the door. But it was impossible not to respect somebody who'd seen the front line and lost comrade after comrade to the hungry, devouring machine of war. And the ones who didn't die, he would've had to patch up and send out to spin the wheel of life and death again or ship them home to try to work out how to live with their permanent and crippling injuries—emotional as well as physical.

He'd never talked about it, never told me how many. He didn't have to.

I handed him the drink, and he took it. He'd been giving Petal a rub on her itchy spot under the collar, but as soon as I sat down, she took up her customary position on my feet.

"What I will say is this," Reyes continued after taking an appreciative sip. "In my experience, while there are a lot of differences in the details, there are really only three ways to deal with loss and trauma. One, you pretend it never happened and try to hide any and all signs to the contrary. Well, I'm not sure if it counts as dealing *with it since there's this big dark hole somewhere in your past that you're avoiding the pain of processing, but it seems to work okay for some. The second is to take a long, hard look at the pain and decide you're going to avoid ever going through that again at any cost. So you shut*

yourself off, sever contacts, and throw your identity into the things you have more control over to make yourself harder to hurt. That works too. I know a few highly successful businesses that have been started that way."

Levi wasn't looking at me. Probably knew not to be too direct. He was better at navigating people than me. He took another sip and rested the glass on his knee.

"The third way, the one I've chosen for myself, is to see that pain, be damned glad it's in your past rather than your present, and take away from it how to cherish the things most people take for granted. Kids shrieking with laughter in the backyard, having no concept of that kind of darkness. The fun and frustrations of spending time with family. The ability to brighten someone's day just by cracking a silly joke. Having a roof over my head and a home I can do whatever I want with. Sitting on my porch with my two overly contented dogs and taking a leaf out of their book in just enjoying the moment. The sun. The birds singing. The taste of a good drink." He raised his glass in acknowledgment.

"And of course, there's that whole wonderful mess of finding someone to share all that stuff with. Share life with. Personally, I'm looking forward to that, and when I find it, I'm going to grab it with both hands and not let it go until something pries it out of my cold, dead fingers. But that's me. And I'm not going to try to dictate what option you choose or judge you for that choice. I'm just suggesting you acknowledge it is a choice, a decision rather than something thrust upon you, and make damn sure you choose what you really want."

He drained the glass and put it down on the side table.

"The thing I am going to judge you for is letting your wounds dictate how someone else lives their life. Dammit, man, you must see that in telling Izzy what she should do and pushing her away if she doesn't do it, you're only escalating the danger to her. If your concern truly is protecting her from harm, then you'd do a much better job of it if you work with her instead of against her. Like you did today." He stood up. "So if you do choose the third option, and if you do love and want to protect her—then stop being such an autocratic ass about it. Thanks for the drink. I'll let myself out."

He was so right it was hard not to hate him for it. But he hadn't gotten to the root of the problem.

You had to be strong to choose that third option.

It was stupid, really. I was used to being strong for others. I'd had to be ever since I was ten years old and told my father would never be coming home. Mom was strong too. But I'd seen her tears and heard her crying when she thought I was asleep and known I needed to be strong for her. So I had.

So why in the hell couldn't I be strong now? For my own sake?

Disgusted with myself, my hand betrayed me and invited Petal up onto the couch.

Izzy should have chosen Levi.

24

SINCE CONNOR HAD NEGLECTED to give me an appointment time for our promised discussion, I decided to pay him a visit first thing in the morning. My hope was to catch him before he could leave for work. Besides, I couldn't deal with this hanging over my head all day. I needed to know the ending of the story—good or bad.

I was a hundred yards up the road when a car pulled out of his driveway. Air leaked from my lungs like a punctured tire until my mind registered it was Mae's blue pickup truck rather than one of Connor's black SUVs.

I might still be in luck. This conversation was best to have without spectators anyway.

Connor's Tudor mansion on its half-acre lot rolled into view. The well-kept lawn was looking especially green after the winter season, and the towering maple and oak trees were beginning to unfurl new leaves. My eyes went to the garage, but I couldn't tell how many cars were inside. Would he be home?

I parked in the circular gravel drive and stepped out into the crisp morning air. Despite the chill, the sun warmed my head and shoulders. Spring was winning. Not giving myself a chance to succumb to nerves, I banged on the bronze lion-head knocker.

The person I'd come to see answered the door. His hair was damp from the shower, and his gray eyes weren't welcoming. A dog—who must be the infamous Petal—on the other hand, was very welcoming.

I bent down to greet her first.

She was, as Connor had so vividly described, brown and medium-sized. She looked like a Staffy crossed with a Labrador or something along those lines. Floppy ears, heart-melting dark amber eyes, and a solid build, currently too thin based on her protruding rib cage. Her "brown" coat was dull but would be the color of rich chocolate with a better diet—except for some random patches of caramel fur and a nasty scar on her hindquarters. Despite her poor condition, her wriggling body, happy face, and lolling tongue expressed her overwhelming gratitude at the simple pleasure of being petted.

I fell for her instantly.

Could I somehow wrangle things to adopt her as my first fur-friend for my looming spinsterhood? The landlord didn't visit that often . . .

"Do you want to come in?" Connor offered.

Petal, after a solid minute of attention, appeared interested in having a sniff around the yard. For her sake, and on the off-chance Connor would derive some peace from the grass and trees, I shook my head. "It's a lovely day, and I think Petal might prefer we talk out here."

Wordlessly, he stepped outside, shut the door, and leaned against it. Waiting.

I pushed aside the idea that he was staying as close as he could to the nearest escape route and started talking. "You've read my letter, so I guess you already know all the reasons I believe we can make this work. I still believe that."

I searched his face, hoping to find some sign of receptivity, but his mask was firmly in place.

Swallowing, I continued on with what I'd come to say. "I want to apologize for hurting you. If I'd known what I know now about Sophia and . . . everything . . . well, let's just say I wish I could go back in time and tell you about my plans with Doctor Dan."

That prodded him into speaking, but his words were not the ones I wanted to hear.

"It's not about that asshole doctor, Izzy. You must know that. I'd forgive you in a heartbeat if either of us believed you wouldn't race straight off into danger again."

"I don't think that's fair," I said carefully. "It's not like I go looking for danger, and I'm working hard to do whatever I can to minimize the risk."

"You can't do enough. That's clear to me even if it isn't clear to you yet."

"That's what I don't understand." My voice was close to pleading. "I mean, there's a risk of loss in any relationship. I'm taking the same risk with you."

"Not quite." His tone was dry yet utterly unamused. "Since I've known you, you've been held at gunpoint three times, shot once, shot *at* on two separate occasions, held at knifepoint twice, knocked over the head, abducted, choked, and had your apartment firebombed. That's not counting all the poisonings. What has happened to me?"

I racked my brain. "You were taken down by a knockout bomb that scrawny scientist guy threw once. And smacked in the nose by Mrs. Fierro's walking cane . . ." I realized the list wasn't nearly as impressive as his and threw my hands in the air. "And you've probably been held at gunpoint and knifepoint and every other freaking point dozens of times, but I wouldn't know because you wouldn't mention it to me. But you can't go through life making decisions on fear and avoidance. *You* taught me that! I used to just lie down and take whatever life threw at me until you made me realize I could fight instead."

"Then I know who to blame for you running around trying to save the world. But I can't stay and watch you get yourself killed. I'm sorry. I just can't."

I was sick of those words. He was the one who'd told me we always had a choice. "Can't or won't?"

"Have you ever lost someone extremely close to you?"

"No," I had to admit. Not on the level he was referring to.

"Then you can't understand . . ." He shrugged. It was an exhausted, defeated motion, and I noticed anew the dark circles under his eyes. "Love doesn't always find a way, Izzy. Not outside of fairy tales. Sometimes the darkness—the scars, the fear, the pain, and all the bad shit wins."

I fought to speak past the lump in my throat, ignoring the tears spilling down my cheeks. He was serious. He'd given up. The man I'd chosen to risk my heart on because he'd seemed so strong, unshakable, loyal—was defeated. Wasn't prepared to fight for me.

"I don't believe that," I said. "Not unless you let it."

Then *I* walked away, hoping the tears blurring my vision wouldn't send me sprawling on my ass and add to the list of injuries I'd suffered since knowing him.

CONNOR

Her tears swept the ground out from under me like a round-house kick to the knees. All this time I'd been so wrapped up in my own pain that I hadn't stopped to think of hers.

I was an idiot. A terrible partner. And who was I even helping in trying to protect myself anyway? If I'd lost her yesterday, the loss wouldn't have hit any less hard just because we'd broken up. In some ways it would've made it worse, knowing I'd chosen to cut my time with her more short. Something I'd inherently known yet was too weak to overcome.

But seeing her tears, seeing her pain, forced me to shift my focus to her instead of myself. And when I did, that dry well inside me began filling up. This was where I always sourced my strength, I realized: protecting others.

"Izzy, wait."

My words came too late, just as she'd shut the door of her Corvette and started the engine.

I dashed after her car as it rolled down the driveway. Thank goodness she didn't drive like my brat of a sister, or I'd never catch her. I was running and yelling and waving my arms like a fool and faltered at the realization I could've been in some corny romance movie. But I remembered Levi's words about his "cold, dead fingers," shoved my dignity aside, and kept running. Petal bounded merrily at my heels.

"Izzy, wait!"

Just before she pulled out onto the road, she spotted me. The brake lights went on, and she got out, a look of bewilderment on her face. Her goddamn beautiful face. The one I'd almost been dense enough to never wake up beside again.

I came to a stop in front of her, suddenly unsure of my reception. Petal had no such fears and dashed past me to dance around Izzy's feet.

Great, I'd been outplayed by a creature who ate squirrel poop.

Izzy squatted down to pet her, so I squatted to do the same, glad for the dog's presence after all.

Now what?

I was going to have to try talking and shit.

Why did the strong, silent type have to go out of fashion anyway? I cursed the sensitive new age movement that changed women's expectations. Dragging her back to my cave would've been a lot easier.

And now I was envious of dogs and *Neanderthals.*

I cleared my throat. "Forgive me," I said. Pleaded really. I would've been willing enough to kneel in the gravel and beg her forgiveness if only I didn't have to find words to do it. "I've been a selfish idiot so wrapped up in my own needs that I forgot about yours."

Her eyes lit on me, cautious, still wet with the pain I'd caused, but hopeful.

Something flickered in my chest. And my next words spilled out a little easier.

"You know, Mom pointed out that I was pushing you away for the very reasons I first admired you. Told me I'd end up with a shallow, self-centered narcissist if I wasn't careful—like Adeline, I guess."

I was rewarded with a flash of humor on her face.

With luck, that humor was about Adeline rather than my poor attempts to express myself. Where on earth was I going with this again?

"The point is, I was wrong to try to stop you from being who you are. I can't fall for you because you're genuine, warm-hearted, and brave and then tell you to stop being those things."

Petal's contented panting filled the quiet as I grappled with the upcoming words.

"Deep down, I knew I was making the wrong call. But it didn't feel like I had a choice."

I swallowed. Played with the dog's ears. Getting shot was preferable to saying the next part out loud, but I owed Izzy an explanation.

"I was focusing on my pain, my fear, all the things I was trying to avoid, and I felt too broken—too gutless—to face any of that again." Would she think less of me for that weakness? I hurried on. "Focusing on the darkness never gave anyone strength. But when I saw your tears, I stopped focusing on myself and all that stuff and thought about you. Not so much the way you throw your clothes on the floor or throw yourself into unwise situations, but your goodness . . ."

I was distracted by her lips, which slanted upward just slightly. Hell. Was she laughing at me?

Dammit if even that wasn't better than crying.

"You're incredible. Your kind heart, your sense of humor, the way you see the best in everyone . . ." I shrugged uncomfortably. "Even when they fail to see the best in you." Would she want to stick with me after everything I'd put her through? "You brighten any room you walk in." The truth of those words hit hard. My house felt lifeless without her. I cleared my throat again. "And I realized I'd do anything to protect that."

Even if she was not-so-secretly amused while I was pouring out my heart.

Even if it damn near killed me.

I drew in a breath to say the three words that anyone—male or female—loved to hear.

"You were right." I rushed on, determined to get to the end so I could stop talking. "We can do this. Find a compromise. Work out a battle plan." She blinked. Hmm, maybe that didn't come out well. Her emotions weren't hidden like mine, but there was such a jumble of them on her face that I couldn't

interpret what she was thinking. "I mean, that is, if you're still prepared to let me try."

I stumbled to a stop. Waited to hear her response.

The first rule of combat is to keep breathing, keep giving your limbs the oxygen they need, but I was holding my breath.

Izzy shoved my shoulder. Her many hours of self-defense training had strengthened her muscles, and squatting as I was, I landed on my ass in the gravel.

Guess I should've kept breathing.

"Of course I'll let you," she said. Like I was crazy for wondering. Petal took advantage of my position to lick my face happily as if saying: See? I knew this would work out. *And Izzy crawled over and straddled me. "Now say it again."*

Shit. Was she torturing me on purpose? I forced my jaw to unclench. "All of it?"

"No, the part where you told me I was right all along."

Seeing her playful grin, the tension I'd been carrying in my chest and shoulders ever since we'd broken up loosened. I lifted a gravel-encrusted hand to tuck her wild, sexy-as-hell hair behind her ear, amazed that she'd still let me touch her. "You were right all along," I told her, then claimed her lips—the ones I'd missed so goddamn much—with mine.

25

AFTER CONNOR AND I HAD KISSED and made
up—several times—the first thing I did was raid the fridge
for a snack and make myself a coffee on his machine. The
second thing I did was insist Connor put on some Vivaldi
so I could bond with Petal over our mutual feelings about
his terrible taste in music.

He refused.

"But I thought our new agreement was that you'll go
along with any crazy plan I hatch up."

"That's not exactly what I remember agreeing to."

We were seated on my favorite sofa in all of his three living rooms—the comfiest one, naturally. My legs were slung
over his lap so I could watch his face while I teased him.

In truth, we'd agreed that I would be respectful of his

fear of loss and work seriously toward increasing my safety—through continuing my self-defense training, utilizing his expertise, and carefully considering what I took on my own shoulders versus leaving to the relevant professionals. I would *always* keep him in the loop, no matter what, so we could face the dangers together, but he wouldn't have veto power. He would push through his fears and respect my wishes, to support me in helping others or doing whatever I needed to do, and celebrate my newfound strength with me. We would work together, on equal footing, and both be better and stronger for it.

But that was less fun. And I knew he was trying to please me after the past two and a half weeks, so I was going to milk it for all it was worth.

"Hmm," I said, "sounds like you should've gotten it in writing then. But I suppose if you don't want to listen to classical music, we can go and announce our getting back together to everyone."

I was betting on Connor liking that idea even less, and judging by his pained expression, I was right.

"C'mon." I took a delicious sip of coffee and leaned down to rub Petal, who was sitting adorably on Connor's feet. "I insist you at least tell me the whole story about how you ended up sharing Petal's esteemed company."

He crossed his arms in silent protest but began talking anyway. "It's not a long story. I was driving to work when she dashed across the road in front of my car. It was a busy road, and she looked in bad shape, so I figured I'd better try to catch her. After some coaxing, she let me approach. I took her to a veterinary clinic. Told them I'd pay for her care. But I hadn't reckoned on them calling the house when I was out and Maria picking up the dog as if she belonged to me. By the time I came home, she was curled up on a duvet in the kitchen. Mom and Maria forbade me from taking her to a shelter while she waited for a new home. So here we are." He fondled her ears, eliciting several thumps of her tail against the floorboards.

I put my cup on the side table and slid all the way into Connor's lap to give him a hug of appreciation. "Thank you for rescuing her."

My gratitude was genuine. But I had a second motive for the hug.

I sneakily grabbed his phone from the couch cushion beside him, concealed it in the sleeve of my jacket, and moved back to my side of the sofa on the pretense of retrieving my coffee. Then I found the appropriate phone app and waited in breathless anticipation.

A second later, one of his classical albums blared through the room's sound system.

Petal pricked her ears.

Connor groaned.

The music climbed to a crescendo.

Petal threw back her head and let out a deep-throated, soulful *AROOOOOOO.*

I stared in shock. Then started laughing.

"She's not howling in protest. She's singing along!"

"What?"

"Seriously. She loves it." I searched for similar singing dogs on YouTube to prove it to him.

"Huh," he said.

"Now you *have* to keep her. She's perfect for you."

"While I appreciate she enjoys the music, I'm not sure Wagner would approve of her vocal accompaniment."

"Wagner doesn't have to approve of it. Only you do. And remember how you agreed to go along with whatever I told you?"

But my nefarious scheming was interrupted by a phone call from Hunt.

———

IT WAS TIME TO LEARN whether I was truly worthy of Etta's respect. Whether I would get away with tranquilizing Hunt, or now that he'd recovered charge of his faculties, he'd kill me.

I hadn't told Etta how I'd fled before he'd had a chance to wake up.

I told Connor now though, just before we stepped through the doors of the 27th Street Community Police Station, and his lips tugged up at the corners the way I loved so much.

Hunt was sitting at his desk, the one in the open office. His gaze slid over Connor and fixed on me.

I locked my knees so they wouldn't tremble.

"I don't recall inviting you," he muttered.

But he didn't drag us off into a private room, which I hoped was a sign he might at least keep his voice down.

Before he could say anything else, I presented the peace offering I'd baked last night. Connor and I had picked it up on the way: a plateful of brown butter pecan cookies. They were distinct enough from the ones I'd made for Etta that he shouldn't catch on, while being similar enough that they should be right up his alley.

He didn't move to take the plate from me, so I set it down in front of him.

Hunt eyed the cookies skeptically. "Are those for helping someone steal Anand's intellectual property? Burying me in paperwork as a result of involving a civilian? Or getting me tranked?"

I hadn't even known he was mad about the middle one. "Um, all of the above?"

He grunted.

I sat down. "Are you going to at least try one, or are you going to throw them in the trash again?"

He picked up a cookie and bit into it like a sullen toddler being forced to eat their broccoli. But he didn't spit it out.

"Right," he said. "Let's get on with this then."

Uh-oh, here it comes. I steeled myself for the imminent tongue-lashing.

Hunt's chair creaked as he leaned back. "After showing Knightley's attorneys what we have, they've advised him to cooperate in the hopes of negotiating better terms for his prison sentence. Which means we've got the whole story. At least as they've seen fit to tell it."

What?

I was so shocked he'd skipped over yelling at me that I could barely concentrate on his words. Had the trank caused a temporary chemical shift in his brain? Had Etta told him to be nice to me? Or was he waiting until he got me alone?

I forced myself to focus.

"We had most of the details correct. Except instead of Anand using his tech invention paired with the Suadere to persuade Richard to take the bait, he was using it *as* the bait. He told Richard all about the microrobots that could inject people without being noticed and convinced him that Suadere applied to the jury at the right moment in the closing arguments would win the trials for him. He just needed four million dollars to make it happen."

Far out. That was one application none of us had thought of.

"Would that work?" Connor asked.

I noted optimistically that Hunt took another bite of his cookie. Maybe that was it. Maybe the cookies had managed to sweeten him up?

"Hard to say. The important thing is Richard believed it'd work and Lyle didn't. According to Lyle, he tried to talk sense into his son, but Richard was in love with the idea that he could get out of the whole mess scot-free. He didn't appreciate his father putting a damper on his parade. Meanwhile, Lyle was furious that someone was trying to exploit the Knightleys' weakness, and worse, that a Knightley would be taken in by it, so he found a person on the dark web who could help. Lyle was told to purchase this specific type of microcomputer, plug it in, and give the dark web contact the access codes. They'd do the rest."

"How did Lyle get it into Isaac's house?"

"He convinced Richard to plug the microcomputer into one of Anand's machines by telling him it was *just in case* Anand took his money and ran or tried anything funny. Lyle said it would allow them to steal all the relevant files and carry out the plan themselves if the need arose. Clearly he had no intention of doing that. Lyle thought those microrobots were pure fiction."

I wondered briefly whether the anonymous dark web contact had thought the microrobots were pure fiction too.

Connor took one of Hunt's cookies. "So how did it all go wrong?"

"Like we figured it did. Lyle had limited means of communication with the dark web contact through a forum, so they agreed on a time for the AI code to be changed and the security mode activated, and Lyle arranged for Richard to be with him during that window. When his son didn't show up, Lyle panicked, hence the half a dozen phone calls we found on his records, but Richard didn't answer. Lyle left a message via the forum to abort the job, but it didn't get seen in time."

"Do we know why Richard went to Isaac's that night?"

"No. We never will since both parties privy to that information are dead, but I'd guess Anand was trying to get the money from him before the trial started."

I squirmed in my seat, uncomfortable that the person who'd pulled off the hack, knowing it would kill at least one person, was still out there. Somehow I'd been so focused on Lyle that I'd mostly overlooked that until now. "Are you going to be able to catch that dark web contact?"

"Lyle's given us all the details he has, but it's unlikely. Anyone taking on assassination assignments on the dark web knows how to vanish without a trace."

Wow. I found it harder to accept than Hunt's matter-of-fact statement implied. But I was ill-equipped for this style of manhunt. Maybe I could tell Damon Wood what we'd discovered and hope Vigilance would take up the cause . . .

Connor rested the hand holding his half-eaten cookie on the desk. "So if Richard hadn't been such a spoiled brat and blown off his father, Lyle might never have been caught."

Hunt nodded. "That's often the case when you're dealing with an intelligent criminal. It's the one detail they didn't plan for that unravels everything and leads to their downfall."

I thought it through and realized they were right. If only Isaac had been killed, no one would've so much as looked in the Knightleys' direction. Lyle wouldn't have made the last-minute decision to bribe Stanley Cox to come forward and explain the otherwise unexplainable double homicide.

And Lyle and then Stanley would never have told us that Isaac was helping clear Richard's name—which had been the detail that led to Mrs. Anand's heartbreaking story and in turn swayed Stanley from his original confession. No, if Richard had lived and the police had questioned him about why he'd been to Isaac's house a couple of times, he could've claimed it was for some AI thing for his new horse racing business, and no one would've been any the wiser.

Even when we *had* managed to piece it all together and convinced Stanley to tell us the real tale, we'd found nothing on Lyle that had a chance of getting him convicted. Only his inability to stay silent before the accusation that he'd murdered his son in cold blood had pushed him to incriminate himself.

It was disturbing to think how close he'd come to getting away with it.

Since we'd made it this far into the conversation without Hunt threatening bodily harm or so much as sending a death glare my way, I felt brave enough to ask something that had been bothering me. "Why would Lyle have a tranquilizer gun hidden in his office, loaded with Xyloxium and ready to go?"

"That, he's refusing to talk about," Hunt said.

Connor must have pondered the same question. "I'm betting he had it there for the precise scenario you presented him with: a business negotiation gone wrong. Rather than kill a person in his office where it'd be near impossible to remove every trace of evidence from, he tranks them instead. Then he pays someone else to make the problem go away for him and never gets his hands dirty."

My eyes were wide. "You mean he might've done that before?"

Hunt had finished the cookie a while ago and now wiped crumbs from his mustache. "He might've done it before, but he's not going to do it again."

I suppose I'd have to be satisfied with that. "What will happen to Stanley Cox?"

"He'll be prosecuted for obstruction of justice. But the judge will take his later cooperation into account when deciding his sentence."

Connor asked my next question. "How did Mrs. Anand receive the news?"

"She was grateful her grandson's killer had been caught. We told her how Isaac died trying to get Richard Knightley's victims the money they'd lost, and she said Isaac left her more money in his will than she knows what to do with, that maybe she could donate some of it to be distributed between them. We advised she wait and see whether the class action pans out first since it's possible the prosecuting firm might find the scam money if they dig deep enough. But it seems like the victims should be counting themselves fortunate either way."

I hoped that would include Stanley. Despite what he'd done, I could summon only sorrow for the man and everything he'd been through.

"What about Isaac's microrobotic hostage-rescue system?"

Connor asked. "Did you manage to recover any of his files?"

I studied my hands.

"Switching the computer off saved a bunch of them from being deleted, although we believe all of them were stolen before that happened. We brought in a robotics consultant who estimates we lost at least half of everything that was there, but she believed a team of experts could cobble it back together from what's left in six to twelve months. The simulation was still accessible, so we showed that to Mrs. Anand as well. She said she'd ensure it ended up in good hands."

The news was better than I'd dared to wish for. But that raised another problem. "Doesn't Tony Callahan own the intellectual property to the files that were salvaged?"

Hunt smiled. "No. Well, it'll need to be officially decided by a probate lawyer, but Anand did it all in his own time with his own money rather than putting it through the business. In an attempt to keep it secret, I suppose. The end result of which means it's a personal asset, and he willed everything he had to his grandma except for a little to that neighbor of his."

Thank goodness for that. But it had other implications too. "Could Callahan have learned that information after buying the stocks and so organized to steal the breakthrough?"

Hunt turned grouchy again. "That's a possibility we'll be investigating. Just one of the many ways having a clueless civilian on this case has added to my workload."

Even with that verbal jab, I felt like I'd gotten off exceedingly lightly. Who knew baking—or befriending your elderly neighbors—was such a useful life skill? We exchanged a few last questions, said our goodbyes, and were walking toward the exit when Hunt called out my name.

"Avery."

I halted midstride and turned. "Yes?"

"If you're ever responsible for a firearm so much as discharging in my vicinity again, I'll find an excuse to toss your ass in jail for another night."

I gulped. That had rated up there in the top three worst nights of my life.

"And by the way"—Hunt looked me square in the eye, picked up the plate of cookies, and dropped them in the trash can—"Etta's are better."

26

I MANAGED TO CONTAIN MY GIGGLES until we exited the police station and then burst into laughter. Which meant I had to explain to Connor why it was so funny that Hunt thought Etta's cookies were better than mine.

Even he snorted in amusement.

Then, since we were already out and about, we figured we might as well return to my apartment and get announcing that we were back together over with. Mae had been hanging out at Etta's, and Oliver had been watching a movie in bed when I'd run upstairs to grab the cookies, so now was as good a time as any.

We mounted the stairs hand in hand, a simple act that made my stomach do a little flip-flop of pleasure. But when

I peeked in Etta's window, her open-plan living area was empty. Darn it. Hopefully Oliver would still be home at least.

It turned out that Etta, Mae, *and* Oliver were in my apartment. They were sitting on the couches with cups of tea in hand, but the television was quiet. Switched off.

What had the three of them been talking about? Etta and Oliver hung out sometimes, but Mae was a new addition to the group, and generally when I came home to find Etta over, she and Oliver were arguing about the TV channel rather than deep in conversation.

All three of them started when we came in, another sure sign that things weren't as innocent as they might appear.

Then they saw my and Connor's clasped hands, and grins spread across each of their faces.

Etta was the first to speak. "I take it you two have finally seen reason and made up rather than had an accident involving superglue?"

"Something like that," I said.

Mae and Etta high-fived.

Huh?

"About time," Etta said, looking awfully pleased with herself. "You can thank us later."

I expressed my confusion aloud this time. "Huh?"

"Did Adeline have anything to do with you getting back together?"

"No? She wasn't exactly . . . the counseling type."

Etta flapped her hand in dismissal. "Of course not. I

mean did she have anything to do with helping Connor see the error of his ways?"

"Um—"

"Oh sit down already, and let us tell you the whole story."

With an inkling that we might indeed want to be seated for this, I pulled Connor over to the sole remaining armchair and took Etta's advice. And here I had been thinking *we* were the ones with the storytelling to do.

Oliver had gone from grinning to looking like he'd sucked on a lemon. What kind of tea was he drinking?

Etta ignored him. "You should tell the first part, Mae."

Mae appeared a little less enthusiastic about enlightening us. But since her choice was putting it in her own words or letting Etta do the talking, she settled her gaze on Connor.

"You know I've been deeply concerned you were allowing your decisions to be ruled by the fear of loss. After Emmett died, I worked hard to avoid modeling that to you and Harper. But his death hit you harder than it did your sister, and then you"—she glanced at Oliver and chose her next words carefully—"experienced your own personal tragic loss, and it took a lot to pull you back from that."

I peeked at Connor and saw he had his mask on, then found that Mae's eyes had landed on me. "You were the first good *personal* thing to happen to Connor in a long while. His business was doing swimmingly, needless to say, but there's more to life than business. And I was worried he was going to throw that away out of fear."

She addressed Connor again. "But where would that have left you, hon? It's like I tried to talk to you about—if you rejected Izzy because she's good-hearted and selfless, what kind of person would you end up with?"

Mae sat back and smiled. "Anyway, I'm preaching to the converted here, but at the time, I was really worried that you'd wind up regretting your decision. A weak or self-centered partner would never suit you, and ending up alone would mean business *would* be all there was to your life. You don't particularly excel at letting your hair down and having fun."

I smirked. That was an understatement.

Mae dropped eye contact and rolled her mug between her hands. "So I spoke with Etta, and we figured that if talking wasn't going to work, maybe pushing you together with a woman lacking Izzy's traits would force you to consider the implications and consequences."

Ohhh, no way.

"Unfortunately, neither Etta nor I knew of an appropriate person to illustrate this, but how hard could it be to find a wannabe actress in LA? Etta asked Oliver if he knew someone who could help."

My eyes snapped to Oliver. *He'd* been in on this too?

His lemon-sucking expression had only intensified.

Etta jumped in, eager to tell her part of the story. "And wouldn't you know it, Oliver knew just the right person for the job!"

"Oh sure," he grumbled, sharing none of Etta's

enthusiasm, "as soon as you said self-centered narcissist, just one person sprang to mind."

Etta reached across their armrests to slap him on the shoulder. "I don't know, it seems like she was more than willing to help you out. Strange after all the complaining you do about her using you."

Realization dawned on me. "Wait. Adeline is *Adele*? You asked *Adele* for help for my sake?"

This was the woman he'd moved to Los Angeles for, the woman who'd broken his heart.

Oliver blushed. "Well yeah, there aren't many people I'd do it for, but for you, old girl, I'll endure a great deal of unpleasantness."

I went over and hugged him. Which made him pat me awkwardly on the back and blush some more.

Then I hugged Mae and Etta too.

"Thanks, guys, I can't believe you'd go to so much trouble—or unpleasantness—for me. For us."

Connor was still sitting on the couch with his arms crossed. "But for the record, we would've been fine without your meddling."

Etta looked at me. "See, dear, this is exactly why he needs you."

"Time for cookies!" I announced. I had some leftovers of the ones I'd baked for Hunt, which brought up another question. "Wait, did Hunt know the real reason Adeline—I mean Adele—was accompanying us when he agreed to that?"

Etta smiled smugly. "Some secrets are made to be taken to the grave."

Mind whirring over the recent revelations, I went to the kitchen, filled up the kettle, and found that *someone* had already eaten all the excess Hunt cookies. Lucky I'd learned from past occasions and now kept a secret stash just for this purpose. Making sure no one was in view to see where I kept it, I extracted the container from the bottom crisper of the fridge, under a pile of vegetables. Oliver *never* raided the vegetable crisper.

I almost dropped the loot when I turned around and found Mae standing in the kitchen.

"Let me help you with all these mugs," she said.

"Thank you."

She pulled me into a sideways hug. "My pleasure, hon. I'm just so glad that Connor has managed to overcome his greatest fear for you."

Wow. I hadn't phrased it that way to myself before and had to swipe my eyes.

Mae smiled.

Then Connor joined us. "Hey, Mom, I was wondering if you wouldn't mind looking after Petal while I'm in Australia. She might like a holiday with you and Agatha while I'm on mine."

"A holiday?" Mae repeated. "That sounds as if you'll be taking her back?"

I stared at him in silent hope, and he winked, actually winked, at me!

"Well, it turns out she likes classical music after all."

Gosh darn it. I teared up again.

When the kettle had boiled, we all sat down and swapped gossip over tea and my secret stash of cookies—a stash Oliver eyed in open curiosity. Worried their cool temperature might give me away, I resolved to find a new hiding spot next time.

A pleasant hour passed.

Just as Connor was beginning to eye his empty mug like he wanted to crawl into it, Etta stood up. "Well, I have a lunch date with a certain police commander to get to. I'll catch you all later."

"Wait," I said. "We're leaving early tomorrow, and I don't know if I'll see you again before then."

She waved away my concern and headed for the door. "Of course you will. I'll be on the plane."

What?

The door banged shut, and we were left gaping at its innocuous gray paint.

"Did you promise her the ticket?" Connor hissed.

"No. I kept hoping we'd get back together."

"Then how come she thinks she's coming?"

I bit my lip, watching in my mind's eye as Etta laid sticks of dynamite around my romantic holiday plans and blew them to smithereens.

"She's always said she'd love to go to Australia. I guess this means she invited herself . . ."

27

CONNOR AND I SPENT a blissful night together, parting only when we had to pack for the trip.

During one of those parted hours, I'd called Levi to tell him the good news and thank him for his part in it. We mutually agreed that I shouldn't be the one to break the news to Connor that Levi was dating his sister. Actually, we mutually agreed that Harper could be the one to deliver that piece of news. And since she hadn't done so yet, I supposed that meant Connor would find out when we returned from Australia. I had no idea how he'd react.

Mae and Petal had driven us to the airport, and now we were seated on the plane. It felt strange to be traveling in business class. The last time I'd flown I'd been flat broke and fleeing from a loan shark. Now I could stretch out—a novelty I'd never experienced on a plane—and based on a quick perusal of the menu, I might even be sad to land.

Connor had warned me the coffee would still be garbage though.

It also felt strange to be setting off to Australia when whoever had stolen Isaac's tech remained uncaught. Especially since the theft couldn't have been accomplished without me. But as part of Connor's and my new agreement, I'd managed to find peace with leaving that issue in the LAPD's capable hands. I'd told Hunt everything I knew, and it wasn't like I had any special abilities that might help solve that mystery. All this hacking stuff was way over my head.

If I was honest with myself, it was a relief to pass the responsibility over to someone else. Besides, I'd been hanging out for this trip before it had been booked.

It couldn't have come at a better time. I needed a break. I needed to go home, away from the secrecy and danger and insanity of the Taste Society. To spend time with Connor as a couple doing normal couple things rather than hunting down murderers, human traffickers, and poison specialists. To reconnect with my family and loved ones in Australia. To recuperate, rethink my life, and get some perspective.

In short, I was looking forward to an uneventful break.

I glanced over at Etta, who had somehow managed to wrangle a business class ticket for herself, citing something about frequent flyer points and raising further questions about her mysterious past. She was talking enthusiastically to her seatmate about the crocodile tour she'd booked and whether she'd be allowed to shoot any with Australia's "quaint" gun laws.

Connor's lips twitched in my peripheral vision. "Think she packed her Glock?"

I sighed in defeat.

Perhaps uneventful was too much to hope for . . .

FROM THE AUTHOR

I hope you loved DUTY AND THE BEAST. That way I can rub it in my brother's smug face since he scoffed at me when I first started writing at the tender age of sixteen. If you want to help me make sure he gets his comeuppance, take a minute to leave me a review or mention this book to a friend who'll also enjoy it. That'll show him.

As a small token of my appreciation for everyone who already did this for other books in the series, I drew you this picture of my brother writing on the comeuppance chalkboard. Enjoy!

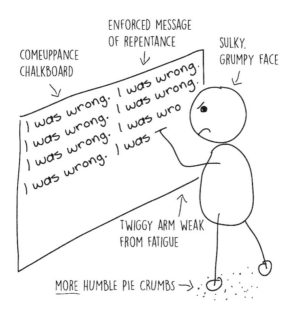

My brother begrudgingly writing out the words he'll never utter aloud

ACKNOWLEDGEMENTS

What would I do without my beloved readers? Oh right, I'd need to get a real job. No wonder I'm so darn grateful for each and every one of you. Thank you.

To my beta team who reads my early drafts when they're like a mangy cat—with bald patches and missing bits of fur all over the place: Tess, Bec, Vicki, Naomi, John, Rosie, James, and Mum. Each book has been better for your love and care (and mange medication).

Special thanks to Mum for ridiculous amounts of brainstorming assistance, endless moral support, instilling a love of words in me from an early age, and still correcting my pronunciation to this day.

A shout out to Tom for sharing your expertise in legal gobble-dygook. Any mistakes are my own, folks. Also, if the producer of *The West Wing* (or anyone who knows said producer) is reading this, Tom is super keen to be a legal consultant on your next project, and he'd be ace at it.

To my proofreaders and final pass editors at Victory Editing—I hope you appreciate that you're the only people in the world I gladly pay to point out my faults. Thank you for being so good at it.

To my incredible husband who brainstorms every book with me, reads the mangiest drafts of all, and keeps me fed while I'm writing on a deadline. Thank you. You are the mythical unicorn of husbands.

And thanks to God who loves me regardless of whether I'm being dutiful or beastly. I'm grateful every day.

Hungering for more?

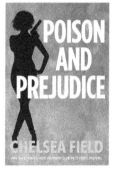

SEE THE COMPLETE SERIES SO FAR AT

CHELSEAFIELDAUTHOR.COM

CONNOR UNMASKED

EXCLUSIVE BONUS SCENE

Want to know what Connor thought of Izzy when they first met?

Read this BONUS scene in his perspective & find out!

CPSIA information can be obtained
at www.ICGtesting.com
Printed in the USA
LVHW03s1810080818
586374LV00002B/328/P

9 781984 348432